An intricate exploration of community and consent, now with ghosts! SANCTUARY is unapologetic about being true to yourself, thoughtful about being kind, and it provides you with new ways of fitting into the world when the world doesn't quite fit. An indispensable book in the new wave of neurodivergent speculative fiction, and a refreshing take on ghost stories too; don't miss it.
– Bogi Takács, Hugo and Lambda award winning author and editor

Andi C. Buchanan's Sanctuary is the perfect mix of heart and supernatural adventure.-
Readers will find their own home in Sanctuary's pages, as they make their way through the twists and turns of this ghostly mystery. Loved it – highly recommend.
– Helen Vivienne Fletcher, author of We All Fall.

With a found-family cast of queer and neurodiverse people, Sanctuary is a wonderful meditation on what we owe the dead, ourselves, each other. Wander this grand old house a while. You'll be in good company, and the door is open.
– Rem Wigmore, author of Foxhunt.

Cover design by JV Arts.

A catalogue record for this book is available from the National Library of New Zealand.

ISBNs:
Paperback: 978-0-473-60048-8
Epub: 978-0-473-60049-5
Mobi: 978-0-473-60050-1

Sanctuary

Andi C. Buchanan

Robot Dinosaur Press

Content Notes

This note is for those readers who prefer to be warned about topics included that might be difficult reading. It does contain some spoilers.

Sanctuary includes physical violence and injury, suicide both completed and attempted, self harm, loss of a sibling, imprisonment (outside the state system), and magical control of a person. There is also discussion of emotional, physical, and ableist abuse of young people, including through therapeutic and educational systems.

Several characters experience difficulties relating to ongoing illness including physical pain and anxiety. A scene in which a character's creative work is destroyed is deeply linked to trauma.

Some characters have had negative experiences with police and the medical system, and others fear these. This leads to avoidance of medical care, and discussion of possible negative outcomes. There is mention of racism and other oppressions, and briefly of slavery (in a historical context).

I have done my best to handle these topics with care and respect. If you choose to keep reading, I hope you can do so in a way that works well for you.

CONTENT NOTES

for those who live with ghosts
and those who leave the doors unlocked

CHAPTER ONE

The ghost of Henrietta Casswell (died in childbirth, 1781, within these very walls) floats by as I'm setting the table for dinner.

My mouth feels dry and I swallow before I speak. I can speak much more easily when there are only ghosts around than I can to living people, but it's still not easy.

"Good morning Henrietta," I say, trying to remember which spoon goes closest to the plate. "Do you want to join us for dinner?"

By the time I've got the words out, she's already halfway through the ceiling—which means halfway into my bedroom. Her legs, skirt, and no doubt many layers of undergarments, though of course I don't look, dangle high above me.

"You're welcome anytime," I say, smiling to myself, but she's gone.

I secretly dream of having a sturdy oak table with carved legs and matching chairs, one that fits the grandeur of our high-ceilinged dining room. In reality, our table is comprised of six smaller tables of approximately equal height (and at least two of them salvaged from skips) shoved together. When my nan died, Dad gave me boxes of her stuff, including more tablecloths than I could ever imagine her needing. I've found a use for them, and they make this creation look as much like a single table as it's ever going to.

I set places for eleven. There are eight of us living people, plus I've set a few aside for any ghosts who may wish to join us. Ghosts don't eat, not exactly, but like us, they know that sharing a meal isn't just about food.

In the kitchen next door, I can hear Araminta and Alison laughing as they cook. I head through to help them carry the food, messaging the house group chat on my way to tell the others to get ready.

It's the last day of the holidays for Holly and Theo, so we've planned a special meal. Araminta has been tracking deals and using her and Holly's staff discounts for weeks to get this together, and the smell wafting through the air makes me hungry already. Theo is the first to arrive, his hair neatly buzzed, skidding across the hallway in those trainers with wheels in the heels that he will not be able to wear at school, so apparently he has to make the most of now, life or limb of the rest of us be damned. Theo's ten years old, Black, and has more energy than the rest of us combined—or at least it feels like it. He proudly demonstrates that yes, his hands do smell of soap, and I ask him to help us carry in food.

The table fills up quickly. There are no two ways about it: this is a midwinter feast. The pizza is topped with roast pumpkin and rosemary, and steam wafts from the pot of beef stew and dumplings at the centre of the table. Numerous other plates are tetrised between them; cheeses and salads and mini tarts. And there's still dessert to come.

I've saved the seat next to me for Araminta and when she arrives, she throws her arms around me, kisses me briefly but demonstratively. I don't move much in response; I'm not like her in that respect, but I can't stop a grin from finding its way to my face, and feeling warm despite the winter outside.

"Would someone like to say some sort of grace?" Alison asks, shifting her placemat slightly so it aligns with the table. She's a thin white woman in her fifties, her pencil-straight hair dyed dark blonde and cut in a bob. "An atheist version like..."

"Secular," Saeed corrects. "Atheist implies that..."

Vinnie throws their hands up in the air, the sleeves of their blazer falling back to reveal perfectly starched cuffs, fastened with silver cufflinks, a white glare against their dark brown skin.

"Please! Food first, pedantry later."

There's as much laughter in their voice as there is exasperation, though, and even Saeed grins.

"Right, fine, I'll do it," Vinnie says at last. "Thank you to Araminta and Alison for preparing this wonderful meal. May we share it with joy and friendship, may Holly and Theo have a successful Spring Term, and may Holly not work too hard."

"What about me! I need to not work too hard too!" Theo insists, looking at Vinnie with indignation.

Vinnie looks at their son with mock-sternness.

"When your report card predicts you an A* in every single A-level and Morgan has to knock on your door each night to check you haven't fallen asleep on a pile of books, you too will receive the same wish."

I ignore them. I'm helping myself to the platter full of mini sausages wrapped in bacon and cheese. It's barely two weeks since Christmas, two weeks since Araminta and I visited my parents' home and celebrated along with my brother, and his partner and baby. And now we're back in our own home, this huge old house that is ours for now only because Denny's property-developer sister has so far found turning it into apartments more trouble, and more money than it's worth.

The fact that tradespeople kept refusing to return after the odd bit of mild haunting probably helped with that.

So for now at least, this is home, and these people gathered around this table are those I share it with. It's like I have multiple families, and I love them more than I could ever find words for, which isn't bad for someone once deemed incapable of relating to people.

Jodie Keane, the most recently deceased ghost to have found refuge here at Casswell Park, joins us, sitting down on one of the empty chairs. Some ghosts are more corporeal than others – exactly why is complicated, but broadly speaking they become less corporeal over time. The older the ghost, the less substantial it is, which may explain why I've never seen a bronze age ghost. And also explains why Jodie, born in 1980 and killed in a car accident that wasn't entirely accidental a little over fifteen years later, is actually sitting on the chair, not just hovering above it with legs bent. Holly, sitting nearest, ladles out some stew for her. Holly's white-blonde hair, normally plaited, is in a loose ponytail which fans out across her back. Jodie doesn't eat, but she seems happy to have been given food, leaning over the steam rising from her bowl. Perhaps there is some part of her that can still smell it.

I'm halfway through a blue cheese, walnut, and caramelised pear tart when there's a knocking sound coming from the main door. We all pause and look up. Denny grabs the fork he's been idly levitating and spinning above his plate, and places it firmly down on the table. I look at him and notice the wrinkles on his face, white skin darkened by decades of sun. He smiles at me.

"That'll be our ghost hunting friends," Alison says with her mouth full. There's a collective sigh.

"Can I shoot them with my nerf gun?" Theo asks.

"No, you may not," says Vinnie. Their words are clear, but I can tell they'd also like to go after the self-styled ghost hunters with a nerf gun – or perhaps something that would cause a little more damage.

"I'll go," Araminta says quickly, already on her feet. I cram the rest of the tart into my mouth and follow her down the wide hallway to the central foyer from which the twin staircases fan out. On our way, we pass the ghost of Tim McCabe (died 1854, Broad Street cholera epidemic) who seems completely oblivious to us. Araminta and I have lived in the same house for three years, been a couple for almost two, and I'm still taking every opportunity to spend snatches of time with her. I wouldn't want it any other way.

We don't use the main door often. It's heavy to open and expensive to get duplicate keys cut for. Technically, it's two doors, rising in the centre to a pointed archway. Both are made of dense wood and it takes a tug to get them open. As Araminta and I pull, I notice Denny has followed us, is waiting a few steps behind with a poker in his hand. I'm comforted by this. He'd be the first to admit that with his lack of motor skills; any attempt to fight the visitors would likely end up with him taking his own eye out. But they don't have to know that. All they will see is a near giant of a man standing quietly with a weapon in his hand. It would be enough to make most people think twice.

As it happens, the only thing to rush at us when we finally get the door open is a blast of ice-cold air. The man standing in the doorway must be in his nineties, supporting himself with a walking stick and breathing as though getting here had almost taken the last bit of life from him. He's wearing Gore-Tex trousers and a jacket even though – for once – it's not raining. Only a few paces behind him is a battered old car, the engine still running and the lights on.

"Can I help you?" Araminta asks cheerfully, her customer service smile plastered across her face.

"You keep ghosts? You keep them safe?"

The man has a posh accent, one my first instinct is to laugh at. Araminta looks at me before answering.

"I guess some people say that."

"I have the ghosts from my family in the car. They've been in my family for generations. I have to go... I have to go into supported living, and noone else can take them. Please, can you look after them?"

As Araminta begins to reply, I edge my way out and over to the car. I peer through the windows, expecting to see ghosts sitting on the back seat. Nothing. I look back in confusion. Then I try the boot. It's open. And in it is a crate of old bottles, all tightly stoppered.

It's an old-fashioned way of carrying ghosts, and not one any of us would be comfortable with, but I try not to judge, especially as these bottles clearly predate the elderly man at our door by a matter of centuries.

Denny and I carry the crate out of the boot. It's not heavy, but it would be too large for me to get my hands around alone. I turn and walk backwards to make things easier for him; I know not dropping things and not walking into things are not in his skill set. Just as I get inside, I hear the car door slam and the car speed up, down the driveway, past the new housing development on what were once Casswell Park's gardens, and then it's gone.

"Didn't want to stay around and chat, I guess," Araminta says with a shrug.

I type into my phone and show her:
>>Did he say who he was?
"Not a thing. He just wanted us to take care of them."
>>It's a lot of ghosts..
But this is what we do.

Back in the dining room, Araminta relays to the others what happened while Denny returns to eating his ham sandwich and bowl of peas. If there's one thing we're all good at, it's making sure everyone's dietary requirements are met, and if Denny wants to eat his usual meal because it's familiar, so be it.

I take the last slice of pizza without guilt. It's cold by now but still delicious.

"Is it dessert time?" Theo asks.

"I don't know how you can even think about dessert after all those dumplings," Vinnie says.

"Second stomachs," Alison replies, knowledgeably. "Both my boys had them. No room left for dinner but plenty for dessert. Make the most of it, Theo, because you'll lose your dessert stomach when you grow up."

"That's okay," Theo says, smugly. "When I'm grown up I'll be able to drive *and* have sex."

Vinnie sighs, raising their eyes to the heavens. "Give me strength, oh Lord."

Vinnie still goes to church with Denny sometimes, even though they've told me they no longer believe in God. Maybe this is why. Maybe they're retaining some hope that the Almighty will aid their parenting.

"I'm going to bring dessert through," Araminta says hastily, pushing her chair out from the table. She's wearing a dress with a square neckline and full skirt, made from green fabric printed with snails. Since she started ignoring her parents' comments that she had to dress in dark colours to hide her size, she's created an amazing wardrobe and finally has the confidence to stand out. "Someone come and help me?"

Dessert is no less impressive than the main meal. There's hot blueberry pie with ice cream, poached peaches in mulled wine, chocolate pudding. I go straight for the cheese board, though. I can only hope that the cheese was near-dated and on special, because otherwise there's no way our collective budget could have afforded this selection. And it looks like there will be leftovers for a while.

The door creaks open and Mallard pokes a paw around it. I reach down and click my fingers, and she cautiously walks towards me before leaping on my lap and settling. Mal was a three-month-old rescue kitten when I first got her, a leaving home present from my brother Rory. Mum told him it was a terrible idea, giving me something else to be responsible for when I was going to find moving out hard enough already. She said he should have just given me a toasted sandwich maker or something, but honestly, Mallard has looked after me far more than I've needed to look after her.

Araminta leans across to stroke Mal's black and white patched fur, her red hair dangling forward over her shoulders.

"Was it the ice cream you smelled? Or the cheese? Sorry about the lactose intolerance, Mal, but we'll open up one of those fish packets tonight, alright?"

I hold the fingers I was eating some cubes of feta with to Mal's mouth, and she sniffs then licks my hands enthusiastically. A trace of cheese won't hurt her.

Mallard isn't the only cat that lives here. Alison has a pair of tabbies, but they stick mostly to her room and the balcony that adjoins it. Mallard, however, has the full run of the house, the long balcony at the back, and the strip of grass that remains of what were, according to the photos Saeed has found, magnificent gardens. They're now a development of townhouses, and it wouldn't surprise me if Mallard roamed a good part of that as well. This is her kingdom, and she knows it.

After we finish dessert, the candles are extinguished, and Theo is sent to lay out his clothes and pack his bag for tomorrow. Holly boxes up some leftovers to take for lunch and then goes to do the same. The rest of us clean up together; putting leftovers in the fridge, washing plates, clearing the dining room. Saeed drags the tablecloths off the table and hands them to me, walking with me down to the laundry. Today's look, as usual, is a mixture of black and brightness; gold nails shining on his mid-brown hands as he grips his black platform crutches and a purple tie – he's dressed up! – over a black button-up shirt. He takes a steady rhythm as he walks, feet and crutches both making muffled sounds on this wooden floor, and I match my pace to his, my arms full of tablecloths.

The laundry room is where the old kitchens were, back when this was the private residence of the Casswell family. It remained that way from when it was first built, in the late seventeenth century, through to the late nineteenth, when it was sold and became a convent. After the war, it was sold again and turned into a boarding school until they moved to more modern premises on the outskirts of town. Casswell Park was in the country too once, just on the edge of town, but now that town has grown up around it, enveloping it. I'm glad of that. I might get overwhelmed with crowds, but I'd hate to be out in the middle of nowhere.

The history of Casswell Park is Saeed's area of expertise. He's got a whole section of the house wiki, the one we use to organise chore rosters and house maintenance, dedicated to his research. Sometimes it helps us understand the stories of those ghosts who were already here when we arrived, but mostly it's an interest project for him. Somehow, he manages to keep it up as well as studying towards a history degree by distance. It goes right back to the house that stood on this site before, partially burned down before being demolished, and we suspect at least one of our ghosts may have died as a result of that fire.

When we reach the laundry room – which consists of a washer and dryer in the corner of a room overly large for them, with twine strung across the ceiling for indoor drying – the ghost of Roderick Lewis is perched on top of the washer, grinning broadly. His hair is typically askew and long enough to push the limits of his school dress code, his face freckled with the start of summer even though it's still the bitter cold of January outside. It will always be the start of summer for him, the looming long holiday. We don't know how he died, not exactly, but we can all take the building blocks of queer teenager, boarding school, nineteen sixties, sudden death, and put two and two together.

I move my head to indicate for him to get out of the way. Roderick, being literate and not too long passed, is one of the easiest ghosts to communicate with – we have some boards set up with letters for ghosts like him to point at when they need to. Right now, he knows exactly what I'm telling him, but he's also fifteen years old and not entirely cooperative. He lingers for just enough time to cause me to start feeling annoyed and then propels himself from the washing machine across the room, landing with a dramatic pose. He hangs out with us as we load up the machine.

I haven't always lived with ghosts, but they've always been part of my life. My dad worked the railways, and his father too, and railways sadly see a lot of ghosts. He took me along, sometimes, when Mum was working nights, to help the ghosts of those killed on the tracks move on, or at least settle down and not be so disruptive if they had decided to haunt that particular crossing or platform.

I didn't know, at least until I started school, that most people don't see ghosts – or don't know they're seeing them, or don't even believe in them at all. They were always normal for me; rare, perhaps – I saw them only a few times most years before I moved here, but just as I seldom saw elephants, it didn't make them any less real. It was accepted in my family that there were ghosts around us, and that we should be polite to them unless they gave us reason to do otherwise.

Then again, there were a lot of things accepted in my family that weren't in the world at large – my being autistic, and not being a boy like I was first thought to be, just two of them. I had the safe and loving upbringing that some of my housemates can barely imagine, but sometimes it made the contrast with the outside world only seem sharper.

It's not that my parents were idealists. They weren't activists either, though they'd both helped hold a picket line when it had become necessary. They were just matter of fact people. If their child was a bit different – and Rory and I both were, in our own ways – then that was simply how it was, and there was no use in fussing over it or wishing things were different.

It was only later I realised how lucky – and unusual – I was.

Saeed and I sit on the bench outside the laundry room, waiting for the load to finish. On a bad day, noise like this is overloading, but today its repetition is comforting. It's easier, too, to talk when I can't hear myself. Roderick floats a metre or two in front of us, striking increasingly bizarre poses. I know it only encourages him, but I can't help but laugh.

"So," says Saeed. "We're going to have to do something about those bottles, right? I'm used to ghosts arriving one at a time, not a whole collection of them at once."

I nod. Saeed is the last person who would mind if I typed the response, but I'm trying to stay in practice by speaking when I can, but not push myself when it's too much. There's just the three of us here, and I think I can do it.

"Tomorrow?" I ask. "One ghost at a time."

"Yeah, that would make sense. One a day maybe. I don't like them being in those bottles, but it looks like it's been a long time so a week or whatever won't make much difference. And if we get too many ghosts at once it might upset the ones that are already here."

When the load finishes, Saeed passes me the tablecloths and I fling them out over the drying lines. We say goodnight when we reach the staircase – while we've managed to get the old lift adequately repaired, Saeed still finds it easier to have a ground floor bedroom. I brush my hand against the wooden rail as I make it up the wide staircase. I like the feel of the wood grain through the peeling varnish. The ceiling is high above my head; this place is grand and I love it, but it is a nightmare to heat. And even though we pay no rent, the maintenance is an ongoing issue for us, surviving as we do on part-time and casual work, benefits, student loans and child support. Still, I wouldn't live anywhere else, and I'm not sure I could; the ghosts need us as much as we need them.

My bedroom is straight off the main corridor, not as large as some but cosy, centred around a wall mounted screen and my collection of consoles. My main telescope is pointed out of the window, even though I usually take it up to the roof when I want to use it; my other one, a family heirloom and possibly two hundred years old or more, is kept safely in a drawer. Round the bed, I've clustered an armchair and a couple of beanbags. There's a bookcase for my games, and a bedside cabinet that holds my laptop, a lamp, meds and toiletries. My clothes go in a built-in wardrobe. After all that, there's little floor space.

Mallard is curled up in the centre of the bed. I sigh. As usual, she's chosen her place and I'll just have to work around her.

There's a knock at the door. Araminta's room is opposite mine, and she's heard me head up. She's dressed for bed already in flannel pyjamas, white with tiny blue flowers all over. Her thick red hair is loose and flames up around the pale skin of her face. We must seem a right pair when we go out; her in dresses as colourful as her hair and me with my near-black hair and clothing that comes only in black, dark grey, or dark green.

"Sleep," I sign with a smile. We've been learning BSL together but so far, I mostly know a lot of words and not very much grammar.

"Yeah," she says. "I'm working from seven tomorrow. Early shift. Means I finish early though. You?"

I grin and sign, "gaming". I'm what they call a night owl. It will be many hours before I sleep, but it's also time for me to be alone for a while. Alone, and in another world. I lean over to Araminta and kiss her gently, my body pressing against hers, and then when she's gone, I shut the door, prop myself up on a beanbag, and settle in for another night in a house full of ghosts.

CHAPTER TWO

Vinnie and I move the crate of ghosts into the centre of one of the unused downstairs rooms, and, together with Saeed, examine the bottles. They all seem to be the same design, though they are filled with imperfections and irregularities. They are old; how old I can't say, but definitely older than the Victorian bottles Dad would occasionally dig up in the garden and keep on a shelf in the porch. Hand blown, I'm guessing. They're a greenish brown colour and near-spherical with a long neck extending upwards, with a glass stopper wedged in tightly with a red substance that I think must be wax.

All of them are covered in dust. I wonder how long they've been left untouched, in an attic or an under-stairs cupboard. But mostly, I'm thinking about how much knowledge of their situation the ghosts might have, captured in their bottles, whether it feels like decades, even centuries, trapped in those tiny glass prisons. It makes me uncomfortable just being around them. Rationally, I know that our plan to release them slowly and carefully is best for all concerned. But there's a slow-burning rage inside of me that wants to smash every bottle, to kick and stomp on them with my boots, to free every ghost from their suffocating imprisonment.

"I wish he'd given us some documentation," Saeed sighs, flicking a fidget spinner between his fingers. "All he said was that they'd been in his family a long time, but we've no idea how long that means, where they lived, why they'd be interested in keeping ghosts in bottles at all..."

That's typical Saeed. We have potentially eighteen ghosts that have not been seen for maybe hundreds of years, and his focus is on some old documents.

"My guess is that whoever captured them was like the ghost hunters," says Vinnie. "They don't mean any harm. They just don't see ghosts as having rights or autonomy; their own interest comes before everything else." Vinnie pauses, turns to me. "What do you think, Morgan? Still keen to go ahead with the one a day plan?"

I nod and give them a thumbs up.

"The only question is," Saeed says, "which one we're going to open first."

It's mid-morning. The low winter sun is finding its way through the windows, and there's a sharp frost still lingering on the grass. Vinnie has taken Theo to school and dropped Holly at her 6th form college as well, allowing her to avoid either the noisy bus journey or the long walk in the cold. Araminta is at work at the Co-op where Holly also has a part-time job. It seems strangely quiet, here in this large house, and the ghosts have been quiet too.

I look at the bottles in the old wooden crate. There are no labels, nothing to distinguish one from the other. I hold my hand out to them tentatively, see if I can feel anything in the surrounding air.

If there's a name for my ability, I don't know it. I didn't even know it was unusual until my teens. Simply put, I can detect lingering sensations attached mostly to places, sometimes to objects. Most of the time, it's nothing more than that. I can walk into a house and know with utter certainty that something bad has happened there. I can be buoyed by the remnants of a celebration weeks later, one I never even knew happened. Ironically, given what people say about autistic people like me, it's probably a form of hyper-empathy, but sometimes there's a bit more to it. Perhaps a dozen times over my life, I've caught flashes of someone else's memory, a brief image lost as suddenly as it's seen, just slipping from my understanding like a half-remembered dream.

I don't talk or think about it much. It's not strong enough to have a significant effect on my life, and outside of this house – where I'm not the only one with an ability not yet explained by science – not that many people would believe me anyway.

I can't even tell for sure if I'm using it now; it's not a strong sense I'm picking up on, in any case. But I'm unmistakeably drawn to a bottle to my right. It feels warm, safe. Something I'm comfortable with. I pick it up. Even if my choice is no better than a random one, no-one else will be able to do better. I turn the glass slowly, thinking I see a wisp of something inside. The glass is misty, as if condensation has formed on the interior.

I don't feel like a saviour. I feel like a captor every minute I hold the stoppered bottle.

It shouldn't affect me so much, but things like this always have. Other people's injuries. Animals in pain. And yes, ghosts trapped behind glass. It's like their suffering ends up wrapped around some part of my brain and I can't dislodge the knowledge of what they're going through.

When I was a kid, people didn't believe I felt anything much because I didn't change my facial expressions as they expected. I can't imagine prioritising choosing the apparently correct facial expression when I'm faced with such pain.

I look at the bottle and nod my head.

"Got it," says Vinnie. "Let's free a ghost."

The room we've chosen does not yet have a purpose, but it's one we've done some basic work on; varnished the floors, replastered the walls, and painted with a rose-pink mis-tint Alison got cheap from a painter friend. I've used it a few times to practice between karate classes. If there's one thing we're not short of at Casswell Park, it's rooms.

In any case, it's the right space for this; uncluttered, unlikely to be disturbed. Vinnie drags in three dining chairs for us; we know this may take a while. I'm still clutching the bottle, as if I'll have broken some promise should I let it go. We thought we'd be undisturbed, but when I go to close the door I see Isobel peeking round the corner, looking worried and perhaps sad in a way I've never seen before.

Isobel was here when we moved in, though we don't know if she died here. Saeed has found mentions of her in the writings of those who attended the school; they all called her Isobel and so do we. By her dress, we've estimated her to be from the early eighteenth century, perhaps twenty years of age, of low income but not in poverty, and probably not a servant either. We're used to her; she strides around quickly and purposefully through the house, although to what end we cannot tell. Perhaps she's forever repeating something she did long ago.

The meek young woman I see now is a far cry from her usual self. When I try to reach out to her, she flees. I wonder if we're making a terrible mistake. But we resolved, right from the start, that we would be a sanctuary for ghosts, for those who need somewhere safe, and so I just hope that by going slowly we will allay Isobel's fears, whatever they are.

We sit in a small circle, our chairs facing each other at an angle. Saeed leans his crutches against the chair, trying a few times before he gets them to stay. We all know that while danger is unlikely, we may still want to make a quick exit.

I kneel and place the bottle on the floor in the middle of our little circle. When I try to open it, the stopper doesn't shift. I pull on it harder, but it doesn't even loosen.

Vinnie hands me a lighter, engraved with their initials. They don't smoke, but I think carrying one is part of their aesthetic, and that if they did smoke, it would definitely be cigars. I flick up the flame and gently hold it to the neck of the bottle. The wax begins to soften, and then dribble down the glass. Hastily, I hand the lighter back to Vinnie and, holding the bottle firmly on the floor, remove the stopper.

Then I sit down.

There's a slight hissing sound from the bottle, and a chill in the air, more than can be accounted for by not being able to heat this rambling and mostly-uninsulated high-ceilinged house – but nothing more than that. We look at each other, nodding, and we wait.

We're waiting some time. Even Saeed doesn't say much. Perhaps we don't want to scare the ghost, but also even he's not really sure what we say at times like these. I brush my hand back and forth against the rough fabric of my trousers over my knee, appreciating the texture.

When the ghost starts to emerge, their movement is slow and gentle, so much so that I don't think we'd notice it if the temperature didn't suddenly plummet. It was chilly in here before; now it's icy, as if I'd been slapped in the face by a strong wind, except we're inside and the air is still. I hold my arms tightly across my chest, burrowing myself into my grey hoodie which feels inadequate against the sudden cold, resisting the temptation to lean forward and see what's happening in the bottle. Ghosts need their space, every bit as much as we do.

He's just a wisp at first, a dull white, like smoke or mist ascending from the bottle into the cold air. Then he grows upwards and we see a form emerge; a head grows, then facial features. My stomach lurches. I can tell this is a child.

He eases himself out of the bottle bit by bit, as if he's reassembling himself as he goes. Shoulders then a torso, arms stiffly by his sides, then his legs come out all at once, ending with two small and pointed shoes, and he's a fully formed boy, about ten years old. He's more transparent than most of the ghosts I know, but many of our ghosts are Victorian or later, and he's clearly from a different era.

He takes a couple of steps back, walking in mid-air, seemingly dazed. He's wearing short trousers with what look like high socks below them, a shirt with a large collar and a leather apron. His hair beneath is slightly askew. It doesn't look particularly fancy except for the collar, but I don't need Saeed to tell me that kids didn't dress like this if they came from poverty.

The boy doesn't look scared and he doesn't look distressed. He's just taking everything in gradually, his eyes wide open, floating just a little way above the ground and turning slowly to see everything around him.

I can't help myself wondering how he died. The more dramatic the death, the higher the likelihood of becoming a ghost; which means that we do see some who died of disease, but many more who met a violent end.

It's harder thinking about things like that when they're children.

Mercifully, and contrary to some popular beliefs, ghosts don't generally appear with visible signs of their manner of death. I've never seen one wandering round with an axe embedded in their head or giant buboes around their lymph nodes. Henrietta has a beauty spot, but I understand that was as much about fashion as it was about smallpox, and in any case it wasn't that which killed her.

"I reckon he's about Theo's age?" Saeed asks Vinnie. "He's a little smaller, but that's probably due to the era he's from."

"Probably," Vinnie says. "The two of them can terrorise us together."

I imagine them running (and floating) round Casswell Park's wide corridors, and I smile. It's not right for someone to die so young, but there's a sort of life for him still. I'm glad, too, that this boy's not likely to get his hands on a pair of ghost-heelys. Small mercies.

We let him move himself a bit, acclimatise. He doesn't go outside the circle created by our chairs – though none of us would try to stop him if he did – but he does try floating upwards a little. He has no real muscles to stretch, and yet that seems to be what he's doing, stretching out limbs sore and cramped from decades or more trapped in that bottle.

I watch him. He's pale and I can clearly see through him. If I were to put my hand through his body – which I never would deliberately without his consent – it would just feel like I was moving through air. That's usually how it is with the older ghosts. The recent ones are more corporeal, less transparent, though still devoid of colour, and while you can move through them it takes effort. It's like pushing your hands through water or oil.

The same spectrum applies to their movements. The less corporeal ghosts can move through walls with ease; the more recent ones find it harder but they are also more able to interact with their environment: they can move an item, may even be able to push open a door.

I watch this ghost-child adjust to freedom after such a long imprisonment. We only have a floor lamp in this room, but we've left it off, so the only light comes from the window, a hazy glow. It's approaching midday, but this side of the house is sheltered and east-facing, so the room is still relatively dim.

After a while, Vinnie looks at each of us in turn.

"We need to work out what to call him."

I sigh and nod. I've been through this process before, and I don't think I'll ever be comfortable with it. I chose my own name – I'm not the only person here who did – and I carry an almost visceral fear of losing it. But choosing them a name is a more respectful solution than calling them by numbers or physical identifiers, and we do our best to get some level of consent. Still, I worry sometimes that we're doing the equivalent of renaming all the footmen James and John and the housemaids Emma.

I grin at the thought. I may be living in a grand old house, but I'm no aristocrat. In any case, I don't think they have many gender-neutral titles.

I do have to push through my discomfort at naming ghosts, though. It looks like we're going to have quite a few needing names over the next little while.

Having established a likely range for the years the child lived, Saeed looks up common names for the era on his tablet. I look over his shoulder. If we read through a list, we might come across the correct one by chance – and he might be able to tell us so.

Some ghosts can tell us their names, pointing slowly at letters. Others can respond when we guess, or sometimes whoever brings them here knows enough to allow us to identify them, even if it takes a bit of research. But for some, there's nothing, and when we pick one, we can only see if the ghost objects.

"Hello," Vinnie says, standing and placing themself in front of the ghost. They speak loudly, clearly. "My name is Vinnie. This is Saeed and Morgan. We are friends. I know it's hard for you to hear us right now. We speak a bit differently to you as well."

The boy frowns, though more in confusion than in distaste, and looks at them, then turns his gaze upwards and out to some point in the distance, way beyond the solid wall that is only a couple of metres from him.

"We know you can't tell us your name," Vinnie continues, drawing his attention back. "We're going to guess some names and see what you think. Is that okay?"

Saeed frantically signals at Vinnie; a ghost in the bottle so long won't understand more recent slang. They swear under their breath.

"Sorry. Is that all right? Do you understand?'

The boy looks blank for a moment and then nods. Vinnie turns to Saeed.

"Benjamin?" Saeed suggests.

The child looks around distractedly, as if he hears and understands Saeed, but can't quite focus on the direction of his voice.

"Benjamin," Saeed says again. There's no recognition in the boy's face, but I'm sure he heard.

"Cecil?"

The child falls into peels of silent laughter and shakes his head. I'm not sure why it's so funny. I mean, I might find Cecil a funny name, but I'm not a ghost with trousers only just below my knees. I look at Saeed, who shrugs.

"Maybe he knows someone called Cecil. Maybe he has a brother called Cecil and thinks it's hilarious that anyone could compare the two. Who knows? At least he's engaging." He turns to the ghost again, who seems to have mostly recovered from his outburst of laughter. "So you're not Cecil. How about Christopher?"

The boy shakes his head and looks towards the window. I lean over Saeed's shoulder and point at names from the list.

"Daniel?" Saeed suggests. "Evan?"

The child is drifting away from us, not because he seems to have taken offence, but with simple disinterest. I understand how his mind must wander; it's the same I often experience when I'm walking outside, when there's too much to focus on so I end up focusing on nothing and wander, not taking note of cracks in the pavement or of cars, of where the footpath ends and the road begins. It's why I don't go further than the remaining strip of garden by myself.

"Henry," Saeed says, almost desperately. "Joseph?"

That name gets his attention. The ghost is suddenly very still and focused, looking right at Saeed. Saeed blinks rapidly in the face of eye contact.

"Joseph," Saeed repeats clearly, a statement not a question this time. And slowly, cautiously, and yet unmistakably, the ghost child nods in recognition.

In the evening I cook up a vegetarian spag bol; tomato and lentils from the cans we have in the back of the cupboard, any vegetables left from our last market trip, and fresh herbs from the collection Alison is growing on her balcony. Name any herb, even the obscure ones, and she can tell you what dish to add it to. My cooking isn't clever or fancy, or even very varied, but I'm good at using what we have. It's just a regular day, so no tablecloths or candles, but we're all eating together.

Araminta is home from work, Holly and Theo from school, and Alison from a trip to the hardware shop. I swear that when she dies it will be that place she haunts, not here, hovering among the power tools or lurking in the garden centre. But she's got us replacement washers for the taps in the upstairs bathrooms and a solar powered light for the section of path where we all keep tripping over in the evenings, so I'm not complaining.

"I hear we have a new resident," Denny says, helping himself first from the pot of spaghetti, then from the pot of sauce. "Yet to meet them though."

"I'm sure you will before too long," Vinnie replies. "Bit shy, that's all."

Saeed fills in the details.

"About ten years old. Late seventeenth century. Well off family, based on his clothes. Name's Joseph – it was either his original name, or he liked it when we suggested it, either way, he's happy. Shy, as Vinnie said, but seems to be doing fine. He's hesitant and a little confused but not actively scared of us."

"How many more to go?" asks Holly.

"Seventeen. Assuming one ghost per bottle, that is. I'm expecting them to be no later than early Victorian, based on the bottles, but besides that, it's all going to be a surprise."

"Looks like this house is going to get a lot busier," says Denny, dropping spaghetti on his shirt and swearing under his breath as he tries to soak up the sauce with a napkin.

"Should we make you some regular pasta next time we have spaghetti?" Araminta asks. Denny shakes his head.

"Look, there's every chance I'd drop that too. A good supply of stain remover is the best option, so just keep looking out for the sales, please."

"Will do."

"Does it bother you?" Alison asks. "The house getting busier, I mean. Do you feel it's getting too crowded?"

"If I didn't like living around ghosts, I'd hardly have given up my council flat and persuaded my sister to let me live in the haunted old house she didn't quite know what to do with, would I now. It was a nice place and all, my flat. Modern. Easy to heat."

There are murmurs of recognition at the last statement. It's still early January, a while until we see the first signs of spring. We're all feeling the cold. It probably doesn't help that while we all enjoy each other's company, we also need a lot of time separate from each other. Even when they're people you don't have to fake being neurotypical with, being around people is exhausting.

We open a couple of packets of biscuits and help ourselves to ice cream for dessert. I make a note to start making crumbles and pie again; no-one ever complains about ice cream, but in this weather, I know that a hot dessert would be welcome.

Afterwards, we hang around talking for a while, and then gradually we go our separate ways, helping a bit with the clean-up as we go. Vinnie and Theo are rostered on today; even though we usually all pitch in, most of us would struggle without a roster to fall back on. In practice, this means that Vinnie is washing the dishes and Theo is zooming back and forth between here and the kitchen with armloads of plates. I hear a loud intake of breath as he scoots in, his arms full.

Surprisingly, no harm comes to either the plates or the child. Leaving them to wash up, we fan out through the big old house, to sleep or read or watch tv, to game or chat online or prepare for the next day. In our separate rooms we are alone again, and yet not lonely.

1703

The ghosts he has captured are lined up in bottles on the shelf of his study. This collection is his pride, what he has been working towards all his life – and yet he knows it can be so much more.

In his notebook; an expensive book, leather bound, with gold lettering on the front, and thick pages inside, he's detailed not just the ghosts he's captured but the ones he hopes to contain within these bottles, the ones he has heard of only in rumour.

There are others who came to this path by twists and turns of interest, but for him, it has been his life's calling. Ever since he saw his first ghost, he's known he will spend his life studying them. He's bringing order to the unexplainable, developing a classification system that treats them with logic, working as a true natural philosopher.

As a boy, he caught butterflies, with a net and a skillful twist of his wrist, pinned them to a board. Many boys have caught butterflies. He knows no-one who is so close to understanding and fully classifying those of the spirit world.

CHAPTER THREE

I 'm woken by my bedroom light gently flashing a soft green throughout the room. I reach for my phone. I'm sure some people would judge me for investing in a WiFi connected, heavily automated lighting system when we can't afford to heat the house properly and some days end up eating just porridge or rice with soy sauce until someone's pay comes through. But it's changed my life. It means I don't lose a night's sleep when I lack the executive function for turning the light off, and I can bring myself out of sensory overload by lying on my bed watching a predictable cycle of slow and gentle colour changes.

These colour coded flashes (turned off from midnight until seven) aren't exactly essential, but I like them. Green means there is a new message on the group chat, and this one's from Saeed.

>> Morning all! Any reports of our new boy Joseph last night? Or any signs he's unsettled? Anything to report?

Saeed must be the only student in the world who voluntarily gets up this early. Especially during the holidays. The light flashes some more as the responses begin.

>> Saw him in the corridor when I went to the bathroom. Seemed a little dazed but that's normal. All fine from my perspective.

Holly proves my theory that teenagers use better grammar than adults when messaging. I was just about to tell myself that maybe that's just Holly, when Alison proves me entirely right.

>> short-trousers boy dropped by my bedroom last night seemed like nice kid all good xx

>> Let's maybe call him Joseph, not short-trousers boy?

>> have you seen his trousers???

>> Yes, but we don't make fun of children because of how they dress, okay?

>> yeah okay no harm intended

>> All good. Anyone else?

This is obviously a sore topic for Saeed, but he's moving the conversation along, and Denny responds quickly.

>> Paid me a visit in my bedroom. Nice if he'd left when he saw me in my underwear, but we can teach him basic etiquette. Otherwise no problem.

>> i nominate V for etiquette lessons

>> Fuck no! Don't you think my raising one ten-year-old is enough?

Saeed interrupts again to bring some order back to the conversation. He's the youngest adult in the house, only just in his twenties, but sometimes he ends up being the voice of reason. Someone has to be, I guess.

>> Ok, sounds like he needs a bit of guidance but is settling in fine. Also, any ghost hunter issues?

>> none I know of

>> Neither. At least these ones seem to be kids who are just really curious, rather than the last lot with all their gear. Figured they could sell footage. Argh!

>> paranormal paparazzi!

>> Yeah. Maybe if these kids grow up and get over themselves a bit they could be okay. I mean, they like

ghosts, we have that in common. They're just not acting like they respect them as people right now.

Saeed brings the conversation back to the topic.

>> Ok, good. If no-one objects, we'll open another bottle today.

>> Sorry, can't help with this one. Have an interview to prep for.

>> Good luck Vinnie! Morgan, you in?

I respond to Saeed with an image showing a black cat raising a thumbs up

>> They have opposable thumbs now??? We're all doomed! Doomed!

>> Don't worry, Mallard will let you live. If she's in a good mood.

I put my phone down and grab my washbag and towels, head for the corner bathroom. It's the smallest of our functional bathrooms, but that means it's usually just me that uses it; no queue and no-one banging on the door as I try to shampoo my hair.

Half an hour and I'm in jeans and a dark green jersey, brushing out my thick dark hair. When I get to the kitchen, I'm delighted to find that someone's already put a pot of filter coffee on. I help myself, gulping it down black as always, and begin to feel functional again despite the early start.

I'm alone until Holly comes through in her school uniform, her eyes tired, grabbing herself some toast to eat on the way, but all around me I can feel the house wake up. Ghosts don't sleep, not as such, but there's a sense in which they're responsive to our patterns; more active when we are, and calmer while we sleep. Tim McCabe, in his too-short trousers and cloth cap, lingers in the kitchen with me for a bit, and I smile and nod in his direction. Finishing off my coffee, I head over to the alcove where Mallard's bowl is. As usual, she's there waiting and meows loudly as I approach as if she's in an advanced stage of starvation, not a cat with eight people to take care of her and as much regular feeding as any cat could wish for.

They say cats are more sensitive to ghosts, but I've never seen that in Mallard. I don't know whether she can't see the ghosts or whether she just sees no value in taking notice of someone who can neither pat you nor feed you biscuits.

Saeed emerges in his wheelchair, dressed in a shimmering gold top and bright purple jeans. His fine, black hair falls smoothly to just below his ears, each pierced with a single gold stud. I swallow, trying to find words.

"You look good. Is it a bad pain day?"

Saeed shrugs.

"Meh. More that I'm trying not to move my leg because my knee keeps subluxing. Joints are the worst. Abolish all joints."

I nod in sympathetic acknowledgement.

"Coffee?"

"Yeah, please."

I pass him a cup and then refill my own.

"You're ready to release ghost number two soon?" he asks, gulping the coffee as if it's his life force. It's certainly mine.

I nod and give him a thumbs up, then point at him. I try to ask 'you?' but the sound sticks in my throat leaving only the mouth shape. But he understands me.

"Sure. Just let me wake up properly first and I'm on to it. Who do you reckon we'll get this time?"

I spread my arms to indicate the range of possibilities. We both know it could be almost anyone inside that bottle. We both know that we'll welcome them, regardless.

Sufficiently caffeinated and our breakfast over, Saeed and I prepare to release the second ghost. I drag two of the three chairs out of the room – we want to release them in a space as uncluttered as possible so we don't overwhelm them.

The process is the same, only there are just the two of us doing it today. I'm not worried. After the success of the previous day, there's no reason to think we're dealing with anything more than a long-dead hobbyist's collection of ghosts. And while keeping them in these green-glass prisons feels desperately cruel to me, it's the sort of cruelty more likely to stem from ignorance than malice. I'm expecting plenty of confusion, some adjustment issues, maybe some expressions of distress, nothing more. And we've dealt with all of that before.

No bottle is calling to me, so I force myself to just pick one at random. I bring it back into the room, take out the box of matches from my pocket – I'm prepared this time – and then I remove the stopper and we wait. There's nothing to even indicate a ghost is in there. I force myself to be patient, even though I sometimes think patience is against my nature. I tell myself the ghost will emerge of its own accord.

If it doesn't, I will have to shake it out, which seems undignified but I don't suppose it's that bad compared to the indignity of being stuck in a bottle for centuries. Gravity seems to apply to ghosts irrespective of how corporeal, but it has only a fraction of the effect it has on people.

I'm twitchy and unfocused. Every second seems drawn out in to minutes. I hear Saeed's fidget spinner like it's a distant, high-pitched whine. Sometimes, I can spend hours staring at a wall, the same scenario or phrase or possibility repeating in my head. Other times, anything other than constant stimulation and immediate response is unbearable, and this is sure as hell one of those times. My whole body is moving, and it's taking all my effort just to stay seated on the chair.

There's still nothing happening with the bottle. Maybe there isn't even a ghost in there. Although... if there wasn't, there wouldn't be any point in sealing the stopper this thoroughly. Then again... what if there had been a ghost but it had faded into nothingness? The thought makes me a little uneasy, a little sad.

Some people think the lack of ghosts from earlier periods of history is a result of the smaller total population at that time. They're not entirely wrong. But ghosts, just like living people, have a limited amount of time on Earth. They fade, eventually, to nothingness. There are variations in how corporeal they are to start with and how quickly they fade, but there are norms. The oldest ghosts we have reliable reports of is about 1200 years old. Six to seven hundred years is a more typical maximum. Over time they grow fainter and fainter until there's little to distinguish them from the air, and then they... go. Perhaps into nothingness. Perhaps into some kind of afterlife, for those who believe in that kind of thing.

I know that, from one perspective, every human is on a path towards oblivion. But that's a thought you can usually put to one side. With ghosts they are fading bit by bit, year by year, and even though it's too slow to notice I still find myself making comparisons, asking myself if they are a bit more translucent than they used to be. Ghosts may not be human exactly, but they are people. People we live with. People who we care for, who are our friends even though that friendship may be a different type of friendship to that which we have with each other.

Sometimes it's hard to know they're fading.

I can't wait for this ghost to emerge any longer. It feels like every part of me is crawling with insects, twitching and alive. I get up from my seat and lean forward, not touching the bottle but looking directly down into it.

I blink a couple of times. There's definitely something in there. Maybe it can't get out, or maybe it's simply choosing not to emerge. I squat down, peering in deeper...

...and suddenly everything emerges all at once, the ghost shooting right out of the bottle and taking his full form almost immediately. I leap back, startled, desperately trying to catch my breath.

Out of the corner of my eye, I see Saeed decide not to mock me. It's a good thing he has some self-preservation instincts.

The ghost is a man, perhaps in his mid-thirties or a little older. He's dressed in a coat with metal buttons close together running up the front, a sash over his coat, and a plain helmet. A soldier of some kind, then. Saeed frowns as if he's pursuing some half-forgotten piece of knowledge and gets out his phone, frantically searching, double checking his suspicions. Then he turns to me and explains:

"Definitely civil war," he says.

I nod. I'd thought as much, even if I'm not that aware of many other wars that happened before the twentieth century.

"What side?" I ask.

Saeed shakes his head.

"That's the messy thing. They basically wore the same type of clothes, very confusing on the battlefield. If I could tell what colour the sash was, that would give me a strong indication, but even that's not certain. I'm sure he'll be delighted that I can explain modern parliamentary democracy to him though."

I have to look at Saeed to check he's joking. It's not always certain with these things, and though he tries his best, he's not always good at gauging people's level of interest – or lack thereof – once he gets going on one of his pet topics. And history, politics, and international relations are totally his thing!

Before we can discuss any further, though, the ghost has moved right through the door. Usually when people say through the door, they mean through the doorway. I really mean through the door. We don't even try and call him back – it's clear he's walking with a purpose and will not be responsive. We'll give it a couple of hours and then follow up.

And with any luck, someone else will get tasked with finding a name for him.

Araminta's got us in to watching a new legal drama. It's not really my thing, and to be honest it's not something I'd usually think of as hers, but we're enjoying it, and it's making good use of my large screen. We've made ourselves nachos – and by nachos, I mean we heated a can of chilli beans and split it across two plates of corn chips, grating cheese on top before melting it in the microwave. We're huddled together in a nest of beanbags and blankets at the foot of my bed, the fan heater aimed directly at us, cuddled up close. I'm always a little surprised at how much I want human contact, having spent so many years rejecting it.

I was scared of bodies once, mostly my own. Scared of their inconsistencies. I liked mechanics, metal and smooth surfaces, easy repair and maintenance, constructions that followed blueprints and well-thought-out designs. I was repulsed, always, by flesh and blood, by squishiness and unevenness. My own, mostly, but the thought of two bodies anywhere near each other was more than I could bear.

It was hard to eat when I felt like that, and often I didn't. I struggled for years with it and I still long, sometimes, to be a mechanical being. I still envy the most non-corporeal of the ghosts; they are draped with shapes of skin and flesh, yes, but nothing squishes or oozes; they are the same consistency right through. It wasn't that I needed to be thin, like people said. I was never scared of fat. I was scared of the complexity of my own body. I was scared of not being able to define myself with clean lines and straight edges, of not understanding how I worked.

It's still hard sometimes, and I find it easier to cook than to eat, but now I feel like I can fold my body around Araminta's and everything feels right.

When the second episode of the night finishes, I stretch myself up.

"One minute," I say.

Araminta nods and settles herself down under the blanket, sleepy. It's almost hard to leave her, even for a moment.

The lights are off in the hallway and I use my phone light to avoid bumping into random cats or ghosts as I go. Holly's bedroom is on the same floor as mine but on the other side, past the central staircase. Like Araminta, she chose her suite for the natural light, but while Araminta needs it for painting, I worry that it might be the only way Holly would get any sunlight, stuck at her desk at all hours.

True to form, when Holly answers my knock at her door, she's red-eyed with exhaustion. Her laptop, one of the few items she was able to take with her when she fled her parents' house early one morning last June, is open and surrounded by file paper and notebooks heavy with equations in different colours. A diagram of the human heart and something that looks like it relates to climate change, every part labelled, are pinned on the wall in front of her desk.

I don't need to talk or type, or even gesture. I just smile and look at the desk. I admit I'm a hypocrite when it comes to the idea of getting to be early – we'll probably be awake at least another couple of hours given that Araminta isn't scheduled on tomorrow. But if I stay up late, I'll sleep late, or catch up a few days later. It balances out. There's no balance in Holly's life, and we all know that that's not going to change.

"I know, I know," she says. We've done this before. "I just have to get through this biology revision..."

I've already picked up her towel and her toothbrush. I don't always feel entirely comfortable having taken on this role – Holly is hardly a small child after all, and she's pretty tough to have come through what she has. But if she told me not to do it again, in the clarity of daytime, I'd stop. As it is, I think she's reluctantly grateful to feel like she can stop without having to make the decision herself. And it's confirmation someone cares for her, which I know wasn't always the case. It's like there's a wordless agreement between the two of us. We know where we stand.

Satisfied that Holly's finally on her way to bed, I head back down the corridor in the dark. I see the shape before I can make out the person; white wisps in the darkness, floating right head of me, in a standing pose in the middle of the corridor, near my bedroom. Her legs are a little apart, her arms folded. She's staring down the corridor at me.

It's not quite as unpleasant as when a living human tries to force eye contact, but it's up there.

Lydia Martin. One of Casswell Park's original ghosts. Most likely to be found on one of the balconies, but she could be anywhere, and tonight she's here. Saeed's found a story that matches her; a servant girl found drowned, likely intentionally, in the pond that was once a central feature of the gardens. If that had happened to me, there's a good chance I'd come across a bit creepy too.

She watches me, unblinkingly, as I slide past her. You'd think that because I live with ghosts, because I've seen them all my life, I wouldn't be scared of them. In some ways that's true; I don't think they will do me harm, or that they're usually malevolent; they're just people, just part of the world we live in. But that doesn't mean I don't get creeped out by them sometimes.

"Lydia again," Araminta asks when I open the door. Mallard has taken my seat, predictably.

I nod, take out my phone and type.

>> And I think something is up with Isobel. Didn't like new ghost.

"Jealous older sibling syndrome? Isobel's one of my favourites. She'll get over it."

>> Y. It's always an adjustment.

I put the phone away, hoist Mallard onto my shoulder, cuddle up to Araminta and hit play on a new episode. Our plates are stacked beside us – I'll take them down in the morning (and I probably actually will; I'm much better at things like that than I used to be). I open a can of cola from the tiny fridge by my bookshelves and offer it to Araminta, then take one for myself, and everything is comfortable and everything is right.

CHAPTER FOUR

A lison has roped us into stripping, painting, and rehanging the doors from the upper level, taking advantage of a spot of crisp, clear weather. I'm not complaining, and neither is Araminta. It's the sort of work that gets you out of the endless loops of your brain and holds the promise of a satisfying conclusion, muscle aches aside.

We're up and dressed early, in old work clothes which means I'm in a jersey with holes in the elbows and Araminta's unusually wearing jeans. She normally exists in dresses, and while they're totally not my style most of them are amazing printed designs in bright colours and homemade, and I love them.

We start with the bedroom doors because we need to make sure they're dry and ready to rehang before the evening, even if we need to take them down again later for a second coat. I'm not sure anyone in this house could handle sleeping in a room without a door – not me, and certainly not Araminta. If necessary, I'll borrow one of the spare rooms we have set up for visitors, but I doubt I'd get much sleep.

We've agreed that Araminta will get started outside while Alison and I get the first batch of doors off their hinges, but when I go to Araminta's bedroom, she's already taken her door down. I'm about to say that she should have waited, that I'd have given her a hand, when I see the sheet taped across the hallway to her bedroom, and I understand.

I have always needed private space. Araminta games with me in my bedroom but only when invited, and she never stays the night. Sleeping together is always a euphemism and never literal in our relationship – and that happens in my room, or sometimes in one of the spare rooms, furniture shoved against the door. Once in the orangerie, our bodies barely hidden behind the outdoor furniture, but we know better than to repeat that particular episode.

Anyway, what I'm saying is that I need privacy, but for Araminta it rises to a whole other level. I've been in the studio part of her suite precisely three times. The room is a brilliant blur of colour, cut-offs of vinyl spread over the floor because they're easy to wipe down. All around are easels, stacks of paint, and sketches pinned to the walls. Different sizes of brushes stored in cups and vases. Aerosols and sponges and boxes of pastels. Floor lamps with daylight bulbs. I know how hard she's worked to build up this collection, saving from her part-time job and benefits, the very occasional sale of a painting, waiting for sales and discounts.

I've never seen her bedroom.

I half-understand why. I know bits of it because she's told me. Her ability to draw was withheld as part of her therapy for years – she was only allowed a pencil after completing tasks for hours on end. Looking into their eyes no matter how much it hurt and not crying. Repeating the same script over and over, because scripting is apparently fine when it's "fine, thank you, how are you?" over and over, and an aberration when you're quoting from a movie. So Araminta always knew that expressing interest in something instantly meant it was restricted, reframed not as a hobby or a pastime or even just her playing but as a punishment and reward, a tool for forcing her into something she never was. Even now there's a deep terror that if she lets on how important it is to her then it will all be taken away, and so she plays it down, doesn't talk about it in any way which could betray her enthusiasm.

She's so careful not to show too much of herself, so any space where she can be herself has to be completely cut off from everyone else.

Sometimes I want a normal life, so I can prove everyone wrong. Even for me – but much more so for Araminta – success has been linked to being like everyone else. I feel like if we could have a normal apartment, with a couple of kids, if I could have gone to university like my brother and had a normal job, then I'd be able to prove everyone wrong who said I had no future.

I think that less and less these days, but sometimes I still wonder if I'm here because I want to be, or just because I can't live alone. I wonder whether, if Araminta had not been treated so horribly, she would want this or would she want us to have a little cottage together; a shared bedroom and lavender round the door. I wonder if she'd even want me.

Sometimes, it's hard to tease out who you are and the shape of the person you've been moulded, even beaten, into being.

I worry about all this sometimes, but right now I'm in the winter air outside of our house with a sander in my hand and I can't think of anything I'd want more than to be here with the people I love and the ghosts I feel bound to protect.

The doors are propped up on a couple of folding tables, a step ladder, and some of the older chairs that are already in a bad state. Tim McCabe is lurking in the doorway, and I can see the face of Jodie Keane in an upstairs window, and through the glass, she looks almost like she could be still alive. The weather is cold, but the air is still enough to have lost its bite, and the sun provides a touch of winter warmth from a clear blue sky.

All the doors are covered with chipped paint and scratches; some of them have graffiti or other damage – this was a boarding school, after all. We've been improving the house bit by bit; this is just one stage among many. We'd love to do a total renovation; pull up the carpets and replace them, add insulation, repaint everything, but there's no way we can afford it. Even repatching the roof has had to be haphazard.

Araminta begins layering the varnish on, evenly and free of streaks. I don't have that level of motor control so I stick to sanding for now. It's a satisfying job, both destructive and restorative. all at once.

I know most people here wouldn't be able to tolerate the noise of the electric sander, but I like how it shudders in my hand, the repetition of noise and movement as I bring it down the doors in long, even swoops. Alison and Araminta both have their noise cancelling headphones on, and probably earplugs under those. I'll need to get mine before too long. People think there's a neat division between sensory avoidance and sensory seeking and sure, some people find their experiences all fit neatly into one category or the other. But for me, it's more a case of every sensory input being intensified. Sometimes I can like something right up until the point it quickly becomes overwhelming.

Which is pretty much how I feel about spending time with people, if I'm honest.

I keep going with the sanding as long as I can, though. I don't have Vinnie's strength or Alison's stamina; I'm a stereotypical pasty-skinned gamer in many ways, but sometimes... sometimes I like doing this sort of physical work. I like the repetition, the movement of it, putting my whole body into something and receiving tangible, physical evidence that I'm achieving something.

We work on the doors over two full days, up early and working until it gets dark. On the second day, Theo arrives home from school a bit before four. He's been declared old enough to walk home by himself, and he's pretty damn proud of it. He's dressed only in his uniform polo shirt and grey trousers – his sweatshirt is tied loosely round his waist and his coat is nowhere to be seen. And to think people hassle me for not dressing for the cold.

"You'd better not have been watching out for me," he says, running up and then skidding to a halt of the soles of his – new – school shoes. Vinnie will be delighted to find those ruined halfway through the year.

"Oh, we have far more important things to think about than you!" Alison says teasingly. "How was school?"

"Miss Rodriguez farted in class. And Nevaeh Tyler put a padlock on the bridge of Jackson Patel's glasses and they had to get the caretaker to come and cut it off."

"Sounds like a brilliant day! Did you learn anything?"

"Yes! How to cut padlocks off glasses!"

"I'm sure that will serve you very well in your future life. Vinnie's at work, they'll be home in an hour or two. Are you ok to get yourself a snack?"

"I'm going to have string cheese and mini carrots and a cookie." He pauses to see if there will be a negative response, testing us. There is none. I think the only food rule I've heard him taught has been to say "no thank you" rather than "ew yuck", which is honestly something I suspect a lot of adults could benefit from.

"Ok," Alison replies. "Out of your uniform first though, so you can wear it tomorrow."

We hear Theo's feet clatter up the wooden staircase, fast and deliberately loud. I turn to smile at Araminta, but she's looking over at where Theo was, distracted. I know she wants children, not now but one day. I also know she's terrified by the possibility. And I'm honestly not sure how I feel.

Theo's soon back, dressed in his tracksuit bottoms and a football shirt, munching very loudly on his carrots and taking a careful look at our efforts with the doors, closely inspecting them as if he's an expert in the subject.

"Going to my dad's this weekend," he says, proudly. "He's got four days off in a row, and he's going to take me to Alton Towers. We'll leave really early and get there before the crowds which means we can do all the best rides without having to queue. We have a plan!"

Theo's father is – as Theo's very proud of telling people – an airline pilot. He flies long haul, which means the time he spends with Theo doesn't usually fit a regular pattern, and not by his choice; I think in many ways he'd rather never be away from his son. That was part of the reason Vinnie stayed so long, wanting to make it easier for Theo to have as much time with both parents as possible – well that, and the two of them are still good friends even though any other kind of relationship may be long dead.

That means that when Theo does stay with his father for a few days, it's all about the quality time. This is clearly no exception.

"That will be really fun," says Araminta. "And you're not at all scared of the rides?"

Theo shakes his head firmly.

"Not even if you go upside down?" Alison asks.

Theo hesitates before speaking.

"No! Not scared of anything... how long though... how long do they keep you upside down?"

"Oh, I'm not sure. Usually just a few hours, I think. Only occasionally overnight."

Theo's eyes go wide and then just as Araminta begins to interject to tell Alison to leave the kid alone, Theo says, "I don't believe you." Swinging his arms to add emphasis, and Alison laughs and admits her lie.

"Seriously, though. If you don't want to go on a ride, you can just say so, it's all good. Everyone's a bit scared of something."

"My dad's not scared of anything."

"Oh, I bet he is. You ask him this weekend what he's scared of. I bet you he'll tell you something."

"Bet me how much?'""

"Oh uh... fifty pence?'""

"Two pounds"

Alison rolls her eyes but holds out her right hand. "It's a deal."

We get back to work. Callum – one of the few people I've developed a relationship with from the paranormal forums – has been messaging me on and off. I slip into a routine of doing some sanding, checking and sending messages, before another block of sanding. There's some activism going on around a haunted asylum that's being turned into a tourist attraction. A lot of the people are coming from a disability rights point of view and don't actually believe in ghosts, but making sure they're safe is his chief concern.

And as I'm someone who is well acquainted with ghosts, autistic, and someone who has social anxiety – and lives with a bunch of people who have similar experiences – Callum is optimistic about the quality of advice and insight I can provide. I think he is hoping for something more philosophical than what I give him, which is essentially a calculation of how many of their ghosts we could offer sanctuary to.

Not long after, Saeed emerges. His dress is more casual than normal, which – intentionally or otherwise – correlates with it being less femme, less dramatic. He's wearing a soft blue t-shirt with a pink quartz pendant, and has some bangles above his wrist brace. He stands and looks at us, an announcement obviously prepared.

"Attention everyone. This is a ghost update."

I turn off the sander, stand up and stretch as Saeed speaks.

"I have checked in with all four of the new ghosts. Joseph, who is if you all recall, about ten years old and from about the late seventeenth century, is settling in very easily and shows no sights of his earlier anxiety. Hannah is late seventeenth or early eighteenth century, probably just a few years before Joseph. She's in her mid-twenties and, unusually, literate. Not just for a woman of that era, but for any ghost. I suspect some with a low level of literacy probably lost it at death, and it's only those who read frequently who retained it, same as memory and some other cognitive functions seem to be depleted. Anyway, Hannah flew straight for any piece of text she could find, as if that was the obvious tool she would use to make sense of this world, and of her new circumstances. So, we took her to the letter boards we use with Roderick and she was able to tell us her name and a few other bits of information. We're working on finding out who she was and if any records of her survive. We suspect she came from a reasonably well-off family, which increases the chances of records. Anyway, she is also doing well – very focused.

"The next ghost, we're calling Lavinia – it probably wasn't her name but she seemed comfortable enough with it. Lavinia's in her twenties or thirties, very old – probably medieval. She's struggling a bit, I think. It may be her age, but she seems a little sad and doesn't know how to speak to me. So yes, a kind word to her if you see her would probably be really appreciated, and of course message the group chat, or me directly, should you spot anything else up with her."

I'm shuffling from one foot to another. I know it's rude but heaps of things are probably rude by some standard or another. And this does feel like it's been going on forever.

"Lastly," continues Saeed, "we have a civil war soldier. He doesn't have a name yet, and finding him one will be our first priority. His dress is quite distinctive, so you shouldn't have any difficulty recognising him.

"While two of those seem a bit confused, there are no signs of particular distress in any of the ghosts, new or existing. I have limited means of talking to them, as you know, but I have spoken to the two ghosts we generally consider most able to communicate, Roderick and Jodie, and they've both answered 'no' when I asked if there were significant issues. So far, I think this whole thing has been a success. So tomorrow we'll release ghost number five, and then take a short break as I know we have some visitors expected over the weekend. I plan to resume next week, assuming no problems crop up, continuing with one release a day, but possibly considering stepping that up to two – though at separate times and in separate rooms. Any objections or questions?"

I smile and raise a thumbs up to Saeed, the sandpaper still in my hand and the dust starting to irritate my nose. There will be more ghosts here, and we will welcome them all.

Kneeling on the floor, I hold the bottle firmly in my hand. It feels heavier than the others. I move it slowly, curiously, keeping it upright. There's something inside it. Something solid.

Something that rattles.

I feel myself wince, imagining being trapped inside a bottle and being shaken against its glass sides. I look at Saeed.

"That sounds like an unusually corporeal ghost," he says. "Uh, try the usual to start with?"

It's become a well-practiced routine. I take out the lighter Araminta brought home from work for me, and melt the wax until the stopper loosens. Then, I take the stopper off the bottle, leave it on the floor, and together we wait.

It's not long before a ghost stretches out. Their emergence is slow, but they seem to be making many smaller, fast movements at the same time: twitching, flowing, flickering. It takes a few minutes before the ghost is person-shaped. I place her at about fourteen. Good quality clothes, but simpler than those I've seen on many of the older ghosts. There's definite fear on her face and she doesn't linger; just as I move to gently approach her, she shoots through the wall and is gone.

I turn to Saeed in shock.

"Unexpected," I say, curling my tongue around each syllable. "She looked really scared."

"Yeah. Much more so than the others. They seemed more... surprised and confused. There was real terror in her face. Still... maybe we'll give her a bit of time alone and then check on her?"

I give him the thumbs up. After a pause, he wheels forward slightly, leans and picks up the bottle, rattling it gently.

"There's still something in there."

He turns the bottle upside down, pokes at it with a finger. He manages to pull the long, fine, tarnished-silver chain out from the bottle, but there's something attached, something that won't quite fit through the neck.

"Can you break the bottle?" he asks me. "We're not going to get it out otherwise."

"Sure?"

"Yeah. We have plenty more bottles. Whatever this is could give us a clue as to who these ghosts are. Where they came from. What they might need."

It's the idea of being better able to provide for the ghosts that sways me. I nod and quickly walk out of the room, keeping an eye out for the newly released ghost. There's no sign of her. I grab a hammer from the toolkit in the laundry and find a copy of a free paper someone will have picked up on a train or something. I spread the sheets of newspaper a couple of layers deep on the floor and then reach up to grab the bottle from Saeed.

Kneeling in front of the newspaper, I tap the bottle with the hammer, gently at first, and then harder.

Despite the thickness of the glass, it doesn't take much for it to shatter. Shards of glass glisten, freshly-broken edges shatter across the newspaper.

I see a flash of something that is a deep red and then it's as if the air is thick and a shadow whirls round and round in front of me. I rub my eyes, unsteady.

I look down at the glass.

And there, right in the middle, is a pendant.

I pick it up, gently, not knowing what condition it's in, but surprisingly it has only a little tarnish and otherwise seems undamaged. It's a hexagonal shape with a large circular hole in the middle, thicker around the internal edges as if it housed a gemstone within them, though there's nothing like that among the shards of glass. Both sides are intricately engraved; one with a series of overlapping circles, concentric with the space in the middle, that remind me of the orbits of planets. On the other side are symbols that appear to be writing of some kind, but not in any language I know of. Nothing about this pendant is like anything I've seen before, but Saeed says it seems oddly familiar.

"Maybe something I saw in a museum once. One moment."

Saeed asks me to hold it so he can take some photographs; he's planning to research where it's from and what the elements on it might symbolise. When he's done, I run my fingers back and forth along the chain. The sensation shudders all through me like the recognition of something half-forgotten.

"Um, Morgan, have you never seen a horror movie?" he asks. Mostly teasing, a little serious. "Because when you find a mysterious pendant in a bottle with a ghost... well, be careful, please."

I laugh and swipe my hand at him, then kneel to wrap the broken glass in newspaper and take the whole package to one of the outside bins. We're not in a horror movie and there's nothing malevolent in these bottles, just ghosts as much in need of a home as we are. And in this pendant, clutched between my fingers, I feel energy and love.

We get by better than some people, in a world where austerity seems to translate to letting disabled people die. But it's been a while since I've had the funds to get Araminta anything to show how much I love her. And this is just perfect.

1704

I sobel cannot start a fire with a blink of her eye like her sister, does not know visitors are coming long before they arrive like her brother does, but she can carry sacks of flour to the cart as if they were as light as feathers. She can leap down to free the water wheel when it gets jammed by sticks or rocks or a stormy night. She has no magic, or whatever it is that runs in her family, but she has the benefit of a broad frame and muscles built up over her fourteen years, and she's as sure-footed as Mouse, the black and white cat who lives in the mill, sleeping by the sacks of grain.

She's also friends with a ghost.

There have always been stories about the mill being haunted; about a man killed by a millstone dropping on his head, a young woman drowned in the millpond, but they're vague tales, devoid of details and tinged with a fear that has never matched the reality for her.

She calls the ghost Tobias, because he cannot tell her his real name but she thinks the one she has chosen suits him. He's never shown any signs of wanting to hurt or even harm anyone, and Isobel has no fear. If she gets a free hour on a Sunday, after church and chores, she sits with him by the stream, laying her head back in the grass, dipping her toes in the water. They do not need words to connect them.

CHAPTER FIVE

I wake up late, am still in my dressing gown when I head to the kitchen to make myself a coffee. There's a smell like warm bread flowing down the hallway. Someone is way more of a morning person than I am.

Alison's in the kitchen, already dressed – and well-dressed at that, in a heavy velvet skirt with a green top, her hair brushed and make-up carefully applied. She's what my mother would call *well put together* on a bad day; today she looks flawless, but traditional. It's her 'mum' look.

"Matt's visiting me for lunch," she says, confirming my guess as she leans against the counter. "He's driving through on a work trip. Haven't seen him in way too long."

"How..." I pause, search again for the words. "How is he doing...?"

Alison swallows a mouthful of scone.

"He's doing well. His youngest starts school in September, would you believe? Scone?"

I help myself to one from the wire rack and suddenly shiver. It's a marked difference in temperature, enough to make me instinctively clutch my arms around my chest.

"You okay?" Alison asks. "My baking isn't that bad, I promise you."

I take a couple of steps further back. The temperature here isn't exactly warm – it's January in a near-unheatable old house, after all – but when I step back it's much more the type of cold I expect. I walk forward to the scones and it hits again. Alison's looking at me curiously.

"It's nothing," I say at last. "Just a weird feeling. Your scones look really good."

I help myself to one and they are: cheese and herb and spring onion, crumbly without being too dry. I know Alison's kids found her transition, especially happening so soon after her divorce, difficult, but things seem to have fully settled down and she has a good relationship with all of them. I'm pretty confident they lucked out when it comes to baking too.

I grin at Alison, giving a thumbs up to indicate – truthfully – that they're delicious.

"Do you want to take some to Holly? She's in the dining room with a couple of her classmates. Working on a project."

I fill up a small plate, and after a moment's thought grab a couple of large packets of crisps and some chocolate from the cupboard; we buy what's on special and stockpile. The dining room door is ajar but I knock gently before walking in.

It's almost as if Holly cloned herself. The other girls may not be the same size or have the same colouring as her, but they all have the same tightly plaited hair and the same expressions of deep concentration. The table is spread with pages of equations and graphs, all three of them with both laptops and graphing calculators in front of them, deeply immersed in their study.

I'm just glad they have found each other.

I leave the snacks and tell them they should grab tea or coffee whenever they want, then leave them to their study. I wonder how much Holly has told them about the ghosts, and if either of her friends will be able to see them. I'm pretty sure she's sensible enough to have warned them; they may be in for a shock if not.

Alison's son and Holly's friends aren't this weekend's only visitors; Saeed's sister Hana is also stopping over on her way back to uni. I'll help him make up one of the spare rooms for her later.

I never would have thought I would be happy in a place with people coming and going; as a child, even my grandmother's visits would throw me off course for weeks. But we make it work, and there's space enough for everyone to have privacy. We have a calendar on the wiki for visitors so there are no surprises and we have the chance to prepare, find out more information, or make ourselves scarce. Bathroom queues are really the only problem; we have plenty of space for the bathrooms we need, but the work required to make them operational needs a licensed plumber and, therefore, money which we don't have.

Saeed and his sister are fraternal twins. They don't look much alike physically, aside from the same mid-brown skin with what Araminta calls yellow-gold undertones, and the same black hair. Their dress separates them further; Saeed's style being some sort of dramatic glam femme while Hana is feminine, but all about clean lines, well-tailored clothes from good quality fabrics, rich but dark colours. When it comes to personality, though, the similarities shine through.

In the evening Denny, Araminta, and I join them, opening a couple of bottles of not-particularly-fancy but entirely drinkable wine, and sit around the dining table talking and drinking.

Hana's major is modern political science, but that doesn't mean she isn't interested in the historical research Saeed's been doing. She sees just enough of the ghosts to be convinced they're there; indistinct, semi-translucent shapes. She couldn't tell them apart from each other, let alone make out facial features or details of clothing; hell, she probably wouldn't even recognise them as humanoid without context, but she knows enough to understand.

She and Saeed talk back and forth, barely waiting for each other to finish their sentences. Saeed talks louder with her than he does with us, verging on combative, but Hana gives as good as she gets. It's clear this style of discussion, almost debate, has been well practised between the two of them.

After a while Hana pours herself another glass of wine and visibly calms her tone.

"Sorry," she says. "Siblings who haven't caught up in so long. Araminta, I hear you're an artist. Is that your work up there?"

I recognise the strategic conversation starter; Araminta's initials are clear in the bottom right corner of the painting, so Hana obviously knows she is. It's a change from her usual semi-abstract landscapes, depicting a range of kitchen equipment – spatulas and lemon zesters and pastry brushes. At first glance it looks like they've been strewn haphazardly on a surface or in a drawer, but when you look closer you realise they're impossible – or they connect to each other in impossible ways. Sometimes they're connected in a way that indicates they must have been manufactured together and thus unusable, but at other times they're almost Escher-like in their illusionary state, defying all known laws of physics.

Araminta smiles and bows her head.

"I try to be. Mostly I work in a shop though. It's hard to make money from art."

Hana nods, taking a sip. She's taken a pen out of her handbag and is spinning it round her fingers. I'll tell Saeed he needs to get her a fidget spinner like his for her next birthday.

"It must be tough. But your work is really good. I'm sure you'll make it."

The discussion carries on about Araminta's art a little more. She's shy about it, but not terribly uncomfortable, as she sometimes can be – I'd shut down the conversation if that was the case. We talk about Hana's study too – she's beginning her Masters, and talking about going overseas for her PhD. Her life feels like high-achieving normality stretching out into the distance along a well-trodden pathway. I wonder what I could have done; I know that it wasn't that I was bad at school exactly, because when I could work alone, was allowed to wear headphones, and wasn't expected to speak, I got good grades. I could never do what she's doing, but I could maybe have done something else, in a different world.

Hana doesn't talk down to me though, and she's happy to wait when I struggle to get the words out, and to carry the conversation when I can only manage a few syllables. She asks me questions about the game mods I've been working on, as though they are just as important and valid as anything she does. Denny vents a little about the ghost hunters, though we haven't heard from them in a week or two. Together we all talk and drink well into the night, though Araminta leaves us early so she can get a full night's sleep before work, and by the early hours of the morning when I head up to bed, I'm comfortable and happy and pleasantly drunk.

In the morning, I get up late (I hold the wine responsible) and most people are either at work or school or engaged in other plans for the day. Vinnie has a temp job, and Alison's messaged the group chat to say she's got a day's work helping this family from America unpack their container and set up their new home.

Alison has this casual odd-jobs business which seems to be the most sustainable way for her to make a bit of money – money she can get away with not declaring, no less – and besides, she's good at it. Being up on a roof, hauling and stacking firewood, or mowing lawns, any of them suits her. Once she was paid quite well to remove a dead mouse from this guy's home – he was petrified of it. We're all precariously employed at most, but Alison is making things work for her as best she can.

Still in my dressing gown, and feeling a little the worse for wear if not exactly hungover, I head downstairs. There's no sign of Mallard so I assume he's already got someone else to feed him. But something in one of the empty rooms I pass makes me pause. There's a ghost in there and I can tell he's unhappy. I walk in tentatively. He's a young man in military uniform, who was able to tell us his name and little more.

Fletcher isn't a ghost I've had much interaction with before now. He's not one who already haunted the house before Denny set up the sanctuary, but he arrived before I did. Now I walk tentatively, gently towards him. He reminds me of someone, the first ghost I ever saw.

At least, the first one I remember seeing. My parents say sometimes they would hear me babbling through the baby monitor as if someone was in the room, and perhaps there was, but the first time I remember was a little after my fifth birthday. I filled in the details later, with my parents' help: my grandma was sick and mum had gone to be with her, taking Rory, so when my dad was called in to work there was no-one else to take care of me. And no-one but him who could persuade the ghost to move on from the railway line.

Sadly, the railways see a lot of sudden deaths. Most of them at least semi-deliberate, though often the coroner will record an accidental or open verdict if there's a hint of doubt. It's not just terrible for the person who dies and their family: it's terrible for the driver, and it's terrible for whoever has to remove the body from the tracks. And sometimes even that's not the end of the story.

They tell you sometimes that the line is closed because the police need to check it out, make sure there was no crime involved, stuff like that. Well, it's half true. This time, the ghost hadn't been problematic initially and they'd reopened the line quite quickly. Then he'd started behaving a bit weird – the usual floating around and wailing. Then, two days after his death, he flew right through the carriage of a late-night express. Initially, most of the passengers just thought the air-conditioning had malfunctioned, but enough of them started freaking out about ghosts to cause a bit of a panic. Something needed to be done, and soon.

Dad strapped me into the back of the old Honda and we drove down the dark roads to the small crossing. Branches brushed against the car. I peppered him with questions: what is a ghost? what is death? did Auntie Janet become a ghost? you know when grandma says dead people go to heaven? well, are they ghosts in heaven or before that? Another parent would likely have lied to me. My parents, well, they weren't like other parents.

"Why is there a ghost here?" I asked, as we pulled up to the crossing.

Dad took a deep breath, and said something like this.

"Well, someone died crossing the train tracks and their ghost is stuck here and unhappy, so we need to help it. That's why you need to be very careful at ungated crossings."

He was doing well at getting more than one lesson into the evening.

At first, I couldn't hear or see anything. I was cold and the ground was wet and I was in pyjamas under my coat. I wanted to go home. But instead we looked down the tracks, together, into darkness. It was a darkness that felt like it could swallow me up.

I remember the ghost approaching all at once. I was overwhelmed, but I wasn't scared. Perhaps that's because I'd never been taught that ghosts were something to be scared of. Perhaps it's because he was scared himself. He was a young man, nineteen or twenty, though I just thought of him as a grown-up at that time. Dad painted his death as an accident, but in retrospect I'm pretty sure he'd intended it. I could tell, even then, what his expression said. It said that there was no point any more.

It's the same expression I see now, almost quarter of a century later, on this same ghost, another young man, who is in an empty room of the giant haunted house where I live.

You'd have your moments too, if you'd died before your time, probably violently, and then you'd been left to linger in this changing world, neither alive nor properly dead, never at rest, while everyone you knew died. Through the centuries, watching wars unfold. It would mess you up a bit.

So back here, back home, a quarter of a century and so many ghost encounters later I sit down on the floor with this young man, this man who died so young, leaning against the radiator, pulling my knees to my chest, and we just sit there together for a while. Sometimes you don't need to speak to understand each other.

We had plenty of time, before I came here, to get this room ready for me. Dad caught the train down with me on the weekend and we added a lock to the door, repainted everything, and he got a friend to get some carpet cheap and help us lay it. I sewed up some dark green velvet-like curtains, floor-length to stop too much heat escaping, and sewed in large gold hoops to hang around a rail. The bed and drawers and shelving I already owned, and I dug into my savings to buy some beanbags.

Mum couldn't get the time off work and Rory wasn't as used to ghosts, so it was Dad who insisted on going to a Travelodge even though Alison offered him a spare room – he couldn't possibly trouble her like that, and bought me breakfast all teary-eyed and proud before dropping me back at Casswell and then driving home.

Other parents might look at me and consider me a failure. They'd note that I'd stayed at home until my mid-twenties, that I had only the most basic qualifications, that I'd probably never go to uni or have what they call a real job, though I pick up bits of money online when I can. They'd be confused about what my dad could be proud of or celebrating, except for getting me out from under his feet, I guess.

And though there were a lot of uncertainties, and still are, I knew from that point on that ghosts were always going to be an important part of my life.

From here on my bed this room feels like home. I don't feel like a prisoner because I can't go out often, even though some people worry about how much I stay at home. It's not like I never go out – I go to karate and sign language class with Araminta; if someone can't drive me to karate, I get a taxi. Araminta and I go shopping sometimes too, or to a movie. If I visit my parents someone takes me to the station and someone collects me at the other end. I make it work. In fact, for someone who can't go out much this is almost the perfect situation for me.

It's cars I struggle with most. They work to rules, or they're meant to, except those rules are vague and some of them are routinely disregarded. I get stressed when I'm around them. They take all my concentration just to try and work out, and if I spend all my energy on that then I don't have any for other things, like not tripping over and not getting lost.

Trains, trains I understand instinctively. If they're not running to timetable, I can bring up an explanation in my head for why and I can map out potential scenarios from that. There are patterns of logic and possibility I can follow, even when there are delays, that simply aren't there if I'm trying to cross a road or even walk alongside it.

Right now, though, I'm home safe, in this space I've created for myself in the middle of a space we've created for ourselves.

It's not static either. From here, lying on my bed with my laptop, zoning out by going through forum after forum – an established way of calming myself and alleviating the sensory overload of the day, so much so it's almost like stimming – I can see how the room around me has changed. It's not just the extra shelving I put in or my new consoles. It's the little things I've collected and rearranged. There's a painting Araminta did of St Briavels Castle – a haunted building now turned into a youth hostel which we visited last year, fulfilling a longstanding ambition of mine – on the wall above my bed. There are a few photos of us both as well, pinned on a corkboard along with some of the family photos I'd printed out and taken with me, and a few pieces of information I need to have at hand and for which, oddly, no app seems to work for storing.

I'm looking up at this corkboard, grinning at some of the goofier pictures of Araminta and I, when I hear a voice in the background.

~ghosts... collected... studied~

The voice comes out of nowhere, distant and indistinct. I'm instantly alert, trying to make out sound among the nothingness. Every noise, no matter how slight, seems suddenly heightened and yet I can hear no further words.

I open my door and look down the corridor. There's no-one in sight. I tell myself that it was just my imagination, that it was just the wind or the creaking of an old building, or that Theo had been yelling down the corridor and my brain interpreted his muffled distant words as something else.

I tell myself that it's just one of those things, an anomaly of the house or of my mind.

I know that it wasn't.

CHAPTER SIX

Araminta and I head out for dinner after our sign language class. It's not something we can often afford but there's a place that does a cheap roti chenai and lemon drink deal and it's much better food than the price would suggest. We're running over the day's vocabulary, muttering words and lightly forming the signs with our hands, trying to commit them to memory.

"I've got something for you," I say as I finish soaking up the last of my curry into the roti. My hands wiped, I take out the pendant which I've wrapped carefully in tissue paper and hand it to her.

"Where... where did this come from?" she asks. She turns it over, looks at the intricacy of the symbols. I tell her the story.

I don't think I'm disappointed by the fact that she knew I couldn't have bought it; mostly I'm just pleased I could get her something.

"It's beautiful," she says. "But... doesn't it belong to the ghost?"

The idea seems unimaginable – it was almost as if it was designed for Araminta. I reassure her that the ghost showed no interest – I might be hiding the fact that we saw no ghost at all, but it's not a lie. She clasps it round her neck – it's an old school hook clasp, and adjusts it into place. It's the perfect length, mid-way between her neck and the low-line of her dress.

I may have come across this by chance, but I don't think I could have chosen much better for her had I had money and a whole shop to choose from. It looks like she's glowing; her pale skin and her cheeks flushed from the cold now almost have a sense of luminescence about them. I bring my gaze back to her face and she's smiling.

It's possible to walk back to Casswell Park but it's cold and on the edge of rain so we wait for the bus that drops us on the edge of the new development, the former gardens of our current home. I'm exhausted. Leaving the house, even only a couple of times a week, takes everything out of me even though I enjoy it. I'm looking forward to the relative peace and quiet of home, or at least the ability to shut my door.

Joseph is hanging out near the front door, around the bushes that are the closest thing we have to gardens. He darts quickly in and out, grinning, and I almost imagine I hear him laughing to himself, or that there's another child with him. It's rare to see ghosts move so fast; I'm more used to the slow, almost disorientated float, the gentle glide past. But he's the youngest ghost we have – at least since the baby incident a year or two back – so perhaps things are different for him. And despite the fact my first thought is that it's past his bedtime (which may be another sign that the end of my twenties is approaching fast) I'm happy to see that he seems to be settling in.

He sees us and we wave to him, and he waves back before hightailing it up a tree. We enter the house and lock up behind us; he'll come in at some point, and locked doors won't make a bit of difference.

When I look up the back staircase, I can see Hannah and Isobel half way up, standing close together. They look like they're talking, except their mouths don't move, engaged in a deeply private conversation. It's a surprise to me to see such a new ghost so close with another, and

I motion Araminta to come with me, to take the main stairs, to leave them undisturbed.

As we walk I can see her smile, see how she keeps looking at the pendant, and it warms me, that such a simple gift – I didn't even have to choose it, it came ready delivered to me – has made us both so happy.

Up the stairs, and we linger in the hallway. I kiss her, our bodies against each other, let her just hold me for a moment before I reciprocate. Sometimes everything just feels perfectly right.

Having relinquished my hold on Araminta – she does, after all, have work in the morning – I'm starting a new game. It's an indie RPG, with surprisingly good graphics, and plenty of monsters to fight. I connect my laptop to the big wall-mounted monitor, drag some blankets over me, and lose myself easily in the story.

It's past midnight when I hear something, and everyone else is likely asleep. It's a distant rattling noise that rumbles below the soundtrack. It takes me a moment to realise it's not part of the game.

I take my headphones off. Nothing. I tell myself to stop being so silly, that if you're going to deliberately live in a house that is not just haunted but actively invites more ghosts in, you can't be easily spooked.

I'm less worried that something is amiss in the house, and more worried that I might actually have to change my sleep patterns. Institute sleep hygiene and all that other stuff, wake up early and go to bed before eleven. Even worse: admit that people who advocate that sort of nonsense are right.

It's over an hour before it happens again and this time the noise is unmistakable. It feels like everything is shuddering around me. I can't ignore it. My game sits paused mid-battle.

I grab my torch – anyone living in a house with electrics as bad as this keeps a torch by their bed, ghosts or no ghosts – and head into the corridor. The rattling rises in a crescendo and then falls to just a distant echo before growing again. My torchlight brings up shadows on the walls. Theo has left an alarming amount of stuff in this corridor for someone with little reason to even be in this part of the house, and it's amazing how even a nerf gun propped up on a table can cast a shadow that looks like some kind of malevolent creature.

I keep walking towards the stairwell. I can feel the vibrations under my feet, coming through the floor.

Rattling floorboards is a bit of a stereotype, frankly, but that doesn't mean it doesn't happen. And I know enough about ghosts to know there's one specific type that does it. We have a poltergeist on our hands.

Percentage of ghosts who are poltergeists: unknown, but low. Denny's speculated that poltergeists are those who had telekinetic powers, like he does, while they were alive. Saeed suggested killing him to test that theory, and for a brief moment I could tell Denny wasn't sure if he was serious.

It might be true that Saeed doesn't *quite* like information enough to kill for it, and if he did I'm confident it wouldn't be any of us.

Anyway, it – thankfully – isn't the ghost of any of my living housemates that stands before me now, but Hannah, one of our newest ghosts. She's facing me, but her gaze is looking intently at the wooden floorboards, causing them to shift and rattle loudly. Her arms, her fingers, are spread out to each side, as if she's using some power through those, and her gown is floating around her, as if in a strong breeze.

When she finally looks up and the floorboards fall back into place, it's not something ghostly I see on her face, but a very human expression. Fear.

From further down the hall I hear a door opening. I jump at the sound, but it's only Alison, in her lavender dressing gown and matching slippers, also carrying her torch. Hannah seems to have frozen to the spot; the floor is still, the house is quiet except for Alison's soft footsteps, but Hannah isn't leaving.

Alison comes around to stand by me, looks at Hannah.

"She looks scared," I say. I've always been okay with facial expressions, but I know most of the people I live with struggle more than I do, and I try to remember to interpret when it's necessary – and where it doesn't make things worse by freaking other people out.

"What's wrong, Hannah?" Alison asks. We know she won't understand exactly, know she's not likely to respond in a way we can understand, but hopefully, she'll know it's an expression of concern.

Isobel arrives through the air all at once, flying with her arms outstretched, at such speed I instinctively duck so I don't have the unpleasant experience of her flying right through my head. She stops, though, right before Hannah, her dress, noticeably simpler when placed in comparison to Hannah's, flares out as if it is subject to the laws of physics in the same way as it was when she was alive. She pays no attention to us, instead moving comfortably to Hannah, and guiding her through the wall to an unused bedroom.

It's a reminder to me that in some ways, yes, we are providing the ghosts sanctuary. But we have to remember it's not a dynamic that always works in a way where we help them. They help us. And they help each other.

With Hannah seemingly calmed and nothing else I can do, I say goodnight to Alison, and head back to my bedroom. My focus on the game is utterly destroyed so even though it's early by my standards I crawl into bed, and stare into the darkness. Mallard finds a space above my hip to settle in and relaxes into sleep.

Eventually, I sleep too, but when I do it's not an easy rest. I find myself drifting in any out of half-waking dreams. Dreams that are honestly the most frustrating, and the most boring that I've ever had. All I can see are words in front of my eyes. There's text written in an ancient hand, leaves of paper floating and turning in front of my eyes. I know that I should be able to understand it, but every time I try to focus, it becomes impossible, the marks of ink on old paper blurring beyond all recognition.

When I finally pull myself from my bed in search of coffee, it's late morning and Saeed is making use of the dining table for a large, printed floor plan, marked with symbols of various colours. Also on the table: half eaten toast which he seems to have forgotten about, a fidget cube which could be anyone's but is probably Theo's, Saeed's laptop, and a library book with the stunningly original title of *Abandoned Mental Asylums of England and Wales*.

I stretch over to look at it.

"Sleep well?" Saeed asks, way too cheerily. I make a noise that I think appropriately conveys firstly that I did not, and secondly that whether I can speak today or not I'm not really interested in it right now.

The coffee in the pot is stone cold. It's tempting to microwave it, but broke or not I still have some standards when it comes to coffee so I clean out the dregs and make a new pot. Sitting down at the table at last with that and some overly sugary cereal, not usually my style but I reckon I need it, I gesture to ask Saeed what he's up to.

"Pittlow," he says. "You heard of it?"

I have. It's the haunted asylum that keeps coming up on the paranormal forums, the one my friend Callum's been talking about a lot. I suppose ghosts anywhere is enough to be of interest to Saeed. He seems to be working with some urgency, though. I look over and find the floor plan to be, as I expected, a historic plan of the asylum itself, perhaps dating back to when it was built. The colours seem to indicate different kinds of ghosts.

"So, there's a company just bought it and is turning it into a haunted asylum tours business."

I roll my eyes. We've discussed these things before. Haunted houses, ghost tours, houses of horrors. Places with websites full of shrieking women in nightdresses, electro-convulsive therapy, shadows stalking the corridors, axe in hand.

It's almost all fake ghosts – let's face it, most people don't even believe in ghosts, and most are literally incapable of seeing them either. Rather than making for a dud family day out, they rely on building up tension and possibility, making the visitors scared of every shadow, freaked out by every noise they hear.

But I've been pretty confident from the stories I've heard that Pittlow is indeed haunted. The ghosts of people who've been through more than enough in their shortened lives. And places like that are bad for ghosts, bad for people who live with them, and bad for people who, like all of us, may well have ended up confined to one of them in another era.

I gulp down the coffee and let Saeed tell me more about Pittlow. For some reason, I don't tell him about the dreams, even though they feel important, even though I'd normally sit and tell Saeed about just about anything. But right now, I have a messaging app open and we're sitting together at the table with no-one else around, and I could tell him anything, except I can't, and I feel more alone than I've felt in a very long time.

1705

The man comes for Tobias on a still summer day, when the river has slowed to a trickle and the work is slow. She has prayed for rain every day this week, and yet still there is none.

He tells her of his work in Natural Philosophy, of the ghosts he has found. She listens in interest, perched on the wall like she was a child or a man. She's never been further than the nearest market town, never known a ghost besides Tobias. He opens up a whole world for her, a world she'd never imagined could be real.

When she watches him capture Tobias, the mouth of the bottle widening and then sucking him in like a fast-flowing stream, it's a wonder at first, but then something feels like it's lodged in her throat and it doesn't go after he's gone, gone with Tobias in his glass bottle.

At night she dreams of solid glass walls, the whole world distorted, her spirit trapped, crushed, contorted. She wakes sweating with guilt that she showed him where to find Tobias. She spends even her Sundays inside now, making work for herself when there is none to do; restacking sacks of flour, cleaning the floor, but her mind is never on the task.

CHAPTER SEVEN

I'm lying on my bed that evening, scrolling through my usual list of gaming sites and paranormal discussions, watching videos from some of the more reputable people who live with ghosts – a small minority of those who claim to. Some of them are on my even smaller list of contacts I discuss Casswell Park with, and some of those have, on occasion, redirected a ghost to us, usually ones whose home is being demolished or has otherwise become unsafe.

Rumours that Casswell Park is haunted are public – and predate our occupation of the house by several centuries. The fact that we offer sanctuary for ghosts, and possibly have more ghosts than any other building in the world, is not. We have considered going public, and we may well do so one day, but it will need to be considered and deliberate, with us prepared for the consequences. For now, there are very few people who know the truth.

Araminta's still at work. I'm comfortable with my own company, stretched out on my thick woollen blankets and the quilt my nan made for my eighteenth birthday. I'm almost asleep when I hear shouting down the corridor.

I lie still and listen for a moment. It isn't playful shouting. Nor is it one of those arguments that break out among us occasionally, heavy with frustration but not with malice. There are eight very different people in this house, most of us very noise sensitive, most of us with significant financial stressors, and some with significant trauma histories; it's actually a wonder that tension doesn't build between us more than it does.

I slip my feet into my boots, not lacing them, grab my torch – which I've learned how to use as a weapon, and is weighted accordingly – and head cautiously along the corridor, taking care to keep my footsteps soft. More shouting; I recognise one voice as Alison, but the others are unfamiliar to me.

Then there's a thump, like something being dropped. Someone being pushed to the ground, perhaps. Someone falling. I speed up, worrying less about the sound of my footsteps and more about Alison and whoever else is involved. I can feel the adrenaline growing, start twitching my fingers as I run the last few metres to the central staircase, and then I pause. The sound is coming from the third floor.

We don't use the third floor. It's only accessible by stairs, no lift, and we're not comfortable having part of our space completely inaccessible to some of us, not if we can help it. And it's far from needed, given that we already have spare rooms aplenty. The attic rooms – once servant's quarters and storage – are barely high enough to stand up in, and the stairs up to them are behind a door that looks like a cupboard, narrow and twisty.

That door is open.

I take the steps two at a time, one hand on the bannister, fully prepared to hit anyone who might come at me from above.

I take in the scene that awaits me. Vinnie and Alison. Two others, young, who I don't recognise. And an open window that on closer inspection looks like it's been forced.

"Ghost hunters," Alison says, confirming my suspicions. It's no surprise that we're having to deal with them once again, though I'd really rather not have to. We've had some issues with them pushing to be allowed in our home, talk to ghosts, take photos. Asking them how they'd like ghosts barging into their homes wasn't as helpful as we wished; they relished the idea. But irrespective, the ghosts here deserve their privacy – and so do we.

Vinnie pushes the smaller of the two in my direction.

"Climbed right up the wall of the house. Would have died if they'd fallen. Think they're fucking Spiderman or something."

"Which one?"

"What?" Vinnie asks.

"Which one? Are you comparing me to Peter Parker or Ben Reilly or...?"

The woman is a skinny wisp of a thing, in jeans and a too-large blue hoodie. Her blonde hair is messy and streaked with green. Round her waist, she has something of a tool belt filled with everything from a torch to a screwdriver to various contraptions I couldn't name.

"Is that really the most important issue you see before you now?" Vinnie asks. It's the same exasperated voice they use when talking to Theo, but there's a touch of anger in there too that's never used when they talk to their son. "Really?"

"I need to know so I can determine whether that was an insult or not," she says.

Vinnie rolls their eyes so hard they almost tip out of the back of their head. I take a look at the guy. He's in a black jacket that doesn't look warm enough for the time of year. His figure fuller than the woman's. Other than that, they're both white with the same blonde hair, and many of the same facial features. I look from one to the other. They could be siblings, may well be.

"Right," says Alison. "You two need to leave, both of you. And you can give me your phones and any other cameras until you're out of the house."

"You're squatters, yeah. You don't own this place. You've got just as much right to be here as we have. So why don't we talk about this nicely and share?"

"Nope." Vinnie's doing all the talking, and I'm not complaining at all. They're still in their work clothes, with their hair freshly barbered – a fade at the sides with just enough length for it to form tight curls at the top. It makes them look very authoritative, which is a little ridiculous if you know Vinnie but exactly what we need here. "We're the legal tenants. And we can guarantee you that the actual owner doesn't have the same level of reticence about calling the police as we do, so it probably wouldn't be to your advantage to get her involved."

"You don't like the police?" says the young woman, her eyes suddenly lighting up. "Maybe we have something in common."

"Nuh-uh. We don't like the police – or at least we've agreed as a household that the police are the last resort, we're not a hive mind – because they perpetuate systems of violence and oppression. You? You don't like the police because they might interfere with you doing whatever the hell you like and damn the consequences. Not the same."

She looks on the edge of tears. "You don't know anything about my life."

"True. And I don't need to. You're going to head down those stairs and you're going to leave via the most direct route, no stopping for your ghost hunting – have you ever considered what a terrible term that is? – and head out of the doorway and down the driveway and back to your homes where you do whatever people like you do on a freezing cold Wednesday evening. The alternative is that I'll lock you out of the window and leave you to head down on your own. It's a long way down, and a lot harder than going up."

I hold out my hands. Two mobiles, a camera. I push them into the deep pockets of my hoodie and hold out my hand again. The girl sighs and hands over two more cameras. Who says you need words to communicate?

We march them quickly down the tight stairway, down the main staircase, and out through the front door. Once we're out on the pavement, I hand their electronics back. Vinnie rubs their hands together, our collective breath forming clouds of moisture in the still, cold air.

"We'll be seeing them again," Vinnie says, with more resignation than bitterness.

Holly and I spend the next few hours going around the house, checking every window and door. She's got a selection of screwdrivers with her, and tightens every catch as we go, and we nail shut a couple of windows where the catch has broken, at least until we can go out and get some replacements. It's only at times like this, when I walk round the whole house or near enough, that I'm reminded just how big this place is. The attic rooms we start with are low-ceilinged but large. I imagine servants in their narrow and uncomfortable beds, spending the little time they got to themselves up here in this space, the rain heavy on the roof.

"All done," Holly says at last, and we head down the narrow staircase to what we ordinarily think of as the upper floor, the one where most of us have our bedrooms or suites. I imagine that when this was a school many would have been dormitories, perhaps four beds each or more if they had bunks, and then how they must have been before the school, before the convent, when this house belonged to a wealthy titled family. I can almost see the grand rooms, the fires burning in all of them, the servants quiet along the corridors, all the way to the late nineteenth century when the upkeep became too expensive and house and lands were eventually sold.

I see Holly looking at me, but I'm not in a state where I can speak right now, so I just smile at her and shrug and we walk on. None of those people in centuries past would ever have predicted it becoming a home to a ragtag bunch like us and a load of ghosts.

As we head down the second-floor corridor, I see Roderick in front of us. It takes me a moment to work out what's wrong. His limbs are pulled out at angles that shouldn't be possible for a ghost, and his face is stretched into a grin that looks more menacing than his usual mischievous one. It's as if there are invisible strings attached to him, as if he were a puppet. I feel myself shiver and I don't quite know why. But as we approach, he seems to be pulled backwards through the outside wall, and then disappears.

Holly is out of words too, and we do the only thing that makes sense: keep going with what we're doing. There's a rhythm to it at least.

The windows are larger here and we check them one by one. Even when the maintenance of this house is difficult, it's satisfying to do, as if we're fulfilling some important responsibility.

We are responsible, after all. Technically, Casswell Park is now owned by Denny's sister Karen; she and her late husband were property developers. They bought it mainly for the substantial lands attached that had once been far on the edge of town but were now a prime location, surrounded by housing developments and less than an hour's walk to the town centre. The development of townhouses, aimed at both young professionals and downsizing baby boomers, was erected; compact and modern two- and three-bedroom units. The fountains that had been the centrepiece were kept and relocated to a park in the middle of the development. It's a nice place – we used to take Theo there to run around and burn off some excess energy when he was a little younger.

That left the hall itself. The long-term plan had always been to convert it into apartments, but the tradespeople they hired to do the initial quotes and surveys kept leaving and not returning. Rumours went round that there was paranormal activity scaring them away. Then Karen's husband died and all her plans were put on the back burner. Denny made her an offer. He'd take care of the property – carry out basic maintenance and pay the rates – and she wouldn't have to worry about any of it. It worked for both of them. And then it worked for us.

Our future here isn't completely secure, but I'm hopeful. Karen has, by all accounts, plenty of money; redeveloping a haunted old house with an abundance of quirks, before you even start considering the ghosts, is not her priority. And I think she feels like, in some indirect way, she's fulfilling the promise she made to her parents to take care of her younger brother, made when she was just a teenager, about a boy they didn't have a label for yet. They knew that not only was he different, but he could do things that couldn't be explained: make pencils float through the air, water flow upwards, marbles roll in different directions, all without touching them. I hope that's as important to her as I think it is, because for now, we just have to hope things stay like this.

We continue our checks. Where bedroom doors are locked, we knock; if there is no answer, we message the occupant to check the windows themselves. Denny's door, though, is wide open. His floor is covered with electrical components and books and smells faintly of oil. In a large tank to my left, Anastasia, Denny's pet corn snake, is curling herself, moving slowly and contentedly. If it were regular burglars we were concerned about, I'd consider her an effective deterrent.

Alison's door is open too, as are the French doors to the balcony, her two tabbies sunning themselves outside. For certain values of sun, I suppose, given how early it is in the year, but it's better than nothing.

It's one of the neater – and more traditional – rooms here. Thick woollen blankets on the bed, a flat screen – though smaller than mine – on the wall, a couple of books and a lamp on the bedside table. Out on the balcony I stroke one cat with each hand, crouched on the ground. I look out over the townhouse development all clean lines and solar panels on the roofs – for all the good they would do you at this time of year. I wonder what Casswell Park's original ghosts think of it; those who would have wandered the perfectly manicured grounds, grown up among the hedgerows and parks, balancing on stepping stones over the streams. I can see the fountain in the park, the one piece of the old gardens amid the new houses. It's not running; it often doesn't at this time of year, but I'm glad it's there all the same.

I make a note to talk to Alison about getting a cat door installed so she doesn't have to leave the doors to her balcony open. It wouldn't be easy to get up that high, but our ghost hunter friends have made it abundantly clear that they are prepared to do what it takes for a sighting of our ghosts.

I'm still feeling an adrenaline rush from the morning's events, still thinking about the ghost hunters. I was into that stuff a bit once, though I had more sense than to call it ghost hunting, even then. But I got my heat sensors and infrared cameras and downloaded scripts guaranteed to be effective ways to talk to ghosts. I hung out on paranormal forums and borrowed just about every book in that section of the library. A lot of it I didn't believe; it made no sense based on my experience of ghosts, but when I found something that seemed consistent or at least plausible, I practically inhaled the information.

But I rarely went out looking for ghosts. A handful of times at the most, and not just because I was limited in my ability to go out alone, but because somewhere deep down I was deeply, deeply uncomfortable with the idea. I've always had a sense that ghosts are like me, that they need both companionship and to be left alone when they need it, and all my experience since has supported that idea.

I think, with a smile, about the ghosts we've released from the bottles, about how much excitement and how much disbelief I could cause by relating those experiences on those paranormal forums. I lurk on them sometimes, post the occasional warning or piece of advice, give an example of a publicly available story that meets certain criteria on request. But I'll never do more than that. It's not safe for any of us.

Araminta has the day off work; she's working all weekend and usually only does three shifts a week; it's what she can do without becoming too overloaded or fatigued, which in their turn make her mental health stuff more likely to flare up. Although trying to make the caseworker who controls her benefit understand that is one hell of a task. I've always been read as disabled in some way, even if people don't understand I'm autistic – Araminta, not so much. It's a mixed blessing. It really is. It means people believe me about what I can't do – but they rarely believe me about what I can.

The only paid work I've ever done is from home, looking through images that have been reported on social media and deciding if they break the rules. I gave it up after a while. The pay is per image, and minuscule, so you have to work fast, and there's only so much child abuse, bigotry, and beheadings you can handle in a day. I think I could work more if people were adaptable with how they communicate with me, but they just assume I can't communicate with them. Part of me hates that, not just because it means things will always be difficult financially, but because it assumes the issue is with me. With Araminta they assume that because she can come across as neurotypical, all fake smiles and painful eye contact, she can keep that up all day, and they have absolutely no clue just how hard that is on her.

She's considering doing an arts management diploma, looking at things like running galleries, and I honestly don't know if that will be easier on her or worse, but for now retail it is. The one blessing of that is that there's no such thing as taking your work home with you, leaving her the time and headspace for her own art. With my near-entirely flexible schedule – as long as I'm not expected to get up early in the morning or anything – things are working out for us for now.

It took a while for our household to work out how to share expenses; all of us have different experiences and none of us conventional full-time jobs. Early on, we devised a formula for equating time and money; everyone had to put in some time and money, but they could balance it depending on which they had more of. We scrapped that soon after. It was good at recognising people's different contributions, but for people like Holly – too busy with school to work much for money or on house maintenance, and ineligible for a proper benefit because her parents should have been taking care of her – it was impossible. But more importantly, we realised that a complex system just wasn't needed. Everyone is here by choice. Sure, we all have off days where we let the cleaning slide and grumpy post-its are left on the kitchen door, but it balances out. Most of the time, we all pitch in what we reasonably can, and keep an eye out for each other.

Araminta is dressed wonderfully as always; a pin-up style dress that's pink and covered with dinosaurs so tiny that you only realise what they are when you get up close. The pendant I gave her is round her neck, and even though it's from such a different time and of a different style it looks like it was meant to be there all along. Her shoes match the green of those dinosaurs and she's tied up her thick red hair in two plaits, and her full cheeks and red with warmth. I don't let myself start thinking about how damn lucky I am, because that's a rabbit hole I'd struggle to escape from, but I do kiss her and tell her she looks beautiful. Which she does.

"Can we go for a walk?" I ask.

I've been feeling a bit stir crazy lately. I'm fine with being home more than most people, especially because there are so many people at home. And maybe because I'm just wired differently in that respect, but even for it me it can sometimes get too much.

"Yeah, but not far. It's too cold."

Her coat, bought on discount, is magnificent; this brown wool with faux fur at the collar and running down the front. I do have a winter coat, but I mostly just layer on jerseys and hoodies, followed by a scarf, hat, and pair of gloves as needed.

At the end of the driveway is a ghost. An elderly woman, not one of ours. She doesn't seem distressed; just lingering. I invite her in but she drifts and doesn't respond. She's still probably looking for us in a way; she's unlikely to be here by coincidence, but as she doesn't seem distressed, I imagine she will turn up at – or through – our door in her own time.

There are a few people around, someone walking home from work, a couple of teenagers chatting with energy drinks in their hands, a kid on a skateboard, but none of them show any sign of noticing the ghost. Things aren't different for us just because we're used to seeing them, attuned for it in some way – though that helps. Some people simply seem to be born with the ability to sense, and in some cases affect, the paranormal, and some aren't. Or, more accurately, it's a spectrum, but one where most people have such limited ability that it may as well be non-existent.

I've had it asked of me – and wondered myself – whether neurodivergent people are more likely to see ghosts. As far as I can tell, there doesn't seem to be a correlation, but it doesn't mean our experiences aren't different either. I've thought about it a lot, and it's why

I've sometimes hidden both that I see ghosts and that I have paranormal abilities – that and the tendency of people to patronise me or send me for psychiatric treatment. They push it into the narrative of what they think autism should be. People like to think we have something to compensate for what they think of as our deficiencies. Our abilities can't be things other people have, like taking care of kid siblings or helping out with the canal path clean-up – or managing the maintenance of a big old house, for that matter – because then they'd have to think of us as people. They're interested in savant skills, those that are entirely disconnected from their own lives: incredibly detailed pencil drawings of cityscapes from memory, every window correct. The ability to recall and play a complex piece of music after hearing it once.

So, I think that the idea that autistic people see ghosts more is not only statistically incorrect, but pretty problematic. But it might be true that we practice it more, or that we notice them differently. The only other connection that makes some sense is the possibility of inheritance, of both autism and ghost sensitivity – unconnected, but occurring in the same families. That may have something in it – certainly both traits are well established in mine.

The ghost follows us on our walk, but she doesn't follow us into the house even though we leave the door open a little as we take off our boots. She'll come in when she's ready.

1698

H is family is not the wealthiest, but he has a sizable income, and – as the eldest son – stands to inherit the family seat and title. Both of those pale in comparison to what is truly important: the pursuit of knowledge, the interrogation of the natural and supernatural worlds, the understanding of the laws which govern the universe.

His most precious possessions are two, and neither of them are items he could sell for much money, were he ever inclined to do such a thing, except perhaps to one of the few who truly understood their purpose.

The pendant was made exactly to his specifications. It's a hexagonal shape with a large circular hole in the middle, thicker around the internal edges for the gemstone that will be housed in there when needed. Both sides are intricately engraved; one with a series of overlapping circles, concentric with the space in the middle. On the other side are words only he can read.

The second is his notebook. Leather bound, thick paper and good quality, largely free of imperfections. Expensive, as these things go, but not valuable compared to the items he grew up surrounded by. To him, it's priceless.

All his notes are in there, careful observations, the development of systems of classification, theories coming together. His life's work.

CHAPTER EIGHT

S aeed asks for a meeting at eight the next morning. I bargain him out to ten. He is a morning person for whom mornings are spent in a shaft of sunlight with a coffee and a book. He likes the crispness, the low sun, being up before most others. Me... not so much, and it's a miracle if I get to sleep before two, so even with coffee I'm not the pleasantest at eight. Or nine. Even ten's pushing it.

I make it, but my hair is still drying. Mercifully, there's some filter coffee left and some croissants Araminta brought home last night – she's allowed to buy near-dated food cheap – and warmed up in the oven they're absolutely fine. We help ourselves, passing round butter and one of the jars of blackberry and verbena jam Alison made in autumn with the foraged fruit she and Denny picked. Vinnie's got a call back about another temp job – a bit of extra money for them – and more than that, because I know they struggle with what to do with themselves when they're not working. Theo and Holly are at school but the rest of us are here, perched around the dining table for this breakfast meeting.

Araminta leans against me and I put my arm round her, looking at her with concern.

"Slept terribly last night," she says. "Again. Or at least, I don't remember sleeping badly but I wake up and I'm still exhausted."

I tighten my arm on her shoulder in sympathy. Saeed swallows a mouthful of croissant and then props up a corkboard full of photos and notes and pieces of string.

"We have a murder investigation going on?" Denny asks. We all crack up except Saeed, who forces a little chuckle but clearly isn't amused by such a reaction to his hard work.

"It might turn out that way if you keep interrupting," he replies, looking pointedly at Denny.

"Yeah, sorry," Denny says. He picks up his chainmail out of a shopping bag and starts working on it, twisting in link after link. It's a hobby he picked up a few years back – and a fitting one for someone who lives in a house that draws to mind knights and battles, even if it's technically a little more modern than that. I asked him, once, how he can manage something that takes such delicate fine motor skills, something he really struggles with.

"Most of all it's a learning thing, isn't it?" he'd said. "I have to do it more to be able to learn. But if I pick one thing and repeat it over and over, I can learn how to do it until it's almost second nature."

Either way, I think now, looking at the glinting links, perfectly evenly formed, he's not just managing but good at it. I think having something to do with his hands helps his focus, as well. It does for me too, even if it's less productive and usually just playing a flash game on my phone. And of course for Saeed, who's rarely without a fidget spinner.

Alison's voice brings me back to the present.

"Go on, Saeed," she says. "Tell us what you know."

Saeed takes a deep breath. He's been preparing for this.

"I've been doing some research on the ghost hunters. I think it's important for us to know who they are, because they're determined to get into the house and they're not going away any time soon. I don't blame them – I suspect we're the most haunted building in the country at this point, and certainly will be if there's a ghost in every one of those bottles. But we are, I think, agreed that not only do we not want them here but their continual approaches are disruptive to the ghosts, most of whom cannot meaningfully consent to this breach of their privacy. And frankly, I don't trust people who try and break into our house to not try and push further than anything we agree to."

Saeed pauses, takes a breath as we nod in agreement, and then continues.

"Right, so the ghost hunters that are currently bothering us, appear to be a pair of young siblings." He points to a selfie he has pinned to the board; it appears to be a young white woman, her blonde hair streaked with green. "This is Keira Casey. She's about nineteen years old, based on the dates she was at school, and is studying nursing. Despite being younger, she seems to be the leader, the bolder one of the two. And her other interest – about which she has a whole blog – is the history of astronomy. She's visiting many historic observatories. Worth a look."

The next photo is grainy and appears to have been taken surreptitiously from a phone camera, probably in our driveway. I hope Saeed hasn't been taking risks.

"This is Logan Casey. Keira's brother, the quiet one, which we all know is suspicious." He looks pointedly at me and I give him the finger as he continues.

"A couple of years older, appears to be unemployed and no real sense of anything else he does aside from looking for ghosts. Every social media account I could find for him is one paranormal link after another, and most of them from not very reputable sites."

"They look really alike," says Araminta. "Definitely siblings."

"I don't see it," Alison says.

"You don't even recognise me half the time," Denny points out. "I still think you have prosopagnosia."

"Nah," Alison says, laughing. "Just trying to avoid having to interact with people."

Saeed continues despite the interruption.

"There are some other biographical details here if you find them relevant. Middle names. Parents. Schools attended..."

"Okay, okay, enough," says Denny, waving his hands. "How did you find this information?"

"Facebook, mostly. That's where Keira's photo came from."

"Fucking creepy if you ask me. Being able to look people up like that."

As if on cue, Henrietta floats through the room. Denny sighs and rolls his eyes.

"Yes, before any of you say it, I appreciate the irony. If Zucker-whatsit was a ghost he'd actually be flying into our bedrooms, not just virtually. But when ghosts invade our privacy it's usually because of their lack of understanding – and they can usually be taught not to over time. It's not their raison d'être. And they don't make filthy amounts of money off it either."

Alison chuckles.

"Clearly you don't have children who are not very good at making the effort to communicate with you but put it all on Facebook. If you did, you'd love..."

"All right, all right!" Saeed waves his arms in a way that I fear brings them dangerously close to dislocating. "Can we maybe focus?"

"Autistic people going off on tangents, what a todo..." mutters Araminta under her breath. I grin at her. Despite the fact that the ghost hunters are making us all uneasy, not to mention wasting our time, the mood is casual and relaxed. Alison lit the fire half an hour before we started; the room is toasty warm and the croissants are buttery and not even a little bit stale. Everything is good until a flaming log comes flying through the air, narrowly missing Araminta's face, and setting Alison's sleeve on fire.

There's instant chaos, but somehow in the midst of it someone persuades Alison not to try and take her jersey off and someone else chucks cold water over it and guides her to the downstairs shower. In the meantime, we get water over the log and then we're stamping on embers that have spread themselves across the floor.

The immediate crisis over, and Alison back in the room in a fresh t-shirt: we all turn and look at Denny.

"Dude," Alison says. She's pretending to be okay but she's visibly shaking. I put my hand on her shoulder awkwardly.

Denny shakes his head.

"That wasn't me."

Alison looks at him in disbelief.

"Look, I know motor skills and spatial awareness don't always come easily to you. I get it, it's not your fault. And dyspraxia and telekinesis are a difficult combination. But we do need to find a way to ensure that doesn't result in GIANT FLAMING LOGS being thrown around the place, because that shit has consequences."

"I get it," says Denny.

"Good. Because I liked that jersey and you're going to replace it." Alison's mostly laughing. Mostly, but still shaken.

"No, I mean. Look, I'm sorry I've caused some of you to have random flying object issues in the past, though frankly if I didn't use my telekinesis things would be even worse. But this wasn't me. I don't know how I do things sometimes, but I always know when I do them. And I swear that wasn't me."

No-one seems to know what to say to that. What had seemed so simple has turned out not to be. Denny breaks the silence.

"But I'll buy you a new jersey anyway."

Alison thinks for a moment. We all do.

"Well, Morgan's the only other living person here with paranormal ability and theirs doesn't work like that. There's nothing new we should know about, is there Morgan?"

I shake my head definitively. I can't find the words to talk about what happened last night, and it becomes harder the longer I leave it. But I do know it definitely wasn't my own abilities at work.

"It could be Holly or Theo?" Araminta suggests. "These things normally develop around the start of puberty. Neither of them are exactly that age, but they're not too far off. Except... they're not even at home. Never mind, ignore me."

"It was a good suggestion," Alison says reassuringly.

"So, either there's someone else around or it's one of the ghosts?" Araminta is working through the possibilities methodically.

"That's how it sounds, yeah, unless one of us has latent paranormal powers – and I feel that if you've reached adulthood and lived in a house full of ghosts for a few years without them manifesting, then chances are they never will."

"A ghost hunter?"

"Fuck, I hope not. If any of them have paranormal abilities that's a whole other layer of difficulty we have to deal with. Not to mention that bringing up all kinds of issues around whether their behaviour is a consequence of them feeling different or... I know how everyone here likes to come up with convoluted sympathetic reasons for people's behaviour rather than just accepting that most people are assholes."

We smile at each other in recognition. Alison's right. And being too trusting, assuming the best, has had negative consequences for me in the past, but I don't think it's something I'd ever want to change.

"The ghosts have been really unhappy lately," Denny says. He blurts it out as if it was something he was holding back on saying and had to be said all at once, but once he's said it we all start chiming in. Some of the things we've noticed are a little hard to put your finger on, or a matter of degree: wandering even more than usual, looking distressed, but once it becomes clear we've all noticed them, they add up.

I notice, and then Denny notices, that Araminta has gone suddenly pale. She's always pale but this... this is almost grey. I feel my stomach lurch, then there's silence, we all turn to look at her.

"Isobel, she's been... she's been really targeting me okay? I thought it was just me, but now everything's been going wrong as well." I can see her starting to cry. I know exactly what is going on for her. I know the type of memories this is dragging up, how small and terrified it's making her feel. I just don't know how to translate that knowledge into actions to make her feel better.

"Can you tell us what's been happening, Mints?"

Araminta bursts into tears, and at the same time cracks up with laughter, taking the large handkerchief Denny hands her, reassuring her it's clean.

"Oh god, don't you start calling me that as well," she says, drying her eyes and choking back sobs. "I don't know. I don't know. It's just things like. She floats above me when I'm trying to sleep, and then when I wake she's right next to me. She pulls faces and mimes violence against me, like she's threatening me, and yeah, I know she can't really do it but still. The other day I was airbrushing a piece and she put her hand between the airbrush and the canvas. She's not very corporeal so it went through, but it shifted the direction just enough to ruin everything... I thought, she's been around here far longer than I have and it's never been like this. I don't know what I did to her to provoke this!"

Other people come forward with stories of other weird behaviour, though it's clear Araminta's borne the brunt of it. I don't mention the strange voice I heard. Even though I tell myself I live with proudly-weird people who fully believe in strange things. I'm not entirely sure why.

Perhaps it would make it more real, that something is seriously wrong.

We're all used to acting like things are normal when they're really not, but when one of your number has just been almost set on fire by forces unknown – and likely paranormal – it's difficult to keep that up. But we try to focus on practical solutions. We come up with some ways to increase our security that don't make us feel too uncomfortable, but we also decide to arrange a meeting with the ghost hunters. There's not much we're willing to compromise, not just because we're stubborn – though some of us are – but because any compromise is not just a concession for us but one for the ghosts, and we're uncomfortable making those decisions on their behalf.

But perhaps, by talking, we can develop a more understanding relationship with them. Personally, I'm sceptical. But we'll give it a try.

That evening, when I've given up the warm fire of the dining room, where we often congregate on winter days for just that reason, for the rattling fan heater in my room, another message comes through on the group chat from Saeed.

> Motion detector's gone off. Going to check it out.

I type.

> Mallard's in here with me, curled up by the heater. Not her this time.

> Probably a tree branch or a pigeon, but given what happened yesterday I'm not taking any chances.

> I'll come join you.

I slip my feet into my boots, not bothering to lace them up, and head down the main staircase with my phone in my hand, greeting Jodie Keane as I pass her translucent form. One day we're planning to get better technology, including movement activated cameras so we can see if it's just Mallard as usual – I swear she does it on purpose. But this time I know it's not her, and it's unlikely to be one of the tabbies. Could be a stray, or one of the things Saeed suggested.

I find Saeed by following the light of his torch; I haven't brought one myself but I don't think we'll be going too far from the building. The bushes are thin and mostly bare this time of year, so it's easy to get a good view from the entrance. We see the ghost only a moment before she sees us and she rushes towards us and then stops, fear in her eyes. Like she wants to come in but is unsure if she can, or is scared of how we may respond.

"I'm Saeed," he says carefully. "And this is Morgan. There are lots of people and ghosts here. Are you looking for anyone in particular?"

She doesn't need us to invite her in. She's a ghost not a vampire. And yet she lingers. I'm not sure if she's waiting out of politeness, or from fear.

It's not the best timing, but when someone knocks at your door – or hovers non-corporeally, as the case may be, the only polite thing to do is to invite them in. With our permission granted, she floats into the hallway and lingers there. I don't think she's hesitating because of anxiety. I think she's connecting with the house, anchoring herself in Casswell Park.

One of the things I've observed about ghosts – and find particularly interesting, given my own paranormal abilities, is how important place is to them. You don't tend to hear about them just idly wandering around the countryside, unless they were already wanderers. Many people think ghosts have to haunt the place they died. If that were true though, so many ghosts would have been destroyed when their buildings were demolished, their fields and forests paved into carparks, their railway lines torn up. If it were true, most of those who live here at Casswell Place would not be here.

They don't need to stay where they died, but I think they need to be attached to a place, what I call anchored.

Finding a new place is a big deal to them and anchoring themselves to it costs them dearly in some form: perhaps energy, perhaps emotionally, perhaps they lose some of their corporeality and thus the time they are able to linger in this world.

We stay with the ghost for a while. I put together the little we know about her. I'd place her in her late twenties, but it's hard to tell. Her dress is dirty and stained, shapeless, the little hair she has left – which appears to have been chopped haphazardly – is matted.

I head upstairs, get out my laptop, and post to a closed list. There's only about a dozen of us on the list, all there by invitation only. People whose interest in the paranormal comes with a commitment to the rights and welfare of ghosts, and who also manage not to engage in stupid stunts. I have a sense someone will know where this ghost is from, that there is information out there that will help her to settle in.

The reply comes two days later, and it's surprisingly from Callum, my friend who is involved in activism around Pittlow. He wants to meet in person. I'm on edge about why, but that weekend Araminta and I catch the train up to the city. I could probably have found a way to manage alone, but I'm glad to have her with me. We lean against each other on the journey up; she sketches the passengers, even letting me see, while I listen to music and watch the countryside out of the window.

We meet Callum in a cafe attached to a public library, about ten minutes walk from the station. He's perhaps a couple of years younger than me, but walks confidently, dressed in a long coat and scarf. He orders hot chocolate, me a black coffee, and Araminta a latte. We introduce ourselves, and I stir sugar into my coffee.

I can talk a little, but it's still a new, unfamiliar, noisy place so Araminta does most of it.

"So," Araminta says. "You know something about our ghost?"

"Yes," he says. "I've been doing some work around Pittlow. You'll have heard of it, of course?"

Suddenly everything becomes clear. Pittlow Asylum. I knew we would end up drawn into it sooner or later.- The woman, the ghost, is in our house and though still skittish she looks to have been growing in confidence with every passing hour. Now Callum gives us a name for her: Florence. He thinks – though he's not certain – that it's her real name, and if so, he's located some documents about her.

"I think if it was now," he says. "She might be diagnosed with some sort of severe post-natal depression, perhaps with psychotic elements."

I wonder if I should ask to read the documents. I wonder if it's okay to do so when I'm pretty sure she can't meaningfully consent. I say nothing. There are no easy answers.

But even without reading them, I now know that Florence must have had a baby.

I try to imagine being a ghost as your child grows up, grows old, then dies. It can't be that unusual a situation – it's reasonable to expect that most ghosts who were older than their mid-twenties when they died had at least one child – but it's the first time I've really given it thought.

"I asked to meet in person," Callum says, "because some of us are doing some activism around Pittlow. We've been trying to talk to the ghosts. I didn't want to put anything online, at least not yet. I've talked to your housemate, Saeed, but I wanted to get a sense of you in person."

I don't understand why people trust those they've met in person more than those they've known online for years, but I know it's a thing that a lot of people do, so I nod in acknowledgement.

"We've been dealing with quite a few issues ourselves. So I don't know how much time I'll have. But you can ask me and see."

Callum smiles.

"That's all I ask," he says.

I'm not sure about activism. My parents were always both union members, and I was taken to the occasional demonstration as a child, but even though so much of what I do is political in a sense – for someone like me, simply existing in the world and refusing to go away is political – what I do is so much quieter than what I imagine activism to be. But I've committed to nothing.

I think of something else too. We've always strongly felt the ghosts dislike being made a spectacle of. That's why we've been so firm on not letting the ghost hunters in. But never has it been made so clear how much the ghosts care about it, how important their privacy is to them.

When ghosts have turned up independently looking for refuge – and there have only been three of them as far as I can remember – have been fleeing the demolition of their previous location, or an exorcism. They've had no choice, in other words. This ghost, is the first I've heard of essentially deciding that a set of circumstances that do not actually threaten her very existence are nevertheless intolerable for her and making the decision to leave.

Callum leaves us with more information – about Florence, about Pittlow, and afterwards, Araminta and I make the most of the day in town, finding an exhibition of digital and game related art, miraculously touching on both our main interests. The gallery is busy and overloading, and we have to take quite a few breaks, but we find each floor has a little dead-end area of space by the lifts where we can hang out quietly. We enjoy ourselves overall. After a quick stop at an art store to pick up a few supplies for Araminta and a clothes shop where I get two of my preferred brand of bras, we eat fried noodles at a dingy but friendly little restaurant before heading home.

It's dark well before our train leaves and, exhausted, I watch our own reflections in the windows. It's been a good day but I can't help thinking of the ghost we've just offered refuge to, whether that refuge is enough, and how many others we may be unable to help.

CHAPTER NINE

S omeone is talking to me as if from a great distance. I'm focused on something else right now.

I squint and look through different panels of glass. Some are close to original – though the orangerie is not quite as old as the rest of the house; others replaced over the centuries since. The quality increased through the years; the newer panes are usually thinner and definitely have fewer imperfections. Each piece of glass distorts the driveway outside in a different way; some stretching it, some magnifying it, some just blurring it...

"Morgan?"

I jump, looking round hastily. I've clearly completely missed the question along with any context that came with it.

"Morgan, they're here. Are you ready for us to invite them in?"

I breathe in deeply, pulling my shoulders up to my ears and then nod. I'm not exactly ready for this, but I don't think there's anything that would make me more comfortable with this.

The orangerie seems to me just a large conservatory and I wonder how it's survived so long, especially with some of the original glass still intact. Saeed has found some pictures from its prime; fruits then considered rare and exotic growing within its glass. How many people, I wonder, first saw an orange, a lemon or a banana, here for the first time? Now this glass extension is a sort of liminal space. Part of the house and yet not. Outside and inside all at once.

Alison has arranged chairs in a circle. She's brought out hot blackcurrant and freshly baked gingerbread which is some kind of miracle and the only thing stopping me from being frozen solid right through now. I sip at my drink and warm my hands around the mug. There's still a light frost on the grass, even though the sun has melted most of it.

Logan and Keira sit next to each other. Logan shakes our hands, introduces himself, and Keira follows. Her hand is warm and fragile, and I try not to be obvious about wiping mine on my trousers afterwards, because I know people sometimes take offence at that.

"Araminta, what happened to your fingers?" Alison asks, pouring out the blackcurrant. Araminta hides them, almost instinctively, but not before I can see they're red and blistered. I can't believe I didn't notice before.

"They're, uh, fine. I burned them cooking. Nothing to worry about."

"Cooking what?" Alison asks, not letting it go. "When?"

Araminta spreads her hands to say nevermind, and as the meeting is going Alison has to let it drop. I feel ill. It's not just this. I've been having more nightmares lately; the book has featured, but what I've seen hasn't been confined to the text. A man mostly in shadow, dressed in a long cloak, carrying the book around rooms that look like our home and yet not exactly, writing in it with thick ink, scratchy strokes of a pen that make me shudder.

It hasn't put me in the best frame of mind for this.

Keira is doing most of the talking for her and Logan both, and she's all smiles and effusive introductions, thanking us so much for taking the time to meet with them. I feel a faint nausea, a fear I haven't felt in a long time. Like I'm being judged by standards I couldn't possibly meet. In a way I've been judged too many times before.

I wonder, as I often do about new people, whether they know we're all neurodivergent, that most of us are autistic. Me, usually, they figure out based on my selective mutism – not everyone with it is autistic but it fits with their ideas of what autistic people are like. But Alison? Araminta who plays up the quirky artist persona whenever she needs to? Denny who's just like you might imagine anyone's grandfather, a man of few words but with specific interests he can spend hours on? I think that the reason so many people are resistant to the idea of a person or people being autistic is because if they accepted us as such then they'd be forced to reconsider whether the same might be true of all kinds of other people in their lives – their family, themselves even.

On our side there's myself, Araminta, Denny, Vinnie, and Alison. Holly is at a study session, Theo staying with his father, and Saeed has gone to catch up with a couple of classmates ahead of the start of the academic year. It would be good for him to have a study group – I know that while correspondence study is the best option for him, he finds it isolating at times, but I'm cynical enough to suspect he may have timed it strategically to avoid this meeting, and frankly, I don't blame him.

As we talk back and forth I feel my chest tighten further. The ghost hunters are communicating as much by looks between each other as by words, looks I don't know how to interpret. They're saying all the right things, that they respect the ghosts and care about their privacy every bit as much as we do. I know they're not quite telling the truth, but whether they're being aspirational or outright manipulative and deceitful, I honestly can't tell.

I often dismiss my anxiety – when most of your housemates have more severe anxiety disorders, it's easy not to notice how much you're affected. Not until it flares up like this, something I haven't experienced in a long time, and now I'm struggling to cope. I don't know who's lying and who's telling the truth, and it's messing with my head. And my inability to tell has been taken advantage of in the past, more than once.

The worries I usually suppress start rushing back and it's so hard to stem them. What if the people I live with – the people I love – secretly hate me and are just too polite to say so? What if it's all a joke? What if they're pretending to be nice to me to suck me in just so they can hurt me more?

I know that isn't how we do things here. None of us could live like that. We're straight up with each other, partly because we need it and partly because that's our immediate instinct, the natural way we behave. If someone struggles to communicate that's something we either adjust to or help them with, not something to be used strategically to somehow beat them.

I force myself back into the present, force myself to look at the ghost hunters in turn, using the trick of looking just to one side of their faces so I can avoid making eye contact without them realising that's what I'm doing. I even talk a little, though Alison and Araminta are taking the lead. Eventually, we reach a conclusion.

The agreement is this: we will ask one of the ghosts if he – and I assume we're referring to Roderick – would be interested in talking to the ghost hunters. If he is, we will facilitate a discussion. Otherwise, they will not push or argue the point, and will not be caught sneaking round here again.

There's one last thing to be talked through. Logan wants us to ask Roderick if he'd mind them recording their discussion, should it happen.

"Absolutely not," says Vinnie. We all turn to look at them.

"Only if he agrees..." Keira says.

"Saeed was telling me this whole thing," Vinnie says, softening their tone a little. "About how ghosts don't really retain knowledge after they become ghosts. The ghost we're thinking of understands what meeting with people means. But even though he's recent enough to have some understanding of video recording, he still can't understand the implications. The internet. How many people could see it and how many copies could be made. He doesn't even really understand how much the world's population has grown."

As the ghost hunters are leaving, and we're standing and stretching, ready to file out of the orangerie behind them, I pause.

"Keira," I say. She turns around to look at me. "You're interested in the history of astronomy, right? I've got something I think you'll want to see. Do you want to wait here and I'll go get it?"

On my way up the main staircase, I feel like perhaps I've been a complete idiot. I'm about to show something that's not just valuable financially, not just valuable to me, but also of great interest to someone who has, among other things, been caught breaking into my house.

But I recognise the expression I saw on her face, the fear that she was being tricked, that she was being offered kindness only as a joke, and then the gratitude that flooded her expression once she realised it was genuine. Perhaps I recognised it because it's crossed my own face so many times.

I take the telescope from the drawer. It's not large; probably just a hobby thing, but it works surprisingly well given how old it is. Its box smells of leather and dust. I hold it close to my chest as I head back downstairs to where Keira is waiting, looking high up at the sky, alone.

I remember what my dad used to say about spiders when Rory got scared of them. That they were way more afraid of him than he was of them. He tried to tell me that about wasps too but I disagree: wasps are just evil. But perhaps it does apply to Keira, if not to all of the ghost hunters.

"It's really kind of you to show me this, thank you," she says as I walk across the gravel towards her.

I can recognise well-practiced speech patterns better than most, but I'm actually pleased that she's making something of an effort. Most of the fury I felt when she broke into our attic has faded in me, and I'm softening towards her despite making an effort to remain wary, to not be taken in. I'm not yet sure if she's a good but misguided person, or if she's manipulative and everything else is an act, but either way I'm warming to her, whether that's a wise idea or not.

I motion her to follow me; I want to get to a low wall where I can put this down before getting it out, and my docs and her trainers crunch on the gravel as we go. We walk around the exterior of the house; along the grass which backs onto the gardens of a row of houses, full with washing lines and children's slides. Looking back at our house, the ivy is growing up the wall again, now sharp with frost, and we will need to pull it back. It's pretty, but it's not at all good for the stonework. A task for one ridiculous day when it's a bit warmer.

One of the things I love about Casswell Park is that even though it's a pain in the ass to do the maintenance, it still makes you feel productive when you work on it. You can always see very visible results of your work.

I look up as we walk and see Mackerel and Anchovy on the balcony, looking quite happy in the winter sun – though doubtless I'll take them a wheat pack when I next heat one for Mallard. They're all spoiled, like many cats are. I remind myself again to talk to Alison about getting a cat door so she doesn't have to leave the door open like that, but I don't think Keira's seen it. I hope not anyway.

Putting the telescope down on the low brick wall, I take it out of its box and after holding it for a few moments I hand it to Keira, and can't stop myself smiling as her eyes grow wide.

She's clearly dressed up for the occasion because rather than her ragged hoodie and jeans she's wearing black trousers and a burgundy jumper. It looks like good quality, too, so soft I have to force myself not to reach out and touch it. She can tell me far more about the telescope than I know; how old it is, where it was likely made, but more importantly she's in love with its shape, the craft taken to make it.

We stand there, both of us, a telescope between us, as if we could be friends. We're divided by so much and yet the fact that ghosts are so important to both of us carries a connection that feels far more important than I could ever have thought it would. And right now, I have no idea what's going to happen next.

It's only minutes after Keira and Logan leave that a car pulls up. Before it's stopped moving, Theo has propelled himself from the vehicle and is charging towards us. I reach out, high five him, and then Araminta grabs him and hugs him and we all pile around and laugh.

"Good day?" Alison asks.

The car parks and Caleb – Theo's father – gets out of the car, grinning broadly.

"Seatbelt stays done up until the car stops. I've told you this," he calls, but there's good humour in his voice.

"Didn't undo the seatbelt though. Slid out of it." Theo is clearly very pleased with himself.

"Yeah, Vinnie will kill you later," Alison remarks.

"I'll call ChildLine!"

"Yep, and they'll tell you to wear your seatbelt as well. Besides, you can't call ChildLine when you're dead otherwise all our younger ghosts would be doing that."

Araminta and I chuckle.

"Imagine," Araminta says. "Referrals to social services to investigate a three-hundred-year-old murder."

"Stop!" Theo says, swinging his arms round with every word. "Stop. Making. Fun. Of. Me."

"Sorry, kid," Alison says. "We're not trying to make fun of you – we're just running with the idea we found funny. But you do need to do as your parents say. They care about you being safe. Do you want to go and find Vinnie now?"

Theo scampers inside, not seeming upset, and Vinnie soon emerges. Caleb is chuckling to himself.

"They say it takes a village – well, I think it takes two parents, a group of their friends, and the ghosts they live in a giant haunted house with."

"He's turning out pretty well," Vinnie says. "All we need to do now is find a way to get rid of those wheelie trainers and we'll be good."

"Yeah... uh... sorry about those," Caleb says, in a way that makes it clear that he's only sorry for any impact they had on him.

Vinnie rolls their eyes.

"He's getting loud noise making toys for his birthday. Very loud. And repetitive. To be kept at your place." They pause. "Do you want to drive back or crash overnight? I heard there's ice on the roads so..."

"Well, if it's no trouble..." he says hesitantly.

"No trouble at all. You can see how many rooms we have. Plenty of space for everyone. We can set up a room in no time."

I used to be intimidated by Caleb.

It wasn't his height and it certainly wasn't his actions. It was that everything seemed to come naturally to him, every word from his mouth seemed as if it was perfectly chosen, and yet without any effort. It reminded me of all my faults, and then reinforced them with anxiety. I'd find myself stumbling, not knowing how to communicate.

Now? Now he's as good as family.

I signal with a thumbs up, a nod, and a pointing down the corridor that I'm happy to get everything set up, and head to a room we use for shared supplies. There's all sorts in there, including an outdoor trampoline which we'll drag out when the weather gets a bit warmer. There's also an accrued pile of spare linen and towels, many of them donated by my and Saeed's parents who seem to think bestowing household goods is the best expression of love. The day dad dropped off a slow cooker big enough to make us all dinner and still have some leftovers for lunch, I decided to agree with them.

The bed is one of the original ones from the boarding school. Nineteen sixties, basic, mass produced, but still functional. The mattresses are of course long gone, and thankfully so. The replacement is foam – we got a batch of ten of them on special, remaindered stock or something. I make it up quickly with the spare linen and a couple of blankets, and leave the towels folded neatly at the bottom of the bed. It won't be the comfiest, but I figure anyone who flies planes long distance has slept on worse.

When I get back, most of my housemates are hanging out with Caleb in the dining room. He's brought us some mochi he picked up at Tokyo-Narita airport. Caleb never arrives empty handed; there's not only a gift for his child but also something for the house. I take the cardboard lid off and place the box on the table, helping myself to one in a green wrapper. It's chewy and tastes of green tea. Not what I'd usually eat, but it's good. We're a family, the eight of us absolutely, but we're also a family that is flexible, fluid at the edges. A family that expands rather than polices its border.

1705

I sobel has seen ghosts all her life. Sometimes they're just the faintest wisp drifting across a room; sometimes they could almost be alive, were all the colour not leached from them. She never got to know any in the way she got to know Tobias, though.

But it's not concern for him that motivates her. It's more fury that anyone could be confined to glass like that, guilt at her role in it and... well she's always dreamed of going on an adventure.

From picking up on village gossip, she knows the name of his house, the nearby town, and that both are some way from here. That doesn't faze her.

She has her bag packed with a spare dress and bread for the journey. She has a little money. She's used to walking a long way, and she hopes there will be someone who give her a ride on a cart part of the journey. She can work for more bread, or for a place to sleep. It's summer, and the world awaits.

CHAPTER TEN

W e've walked this house in pairs before. Usually it's for doing a detailed check for damage or a maintenance view. We did it once when a child was missing from one of the houses behind, just in case they could have got in and hidden in a cupboard or something – they were fortunately found in a neighbour's shed, cold and hungry but nothing worse.

Today we're walking the house in pairs again, checking for damage and conducting, as far as we can, a census of the ghosts. We're moving from each corner through to the centre, checking every room, noting down any changes to the house, any evidence of anything wrong, and – most importantly – checking up on the ghosts, making sure they're all there, and looking for any signs of injury or distress.

Saeed and I are downstairs, starting from the laundry rooms and working our way towards the staircase in the middle. I'm uneasy in a way I haven't been since I settled in and began considering this my home. I'm jumpy, conscious of every footstep on the creaking wooden floors. My chest feels like it's been pulled tight and the tips of my fingers tingle with tension.

But there's nothing amiss in the laundry rooms unless you count a load of Denny's clothing, which has been sitting in the washer damp for too long and is making the place smell musty. I pour in a good measure of detergent and turn it on for another wash. Saeed sets an alarm on his phone so he can remind Denny to go and get the clothes out when the cycle finishes.

The first two rooms, one set up as a spare room, but both largely unused, are similarly uneventful. But in the third, we find a ghost, Joseph, the one Alison can't resist referring to as Trouser Boy. That's usually a joke but no-one's laughing now. There's a hollow right through Joseph's head, taking out most of his face. Where his eyes and nose were is just nothingness. He's standing blankly in the corner. I'm not good at interpreting facial expressions even with people who have faces, but I can assume he's not doing well.

When I move over to try and somehow comfort him, he walks upwards and through the ceiling, as if climbing an invisible staircase.

"This makes me uncomfortable," I say.

"Same," replies Saeed. "We know ghosts can fade, and it's sad and everything, but it's normal. Inevitable. But they don't just lose parts of themselves. We've seen the fading be more pronounced in one part of the body – typically the lower extremities – than the others, but it's a gradual change. They don't just... lose a limb or something. Not unless it happened before or at their death, anyway. And I've never seen anything like whatever happened to Joseph."

I nod.

"It's one thing to be without limbs," he says, and he's babbling now. "Sometimes I've wished I could dispense with mine. But it's like these have been forcibly removed..."

I message the group chat.

> Just found Joseph. In a pretty bad way. Let's just say half of his face is missing. Oh, and his head and brain.

Didn't want to stick around. Think he's heading your way V.

> Just seen him. If you ever wanted to know what a face saying "wow that's cool" and "holy shit that's terrifying" looks like you might want to take a look at Theo right now.

> shit

I don't have a better response than that right now. I feel for Theo, who has been thrilled to be considered a full participant, making up one of the pairs together with his parent. I know Vinnie doesn't really feel okay about it either, much as they're making light of it right now. Joseph and Theo are the same age, more or less. It's hard enough to think of a kid that age dying – but then being imprisoned in a bottle for centuries, and then having your face and half your brain cut or blown off... well, that's not a nice thing to be confronted with.

Two rooms later we see another ghost. I recognise her as the girl we released from the last bottle we opened. But I have to recognise her only by her dress, because she has no head. Atop her shoulders there is nothing. She reaches behind her back and brings out a head. Ghostly, non-corporeal, recently severed; bone and veins still visible and glowing, she holds it grinning above her neck.

I know whose head it is. It's Holly's head. Severed and ghostly.

I've been seeing ghosts all my life. I've never screamed in response to one before.

I scream now.

Saeed emerges to my scream. As soon as I recover myself I ask Saeed if I can push him, he says he agrees the situation calls for it, or I could just go on ahead. I tell him, with all the humour I can muster right now, that I might leave him alone to be eaten but there was no way I was heading into whatever had happened by myself.

Then I grabbed the back of his wheelchair and found strength and speed I didn't know I had to propel both of us down the corridor, past the staircase, turning again in the next part of the corridor, then somehow flinging us around and smashing through the closed, but mercifully light, doors with my back. Bringing us to a halt, I let go of Saeed who wheels himself towards Holly, Alison kneeling beside her. I can see her shape on the ground, her blonde hair – not much darker than that of the ghost version of herself – fanned out on the wooden floor, but I don't look any closer.

A quick exchange of shaky words with Alison reveals that probably a few moments before the ghost revealed Holly's head to me, Holly had collapsed to the floor, shaking; perhaps experiencing a seizure, perhaps something else entirely. Alison had just been in the process of loosening the clothing around her neck and putting her in the recovery position before going for help when Saeed and I had arrived.

"She'll be okay," I hear Alison say. Then Saeed's voice asking if he should call an ambulance. I'm useless.

I can hear Holly burbling. Alison reassuring her. The burbles become words. Holly is alive, at least. I can't look at her. I'm ashamed at how self-absorbed I'm being, but I can't bring myself to go any closer. I can feel the tears running rapidly down my face, and shaking and twitching in every muscle, but this doesn't feel like crying.

Slowly I turn, force myself to open my eyes. Holly looks ill, but largely unharmed. At least her head is firmly attached to her body, I can tell that much. Looking closer, though I try not to stare too obviously, I can see marks around her neck; not deep cuts, but more as if something had been tied, someone had tried to strangle her.

Alison holds one of Holly's hands and I take the other instinctively. She looks more sick and dazed than distressed, though.

"I'm going to see if Roderick knows anything," Saeed says. "Denny, can you help me look for him?"

Denny returns with Roderick, followed by Saeed who carries one of the posters with letters of the alphabet that enable more communication with the literate ghosts. I've never seen Roderick looking so serious before. There's still a hint of mischief in his expression, but even he seems to be sobered by the situation.

I make a brief calculation in my head. He'd be in his sixties now, easily, my father's age. I imagine him still retaining a little of that youthful mischief as he grew up, delighted when his first grandchildren arrived, aiding them with pranks and mischief to the despair of their parents who will, typically, have been his opposites; serious and quiet.

There are a lot of poignant might-have-beens when you live with ghosts.

Roderick thinks for a minute and then begins to point slowly at the letters. Saeed reads them out loud.

G

H

O

We – almost inevitably – only get three letters in before Roderick hesitates, starts to drift off. He notices something – something we may not be able to see, and smirks in amusement.

"Roderick, please," Saeed says desperately. "Please focus. We really need your help here."

Perhaps surprisingly, Roderick does snap back into focus.

"We're going to assume that word is ghost. Is that right, Roderick?"

He nods in response and begins pointing to the letters again.

E

A

T

The remaining letters come flowing quickly, almost too fast to sound them out as we go.

E

R

GHOST EATER

Ghost eater. If I'd wondered whether there was a worse term than ghost hunter then I think I've found my answer. But to be sure, Saeed asks Roderick again. We've found in the past that either/or questions are best when we really need to get answers from ghosts. Open-ended questions are hard for them to answer. If we ask them a yes/no question they feel emotionally inclined to say yes, especially if they sense you're stressed or unsure. So we offer Roderick a choice.

"Roderick," says Saeed, his voice clear and deliberate. "Did you say Ghost eater or Ghost Hunter?"

I hold out my right hand as Saeed says 'eater' and my left as he says 'hunter'. Roderick points with a confident expression to my right hand.

It's Alison who speaks next.

"Roderick," she says. "This ghost eater. Is he a bit like a ghost himself...?"

Roderick shakes his head and then shrugs, but points out some more letters.

B

O

O

"Very stereotypical for a ghost," Denny whispers to me. I shush him but laugh despite myself. I'm glad I can still laugh.

K

BOOK

"What book, Roderick?" Alison begins to ask, but as she speaks the words, Roderick is drifting off, diagonally up and then through the high ceiling. We could run after him, but by the time we'd get along the corridor, up the stairs, and then along the corridor to the room above, he could be anywhere. And if he either doesn't want to or is struggling to talk to us, running after him is unlikely to yield the desired result.

I try not to be angry. I'm not angry at Roderick, but I can feel a little anger at the situation creeping up inside me. All ghosts are like this to some extent. I'm not sure if it's an attention issue as we understand it, or, as some have suggested, they're partly in this world and partly in another, meaning they have to switch their focus between the two. It's understandable, but when you really need something and can't get it, it's hard not to be frustrated.

I take one of my anxiety meds, finally start to calm down. I sit on the floor and look all around me. We've often felt overwhelmed by this main hall – it's an amazing space but beyond our capacity to do much with. Most of it is two storeys high, which would necessitate scaffolding for significant repairs, and that's just for starters.

And yet in its day it must have been glorious. If you look up you can still see what's left of the high arches and ornate ceiling plaster. A floor – before it was stripped back – fit for dances. I wonder if some of those who are now ghosts danced here, courted, met lovers. I wonder how many spent those evenings sat along the walls, never asked to dance except from pity or as a joke. I wonder how many young women were dancing with men while looking only at the other women, men looking at the other men.

Denny has brought Holly sugary tea and some paracetamol and Araminta has dragged through a chair for her, and at this point she's just looking very tired and a little dazed. When we tell her what we saw she starts laughing nervously and then tries to make light of the whole thing, tugging at her head to demonstrate that it's well attached. But I can tell she's terrified. The only mercy is that she didn't have to see her own severed head.

If anything, though, I'm more worried that the marks on Holly's neck might have been something she did herself rather than something paranormal. I'm surprised by how stressed I feel about it. Suicidality isn't exactly new to anyone here. It certainly isn't to me. And yet I'd fantasised that by getting here so young, Holly might have been spared the worst of the self-hatred that people like us inevitably find permeates our lives. That was naïve. In many ways, it seems she's had it harder than the rest of us.

It's been different for all of us. Diagnoses – of autism or ADD or the now-defunct Asperger's Syndrome – at different ages, coming out as queer of one stripe or another. Even seemingly similar experiences have had such different effects. Araminta and I were both diagnosed young, something that wasn't really possible for most people of Alison and Denny's, even Vinnie's, age. For me, even though things weren't always easy, it allowed me to understand myself and sometimes get the support I needed. For Araminta it led to years of intense and exhausting corrective therapy, the devaluation of herself, active abuse under the vague guise of treatment, and denial of her humanity to the point that even she doesn't think she's human much of the time.

I was, if nothing else, always around someone who got me. I never had to wonder why I did things a particular way, and I was usually spared punishment when I could not do the same things as my neurotypical peers. But though my parents protected me from the worst of it, people's assumptions had a lasting effect. Whereas Araminta was told she could do everything – and assumed to be disobedient when she couldn't – I wasn't even given the chance to do many of the things I could have done.

But right now, I have to turn my attention to the issue at hand, working out who could be responsible for causing all these problems we're now faced with. I mentally run through possible suspects and other, less human, forces.

It may be a premature conclusion, but I think very little of what is going on is because of the ghost hunters. Certainly they've proven to be determined and pushy, not so good at respecting other people's boundaries. But they also all seem rather naive and non-malicious, motivated by interest, curiosity, and perhaps the prospect of online fame. They may genuinely not understand the harm they can do to those ghosts, or they may not care enough, but this level of destructiveness just doesn't seem to be like them. No, this is something else entirely.

I think this can only be the work of the ghost eater.

1706

I sobel had a plan: she was going to rescue Tobias, perhaps give the one who caught him a piece of her mind, and then head back home.

She didn't expect to stay.

She doesn't know exactly what she is here: not exactly a servant, not exactly an apprentice, but she does know she can see ghosts more clearly than the man she works for, more clearly – he says, in a rare moment of praise – than anyone he's known.

She has a room at the end of the house – a guest room, not a servant's room. The rest of the family here are polite to her, but mostly ignore her, unsure how she fits into the structure of the house. She's well fed and has comfortable sheets and warm baths every week.

That's not why she stays. In those laboratory rooms, a whole world has opened up for her. She's learned to read, letter by letter, and then to write. She's slow at it but getting faster. She's learning about ghosts and alchemy, about the stars, about how there are other worlds like this out there in the sky. She's learning natural philosophy, about experimentation, Newton's Rules for Science, eliminative deduction.

She does believe, one day, that she will set Tobias free, smash the carefully labelled bottle that is kept on the shelf, and she tells herself that that's the only reason why she's here.

She wonders if her discomfort with the collection of ghosts is a failing on her part, a foundering of rationalism. She has every interest he does in learning and classifying, but she cannot endorse keeping them in those labelled glass bottles forever, never to see the world again.

There's worse. One day in winter, when snow drifts are piled up to the house, he asks her to assist, holding the bottle that contains the ghost of a girl not yet quite grown. He begins the incantation, lighting the carefully prepared composite that will give the right density of smoke. The ghost emerges, as she is used to by now, a young face, a head with braided hair, rising from the lip of the bottle. But instead of continuing to pull her out, he takes a knife she has never seen before from the table, mutters a few words of an incantation, severing the girl's head from her body firmly at the neck.

Isobel drops the bottle.

CHAPTER ELEVEN

Half of us wolf down our dinner as if we'd been starved for days, while the rest of us pick at it, swirling chilli and rice round our plates, unable to eat much. Only Vinnie is absent; they've taken the crate of bottles to Caleb's apartment for safekeeping, anticipating that the ghost eater, as we're now all calling whatever malign presence seems to be stirring up trouble in this household, might do something terrible with them if he's given the opportunity.

The rest of us decide that we want to keep watch overnight. We'll do it in pairs; even I've seen enough horror movies to know you don't keep watch in the haunted house at night alone. Even when that haunted house is the place you feel safest.

I'm one of the ones who isn't really eating. Everything feels different for me at the moment, as if the whole house has come to life. I'm feeling energy emanating from its walls, from the shapes of its rooms, from its very existence.

When I finally force myself to eat at least some of the meal, I do so in silence, only nodding or laughing at what seem to be the appropriate points in an ongoing argument that diverts along tangents including the X-Men, the 1812 overture, and whether it was unfair of Alison to name one of her cats Anchovy.

"I know Mackerel's named after a fish too," says Saeed. "But that's for that pattern of markings, right? An anchovy is just a fish."

"Cats like fish!" Alison insists.

"I like music," Denny says. "Would still be fucked off if my parents had called me guitar."

Alison shoots daggers from her eyes at him. Not literally. It would be a useful power if she could.

"I thought you'd be on my side."

"Not when it comes to giving your cats terrible names. I like any animal more than even my favourite humans, remember. Even cats named after ducks."

I know he's trying to wind me up. I know I shouldn't rise to it. Yet here I am, instantly on my feet, glaring at Denny.

"Holder of the world speed record for steam locomotives." I enunciate each word clearly and loudly at Denny. "Not a fucking duck."

"Yeah, yeah, okay. Just checking you were still with us," Denny says while Saeed mutters something about autocorrect. I laugh but as soon as I sit down I'm starting to zone out, as if I'm in a hundred different worlds all at once, and the people around me are far away. I feel other presences, whole histories bearing down on me, overlapping, so strong I can't pick any one thing out. The room seems to be spinning a little.

Things aren't usually this intense. I've always had this ability, but normally it takes a lot to set it off. Places where there has been extraordinary violence. Very old places. Places where there have been a large number of people experiencing strong emotions – it's been set off by sports stadiums, even music venues. But now... now it's everywhere. When I walk outside I can feel it in the trees, even in the blades of grass. Everything is heightened, to the extent that it's almost as great a change as if I'd gone from no ability at all, to this.

There are a lot of unknowns, but I know something is changing. Not just for the ghosts, not just in those around me, but in me.

After dinner I wander round the house a bit, but I feel like I'm getting pulled in one direction. I stop fighting whatever invisible force is working on me, and end up in one of the unused downstairs rooms. It's empty with an unvarnished wooden floor and chipped blue paint that likely dated from when this was a school, the room itself perhaps a classroom. Initials engraved into the wooden window frame support that hypothesis.

I sensed something slight in this room the first time I went into it, the knowledge that something significant had happened here. It was likely to be a death or an act of violence; it didn't surprise me given the size and age of the house, that it held unpleasant secrets. Saeed had a quick look through his records but there was nothing, in particular, to tie it to. I'd nearly forgotten about it...

Now, though, it's not just a room that provokes a sensation. It's as if the walls are vibrating. As if everything is alive, as if energies of the past are as strong as they ever were and they're all running through me. Once I had only a vague sense that this room had a past. Now it's clearer than anything like this has ever been for me.

Somewhere in my mind's eye, I get a definite, if fuzzy, image. I don't know whether what happened was deliberate or an accident, but I can see metal cutting through flesh, blood spreading out across the floor, soaking into the wood, dripping through the gaps to the earth below...

It doesn't scare me that it happened here. I know terrible things have happened at Casswell Park over the centuries, as they have in any house like this.

It does scare me that it's suddenly become so much clearer to me, and I don't know why.

I know that I'll find it only too easy to fall asleep if we stay in my room, and Araminta's is, as usual, out of the question, so we set up a base in the spare room next to mine. Holly is with Saeed in his bedroom, Vinnie and Theo in the living area of their suite, and Alison and Denny in the main hall. Between us, we're pretty well spread out through the house. We've set up timers to ensure we walk around our sections on a regular basis.

Araminta and I are stretched out on the lower bunk of the boarding school bed. She's brought her laptop, logged in on a guest account because me glancing at her browsing is another source of anxiety for her. I've gathered together sugary snacks and a bottle of Coke Zero, meaning we have everything we need in order to keep us awake all night.

Even past midnight I'm wide awake, but Araminta is yawning. She'll be calling in sick later – fortunately, she's the only one of us scheduled to work this Saturday. She's also seemingly immune to almost all illnesses, so aside from the occasional bad anxiety attack, she can save her sick days for hangovers and the weird things that happen when you live in a giant old house filled with ghosts.

Jodie Keane drifts through the room. I make a note but it seems like typical ghost behaviour so no need to do anything else. Another half an hour passes with nothing to report. We each do a walk up and down our section of the corridor in that time. I see what seem like lingering shadows on the hallway, but dismiss them as tricks of the torchlight.

It's just when we're beginning to think everything is fine that I hear wailing somewhere in the distance. I open the door and a ghost flies down the corridor so fast that I can't even tell who it is, bringing with them a thick draft of cold air. I like to think I'm completely comfortable with ghosts, and most of the time I am, but something about this evening is starting to creep me out.

The hours drag on. Jodie walks through the door – literally walks through the door, not just the doorway

– twice, long strides and head bent low, but when we ask her if something's wrong, she doesn't seem to have heard us. Later we hear screeching, loud and shrill and terrifying. I go to investigate it, my feet feeling heavy, torch in one hand and phone in another. In the next room I find Tim McCabe pinned against the wall, his body stretched and contorted in ways I didn't think were possible even for ghosts. Nothing I can do comforts him, but he stops eventually.

We circuit the corridors again. The shadows are growing. It's only when I walk with Araminta that I start to realise what is happening. I ask her to stop, walk again, change which side of the hallway she's walking on. I can't deny it. She's shedding shadows as she walks, patches of darkness peeling off her and layering themselves up in the corridor.

We type the observations up into the shared document Saeed created so we could refer to it later, and to stop the group chat becoming overloaded with this stuff. It's all we can do. It's looking like everyone else in the house is having similar experiences. We pass even my preferred bedtime, and it's hard to tell what is ghosts in the background, what is my exhausted imagination, and what is just the wind.

I've a bit of a sprawling project – or at least a collection of notes – about communication with ghosts, and about how ghosts communicate with each other. My idea – what Saeed would call my hypothesis – is that almost everything ghosts do is a form of communication. That applies to wailing, to poltergeist activity, even to much of their movement, as well as the more obviously deliberate forms of communication. I find it odd that even many of those who obsess about ghosts, who devote their lives to understanding them, seem unwilling or unable to understand this, much less to make anything more than a basic attempt to interpret that communication.

The first message to come through on the group chat is from Denny, and it's uncharacteristically panicked.

It would be wrong to say Denny is uncomfortable with computers. If they have no more than two colours and are operated by a command line input, then he's as comfortable with them as if he were cradling a child of his own. But anything more than that makes him overloaded and anxious. He can cope, but it never comes naturally, and everything he does is carefully considered, even messages to our sometimes-ridiculous group chat. You can almost hear him asking himself in his head: is this the right thing to say? the right place to say it? is my grammar absolutely impeccable?

I'm saying this to make it clear that getting a message from him that's been written quickly enough to have an obvious typo – let alone two - is a sign that something has happened. And I get that message now.

> somethng wierd down here

Araminta and I both stand up instantly, her gulping down the last of her glass of coke – we're going to need all the caffeine we can get – and grabbing my phone, messaging as we walk out into the corridor. Already the correction comes through and I smile at it despite my worry.

> sorry weird
> can someone get down here
> mints and I are on our way. Weird how?
> Did you just call me Mints???

Araminta is right behind me with her phone out also, chuckling in indignation despite herself.

"Can you not?" she says aloud.

I laugh despite myself, and more so when Vinnie's message comes through.

> ghost weird or other supernatural weird or that one time Saeed made special brownies weird?
> maybe ghost?
> not like usual ghosts though.

I feel sleep dragging down at my eyes. Despite begging a zopiclone off Saeed, I slept terribly the previous night, shaken awake again and again by the thought of Holly's ghostly severed head. I can't even begin to explain what I saw, and the lack of any kind of rational explanation means I simply can't put the matter to rest, can't let go. I keep wanting to go to Holly's room to try and placate my fears, check she really is safe and well.

I force myself not to. Holly may technically still be a child, but unlike Theo she's not just on the cusp of adulthood but also here independently. Sometimes she's more of an adult than the rest of us – it's her who will replace a washer or a fuse, not to mention reminding us that bills are due or noticing when we're low on milk. We watch out for her, of course – a bit more than we all do each other – but the last thing she needs is to go from abusive parents to overbearing and fretting flatmates.

Denny's messages direct me to the blue-painted room I seem to be so drawn to at the moment. Denny is inside and Saeed is not far behind Araminta and I. And there's someone else, not quite a ghost and not quite a person. I may have never seen him before, but there's no question in my mind that this must be who we've been warned about. The ghost eater.

He moves quickly, darting around the room as if he were a cat in pursuit of an oversized, fast-footed mouse. I catch glimpses; his black cloak, curled hair, buckled shoes, piercing eyes...

I'm not scared at first. I'm good at rationalising my fears away and I do that now: he isn't scary and he doesn't look particularly strong. I'm not scared of ghosts and I'm far less scared of people than I used to be, so there's certainly no reason for me to be scared of someone who appears to be somewhere halfway between the two. But as he approaches, I can feel anxiety starting to claw at my throat. It's not that I fear he will hurt me, but because how I react may change things for so many other people, people both human and ghost who I love, who I feel responsible for, and I'm so scared of fucking it up.

I hear Saeed behind me and I scream at him to stay back. Of course, he does no such thing. The person, the ghost eater, the man who is not exactly a ghost, is approaching, and then it all happens at once.

When it happens, it seems like it's in slow motion, but so is everything else; my thoughts, my reactions, even the movement of my arm. The ghost eater takes a few steps back. Foolhardily, I step forward, protecting Araminta, which seems to enrage him further. He launches himself at me, and then he's through me, sharing space with me, his molecules and mine intermingling.

I feel icy cold, and I feel intruded upon. I'm fighting to get him out, get him away from me, flinging my arms desperately, but it's impossible to get a hold on him when there's so little differentiation between us.

Then, and the whole thing must only have taken seconds, he's moved past me. At first, I think he's won. Then I realise it was never about me at all. He's going for Araminta.

I move to try and fight him but my stomach lurches and I vomit on the wooden floor, fighting to stand up properly but being waylaid by the betrayal of my own body.

The ghost eater launches himself towards Araminta, his hand outstretched, his fingers wrapping around the pendant, trying to grab it from her neck.

He's not corporeal enough to snatch it, but it doesn't slide through non-corporeal fingers either. I reach out to Araminta as he pulls on her and she struggles to balance herself.

And before we can properly react, he's gone. I don't know exactly what we're dealing with but I know this much: the last bottle we opened has unleashed something we couldn't ever have predicted, and he wants something from us that we can never agree to give him.

While I'm still in shock, Araminta's instincts are clicking into place. As I stare, she grabs her phone and a torch and tells me to wait; I hear her footsteps light but fast along the corridor. Soon everyone is nearby; Denny and Alison scanning the corridor outside, Araminta telling me to sit down and getting my water bottle for me, Saeed frantically researching as much as he can on his tablet.

There's no use going after the ghost eater. He's not human and he's not even a ghost. He casts a shadow unlike any ghost but he's not fully corporeal either. We don't know how to fight him or how to bargain with him; we don't even know what is anger, what is confusion, what is calculated scheming. I wonder even if the pendant was once his, perhaps he thinks we stole it from him. Perhaps he doesn't understand how much it is Araminta's, how much it is my gift to her.

I bring up the group chat. My hands are shaking and I keep hitting the wrong keys. We're all here, but I can't say words out loud right now.

I laugh, and it comes out like an odd gurgle of sounds. Damn millennials all looking at their phones rather than talking to each other. Except some of our number are in their fifties and one is only ten – I'm not sure if there's even a word for his generation – and they're showing me every bit of love and care and understanding I need. Plus, all of us are interacting with each other, and given that we're all supposed to have diminished social skills or something, that should rightfully be considered an achievement.

We piece together what we can. That this is the ghost eater who Roderick spoke of, and he was likely contained in the bottle we most recently opened and let out when we unsealed it. We're not sure exactly what he is; he has some things in common with ghosts, but he's not only physically distinct from any ghost we've ever known but he seems to behave differently too.

There's a lot of folklore about ghosts wanting revenge or holding a grudge. It doesn't happen in reality nearly as often, but when it does it manifests more as an obsession than a calculated plan. They keep returning to someone or something, and they can certainly make someone's life a misery, but there's little calculation or planning to it, and unless you personally murdered them, they're unlikely to act with malice towards you.

This is different. The ghost eater is strategising. He has a plan and he's working towards a goal. I know part of that goal, or one step along the way, is getting hold of the pendant. But there are still many unknowns. Is the distress he's causing the ghosts an intentional part of that plan, or an unintended side effect? Why, specifically, are they appearing injured or missing body parts? How can we stop him?

We all know one thing, though: the community we've worked so hard to build is under threat. And it's not really clear what the attacker is, how we can fight him, or what our chances of success are. And this makes me far more uneasy than my direct encounter with him. All my muscles ache and I'm struggling to focus.

"You should probably stop wearing that pendant," Saeed says gently, cutting through the silence.

Araminta nods, but she's looking at me rather than Saeed.

There's something between me and Araminta now, that's not just love but something older, deeper, and we both know that pendant's not coming off. It crosses my mind that it's enchanted me in some way, that there's something evil about it, but it doesn't feel like it. It feels like it's perfect for her, and it connects us in a way that neither of us knew we were missing. She tucks it into her dress, subconsciously, and as she does I can see a burn mark, just below her neck, where the pendant sits.

CHAPTER TWELVE

As I inhale from a mug of coffee, and push porridge around my bowl, Araminta shows me the photo she took the previous day. It's a soft blur, patches of pale flesh colour, red and black, a roughly humanoid shape, and no more. I sigh at the inevitability of this result. Ghosts never photograph well. Sceptics call it convenient; those who know it to be the truth suspect it to be something to do with the light frequencies that change as they lose corporeality. What we're faced with may not exactly be a ghost, but it's got plenty in common with them, and this is just one more thing.

I shrug.

"Better than nothing. Thanks for trying."

"That's not everything. Someone else came for my pendant."

I'm on my feet in no time, horrified.

"What? Who? The ghost eater again?"

Araminta shakes her head. "No, Isobel. She wasn't... I mean, she was kinder about it, but she clearly wanted it. Or at least wanted me to take it off."

"Maybe you should...?" I start to say, uncomfortable though the thought makes me, but she shakes her head and clutches it with her hand. I know that look. It's the stubbornness that she has used to survive things much worse than I've ever experienced.

Saeed starts to tell me about his, mostly dead end, research attempts. He's eating more enthusiastically than me: cornflakes and fresh fruit along with the obligatory mug of coffee. And as he does so, Araminta slips out of the room and within just minutes she's back carrying a blue tote bag. Then she perches on one of the stools at the back of the room, takes out a book and a case of pencils, and begins to draw.

It's rare for her to do any kind of art in front of us, but she's so focused now she's almost in a trance; working in her hardbacked sketchbook with a soft pencil, broad strokes for the basic outline and then building up detail bit by bit. Despite knowing I'm about to come face to face with the image of the person who terrified me last night, I love watching her. It's like watching a side of her that's so important to who she is and yet I rarely get to see.

Next, she takes a pack of well-worn coloured pencils from her bag and starts adding in the colour. It's not a neat and detailed colouring, not like colourising a comic, but more patches of colour spread across the figure, giving a general impression. If I look close up I see little more than a series of scribbles, but at a distance and I see she's captured him exactly, not just how he looks, but the implication of how he moves.

"This is incredible," I say, and Araminta shrugs uncomfortably.

It's hard to find words to describe what I see before me on the page. I don't know what he is or where he's from. He's not human, at least not in the way we are, and he's not exactly a ghost either, but he has both a humanoid shape and features. He's more corporeal than a ghost, but perhaps the most significant difference is his colouring. When you first become a ghost you retain a little bit of colour, chiefly in your skin and hair; you look pallid but not deathly pale. That leaches out slowly over the duration of a few months, two years at most. This person, whatever he is, has something else going on.

I take in his features slowly, one by one. He presents as male. His flesh is slightly darker than mine, but he's still clearly white. He has no obvious mark, and he comes across as neither tall nor short. He's dressed in what I'd call black trousers, though they don't look like any kind of modern trousers. He wears some sort of blue tunic under a thick black cloak lined with red.

Looking down, I see his black boots, fastened together tightly with ribbons. I'm reasonably sure his hair is a wig, and not a very good one at that, but that's not for me to judge.

"Well done, Araminta," Saeed says. "We can definitely work with this."

Alison has joined us quietly.

"You're saying all these colours were clear?"

I nod.

"Yeah," Araminta responds. "At least, I'm pretty sure I've remembered them right. He certainly wasn't colourless like most ghosts."

"And how solid was he? Could you see through him?"

"Not very. Maybe similar to Henrietta?"

"About sixty percent opacity," I suggest.

"Yeah, no clue what that means," she says, but there's no harshness in her voice. "Similar to Henrietta is what I need. So we're looking for someone that's both like a ghost but not. And also casts shadows."

Saeed takes out his phone and takes a few careful photos of Araminta's drawing.

"I'm going to do some research," he says. "I'll let you know how I get on."

The shadows are still piled up in the corridor and nothing we do shifts them. Patches in constant darkness even when we shine lights directly at them. I try to distract myself. I try not to worry about any of this.

When I'm feeling stressed, everything gets cleaned. Hardwood floors in the communal rooms are mopped. The guest linen is rewashed, reorganised, and an inventory made in the house wiki with a printed copy pinned to the airing cupboard door. I take out all our herbs and spices from the cupboard, pouring those still in packets into glass jars, making sure they're all well labelled. Next on the list is reordering both my own shelf of books and – much more challenging – our communal collection, which consists of three bookcases, each taller than I am and all of them full, one to the point of being double stacked.

My own collection is a bit of an odd mix. I don't read much; visuals make far more of an impact on me, but what I keep is really important to me. Sometimes I don't even know why; there are books of poems that I memorised instantly and made every hair on my arms stand on end, and others that I saw in the shop and instantly fell in love with. Most were gifts though, carrying memories with them. But there's something more than that today.

It feels like the books are alive in my hands. They don't move, exactly, but there's a heaviness to them, a responsiveness to my touch that I'm not used to. I pick up the oldest book I own. It's not sentimental; it's a copy of Alice in Wonderland I got second hand because it was so beautiful I couldn't not buy it. Illustrated with these hazy, dreamlike pictures, gold edging on the pages, thick paper that felt so good between my fingers. But it's not just these things I feel when I pick it up now. I feel it charged with history, decades running through it, this sense of all the people who read it before me.

When I pick up the inscribed copy of See Mouse Run, my favourite book as a small child, the one my nan gave me for my second birthday, it's so overwhelming that I start sobbing. It's not that I miss my grandmother, though

I do. It's that this one book seems to hold the entire emotional weight of our relationship and I feel it flow into me. I'm feeling completely overwhelmed with emotion right now. All these things are happening at once and I'm not sure how connected they are. I know, though, that the worst of them has to be any threat to my friends, to the people I love.

I move away from the bookcase and tell myself that it will be fine. I tell myself that we've been through worse. And we probably have. A few years back we had a ghost who saw a resemblance to those who murdered her in all of us. And while her consequent aggression was limited by her non-corporeality, it still got to us emotionally, all of us eventually. We also had a ghost baby who wailed all through the night, so loud the walls started to vibrate. We handled that. We're handling the ghost hunters. We'll handle this. We like to have plans and predictability, but we're also well used to things being a bit weird and not having an immediate blueprint that allows us to solve them. This isn't the first time, and it won't be the last.

Meanwhile, Saeed is researching, the ghosts are reacting to whatever it is, and sooner or later there will be a place for me, but right now it's time to distract myself with more household chores; I'm never so motivated to complete them as when I'm trying to avoid something else.

I begin sorting through my basket of clothes that need mending or stain removal, anything beyond a basic wash or iron. There is work I can do now, and other things I can bribe someone with more sewing skills, which mostly means Holly, to take care of. Growing up in a home with strict gender roles was awful for her, but she emerged from it with a few skills; the cleaning and sewing she was expected to learn, but she's also really good at basic DIY because she watched and learned what her brothers were taught as a sort of quiet defiance. I learnt a little of each, Rory and I both did, but I reckon my fingers are built more for operating a console than a needle and thread.

I put together a bag of clothes that need stain removal – even wearing only dark colours doesn't completely eliminate the need for this, and head down to the laundry where I begin to soak them. Just as I'm in the middle of this, the phone in my pocket vibrates. It's from Saeed, and he's found something.

Saeed's bedroom is twice the size of mine, and yet bursting at the seams with books and clothes. It's dominated by a desk and two large bookcases; there's a single bed in the corner, with a clothes-rack next to it to supplement the built-in wardrobe. There's also a small dressing table covered with make-up and lotions, and scarves hanging from a hook on one side of its mirror. His wheelchair, which he uses on some days but not most, is stashed half under the clothing rack, with an assortment of clothes, most of them sparkling, draped over it.

"You have something to show me?" I say.

"Yup. Come and look at this." He's leaning against the high back of his chair and grinning widely. I find a stool under another pile of clothes and clear enough space to put it down by the desk. Meanwhile, Saeed slides the laptop into its dock so I can see the screen on the larger monitor. Then he brings up an image and sits back, lets me take a look.

I don't know much about art. I go to galleries with Araminta sometimes and I enjoy a lot of what I see but I wouldn't have a clue what I was looking at unless she tells me. Araminta would be able to look at this picture and identify the era, the techniques used, perhaps even the artist. I can deduce that it's a portrait, and that it's old; that's about my limit. Hopefully, it's more the content that Saeed's showing me; if he was looking for comment on some artistic technique or school, he would have been best off talking to Araminta.

I look at the man portrayed in the painting. He's young, perhaps in his early twenties, dressed in a wide-lapelled jacket with a white shirt. There's something dramatic and fancy looking at the collar of the shirt, though I'm not sure if it's a cravat or scarf, or part of the shirt. His hair's long and has been curled. Below his trousers are black shoes with large buckles.

The backdrop is one of fields and distant hills; it could be anywhere, or perhaps entirely of the artist's invention. But it's not the scenery I recognise; it's the man. All the images come together: the one from my memory, where he tried to take Araminta's pendant, the one Araminta drew, and the one right in front of me here.

He's younger, yes, and a good bit better looking – but I remember that story about Cromwell, about how painters always painted their subjects in the best light. The FaceApp and Instagram filters of their day, I suppose. Irrespective, I'm confident that if it's not him then it's at least a very close relation.

"Where did you find it?" I say at last, trying to take everything in. I'm sure Saeed can tell by my face that I recognise the man in the picture, confirming his conclusion.

"In the collections of the National Portrait Gallery. They've digitised a load of stuff and made it available on their website. A sort of virtual gallery. It wasn't actually what I was looking for; I was seeing if there was any record of an event that related to what we saw today."

"Hang on," I say. "You were looking for something about Casswell Park? He's connected in some way? I was assuming he'd come with the bottles from somewhere else entirely."

"It's odd isn't it? I'm not a hundred percent sure what the connection is. It might just be a matter of location that meant he ended up here – he just didn't go far and then the man that brought him here just went for the nearest suitable place. Or maybe he knew far more than he was letting on. I mean, he made it sound like he just needed someone to take the ghosts, like he was surrendering a cat to the RSPCA, but maybe there was more to it?"

I think for a bit.

"Is there any way we can trace that man?" I'm asking myself as much as I'm asking Saeed.

"We didn't really get much information," Saeed replies. "And I don't want to stereotype but I'm not sure we'd have much luck finding him on Facebook."

"Ha! If you listen to Holly she'd tell you that Facebook is just for old people these days..." I feel relaxed around Saeed and his enthusiasm is almost infectious... I'm on the verge of babbling. It's not often I can talk this easily, but when it happens it's hard to shut it off.

"And I guess we count as old huh?"

"You got it in one. But I'm thinking. He's probably local. How many care homes are there around here? We could start there. Perhaps pretend to be a relative?"

"A relative who doesn't know his name?"

"Well, we could turn up with a couple of ghosts and scare someone into telling us... which would both be unfair on underpaid and likely immigrant staff and exploiting the ghosts for our own ends. Yeah, yeah, I know. Still, there's got to be some way of going about it..."

"It's a shame we don't have cameras on the motion sensors yet. We could have caught his registration plate."

"Hindsight," I say, savouring the word. It's not one I'd have reason to say often.

"Anyway," Saeed says. "Back to this guy." He points at the screen and his finger braces glint in the light. "His father owned Casswell Park. They were titled – it's too early for them to have this much money and not be, really, but they weren't one of the super established old families. The inheritance laws were pretty clear at the time. The word for it was primogeniture. Basically, everything went to the eldest son, very few exceptions. They wouldn't split it up between the children, although the girls would have a dowry paid."

"So he inherited Casswell Park?" I ask.

"No, he didn't. His younger brother did. That's what's so odd."

I think on this for a few moments.

"Ok, so... his father liked the younger one more or something?"

Saeed shakes his head. "It was a big deal to go against those inheritance norms. Like, really big. You didn't do it out of vague preference. So I'll show you what else I found."

I'd thought Saeed had called me through as soon as he had found something. Of course I was wrong – it was a ridiculous assumption in retrospect, knowing Saeed as well as I do. It's not because he's been hiding anything from me, but because he was so deep in research that there was no way he could have executive functioned his way out, no way he could have veered from his trajectory. It's one of those things that is sometimes a strength, and sometimes a disaster.

"You've found a bunch more stuff, haven't you?" I ask, smiling. Saeed nods, scrolling through documents.

"One moment," he says, and I wait as he gets everything organised. He clicks through an alarming number of open windows and tabs – even my custom-built gaming machine would struggle with that amount of processing, so it's a surprise his laptop is still functioning. But he gets there.

"Right, so," he says, and as he talks he moves through documents, evidence to illustrate his points. "I've come across this guy before. There's no official or detailed record of his life, and the assumption of family members seems to be that he died abroad."

"Anywhere in particular? What was he doing there?"

"Tax evasion, probably. That or somewhere with a non-extradition treaty."

"Really..." I catch Saeed who's laughing at me. I pretend to swipe his face. "Saeed, seriously, where was he?"

"We don't know. There are a few statistically likely options given the era. We're talking about the early years of the British East India Company, for example. Or there was what they called the Grand Tour. Not that car show. Young men, usually, went on a sort of chaperoned gap year to see the great treasures of Europe. He was a bit old for that, but perhaps he could have been chaperoning someone else, or taking the trip he didn't have the chance to take when he was younger. There are comments he was uninterested in business or making money for the family – which is actually a good thing because otherwise my mind would go to the slave trade."

"Ah. Shit." I say.

"Yeah. Unfortunately a lot of well off families of this era were getting their money that way, and I haven't found anything that directly links the family of this house, but it won't surprise me if it comes up. It's statistically unlikely he was an explorer, to use the nice word because wow is the idea of exploration problematic, but this is the right time for them. And given how weird this whole situation is, I'm not sure we can base our assumptions on statistical likelihoods really. More importantly, we don't find any mention of his death until two generations later. It doesn't seem to have been recorded at the time. Maybe the documents went missing, but it seems more like he went overseas and people just assumed he'd died there. Perhaps they didn't want to think about him, perhaps he just disappeared. And those later references, they make it sound like he was disgraced in some way, which could mean some sort of sexual exploit or scandal, could mean something financial, something that brought shame upon the family name..."

"...or it could mean ghosts?" I ask.

Saeed smiles. "You've got it in one."

CHAPTER THIRTEEN

That night snow falls heavily. I fancy I can hear it shifting faintly on the roof above me, see the glint of the white reflection around the edge of my curtains. Or maybe I can't sense any of those things at all, but I somehow know all the same. I tug open the heavy curtains. I don't use the balcony very often, being a creature of darkness and screens, but today I slip my sockless feet into my boots and walk out.

Everywhere is thick with snow; the townhouse roofs with their solar panels, the square church tower to the right, and the town centre beyond. Looking below, I can see it thick on our driveway and our strip of garden. It will also be heavy on the roof, and I worry, briefly, about damage, knowing how we desperately struggled to get the money together for the last batch of repairs. But then I cast that thought aside. I love snow, and I'm going to enjoy this snowfall.

I take a little from the rail, place it on my tongue, and smile.

Then I'm throwing on clothes: hoodie, scarf, gloves, squeezing my feet into thick socks and into my boots, and then heading downstairs. I'm a kid, deep down, and at Casswell Park I don't even need to hide it.

I'm met by the only person happier than I am at this state of affairs: Theo. He greets me with a hug, punching his fist in the air as his update becomes almost a chant.

"SCHOOL. IS. CANCELLED."

"All schools?"

"That's what the website says."

"We'll make sure we confiscate Holly's laptop and books. Right now, though, I'm heading outside. You coming?"

But he's already racing ahead of me. We tug at the main doors until they shift and then we fling them open on this freshly white world, with the cold air racing in on us. For a while, just for a while, I forget the trauma of the past few days, forget the image of Holly's ghostly severed head, which I've been unable to shake from my mind's eye. Just for a while there's thick snow on the ground, snow and heaps of potential.

I'd like to say I got the first snowball thrown, but Theo, inevitably, is quicker than me. My cheek smarts with the impact, and then the frozen fragments begin their slide down my face and the outside of my hoodie. I regret not wearing something truly waterproof, but it's a bit late now. While I'm bending down to make one of my own, another snowball clips the top of my head. But when I retaliate I'm surprised at how good my aim is, catching him square on the nose and following up with one in the centre of his chest straight afterwards.

I feel a little guilty, but just as I try to formulate an apology he's laughing and throwing more at me. Holly and Alison appear soon afterwards, Alison almost steering a reluctant Holly outside to the snow. She looks younger than she is, in a too-small pink puffer jacket. She hasn't managed to get any kind of benefit yet, not if she wants to stay at school, so what she gets from working one or two shifts in the shop is all she has. We've reduced what she pays into our collective account, but I suspect she's still struggling.

I don't get much on my benefit, but I had a starter pack of stuff when I came here, and my parents help me out a little when they can: clothes and shoes under the guise of birthday gifts, shopping trips with my mother that she says are making up for lost time, the lost time when I wore boy's clothes and hated shopping. I dress pretty androgynously now, but my clothes mostly come from the women's racks and I've dealt with my anxieties around clothes shops. So I manage. For Holly, though, there's none of that to fall back on – and, being younger, she's determined to prove her independence, that she's doing okay without needing anything from anyone else.

I wonder if we can work out a way to help her in a way she'd accept. That's for later, though. For now...

I fling my next snowball at Holly, intentionally getting her in the shoulder rather than the face. She looks shocked for a moment, and I worry I've misjudged, but then she's laughing like the rest of us, running and ducking behind a wall, getting her own ammunition supplies together and then hurling them in quick succession at me and Theo, and then before I know it all of us are in this massive disorganised all-directions snowball fight, Araminta and Denny joining us. Denny's in an old bomber jacket that doesn't look warm enough but he doesn't seem uncomfortable, and Araminta in an olive green coat. Like most of her clothes she sewed it herself. Shops that stock her size are annoyingly rare and expensive, so once she realised she had a talent for sewing it became a valuable skill for her.

We lobby the snow back and forth. Often, I feel self-conscious when I'm having fun, like someone is going to call me a freak – and sometimes they do. For us, adulthood is not something we reach but something we have to earn – often working to higher standards than other people – and revocable any time. There's so much pressure to internally police our every move and expression. But right now... right now, I don't care. Right now I'm loving every moment, burning through energy and yet always finding more.

I realise Theo has been making snowballs twice as fast as he's been throwing them, preparing for some kind of rapid-fire assault. The game is changing. Even some of the ghosts are out here, more relaxed than I've seen them in a while. I notice – too late – that they're the colour of snow and you often don't see them until you're right beside them. A few of them join in; they come swooping at me just when I'm about to throw a ball, putting me off my game, or they'll dart from side to side, confusing me about who is where. Sometimes it seems like despite all our best intentions there's such a division, such a marked line between us and the ghosts that it can never be breached. And then sometimes, sometimes we all play together and it feels more natural than we could have guessed anything ever would.

Later, when I'm a bit more tired, Vinnie and I talk quietly as Araminta and Theo volley snow back and forth at each other. We're leaning against the glass wall of the orangerie, Vinnie – having recently taken up vaping – blowing clouds of smoke that smell of pecan and vanilla.

"I've been wondering," Vinnie says, nominally to me but more to the universe in general, "whether it would be better for Theo to spend more time with his father. Perhaps with his grandparents when his father's working. Things have been pretty unsettled here, yeah."

I nod in affirmation as Vinnie puffs out a cloud of smoke and then continues.

"I know he seems all energy but he's been sleeping so badly. And whatever happened with Holly – look, I'm as protective of her as anyone and she's vulnerable in some ways, but she's tough, really tough, in others. But Theo's just a child. And he's been getting into trouble at school."

I nod in sympathy, feeling a bit out of my depth.

"Actually been misbehaving? Or are they just interpreting autism stuff as that?"

Vinnie shrugs.

"It's hard to tell. I can totally believe he's disruptive, but he's a good kid. Kind. There's this whole thing where they see Black kids as older than they are, and it can happen all of a sudden, just like that." They snap their fingers. "Suddenly what was a cute kid horseplaying and messing around becomes violence, and disobedience, and a whole big deal. Maybe that's what's happening, or maybe he really is acting out because he's stressed."

I dig my hands in my pockets, the scented smoke all around me. "I don't want him to be stressed," I say. "But..."

"But this is his home." Vinnie finishes the sentence I cannot. "Yeah. It is."

The snowball fight continues, off and on, through most of the morning. As we start getting hungrier, Araminta says she remembers something about putting snow on pancakes.

"You can't do that in the town," Denny says. "The snow round there's filthy."

"Oh yeah sure," replies Vinnie. "No weird smells or defecation or poisonous plants in the country then."

It's a ridiculous topic to be pulled into an argument about, and yet we all are. For Alison, the seed has been planted and she heads inside to begin making oatmeal pancakes. After a little while she calls in Araminta and I to help and we roll up this huge stack of pancakes with tinfoil around them so we can eat them with our fingers, then we fill them with hot apple sauce and bring them out on trays and all stand around in the snow and the cold sun, eating these amazing pancakes as if we hadn't eaten in years.

The last one of us to emerge is Saeed. He hates snow, viscerally. I had thought it was because it made moving around for him even harder and increased his injury risk, and that's probably part of it. But, as he explained to me last year – when it didn't really snow but kept looking like it was going to, it's mostly sheer annoyance at how excited his mother got whenever it snowed.

"It was embarrassing. We had these matching hats and scarves – matching designs, different colours, and mine was navy blue, if you can imagine a colour so unsuited to me."

"Pretty sure everyone's parents embarrass them," Araminta had said.

"You don't understand. She had this photo of her grandmother and her siblings back in the valley they lived in in Pakistan – well it's Pakistan now, anyway – playing in the snow and she'd make us pose and recreate it, and then she sends it out to all the relatives and put it up on the fridge."

We've all heard this story before and Saeed never ceases to be frustrated by how we never see this as quite as much of a valid grievance as he does.

But this time's he's out here with the rest of us all the same, helping himself to one of the last pancakes. I stand next to him, idly dripping melting snow down his neck. I'm not going to risk overbalancing him or exacerbating his pain issues by dragging him into a snow fight but he's sure as hell not getting out of this scot free.

"Hey, can I take another look at your pendant again?" he asks Araminta. She unbuttons her long coat, while I send another cascade of ice water down Saeed's neck.

He pauses, turns around. "Could you stop that?"

"Sorry," I say, not sorry at all, but doing my best to look innocent. He rolls his eyes and looks closely at the pendant. I can hear him muttering to himself though I can't make out any words.

"Oh, you will be," he says, grinning at me. "Thanks for this, though. I should have something to show you guys soon."

Araminta puts the pendant back inside her clothes. I look out at the snow-covered houses across the road, and beyond them to where I can see the sunlight bouncing off the snow on the church tower and the tallest trees.

I'm back in Saeed's room to hear details of another round of research. I've changed my clothes entirely; my soaking socks and jeans are in the wash and my shoes are drying upside down on top of a radiator. I'm in the next step up from pyjamas; comfy trousers and a loose long-sleeved t-shirt. I've been wearing a small blanket round my shoulders but Saeed's room is warm and I soon take it off.

"So, what revelation do you have for me today?" I ask.

Saeed's face in response to my joking question indicates that this might actually be a significant revelation.

"This," he says, bringing up a document and scooting his swivel chair back to enable me to take a closer look. It's an image of a young woman, probably pencil drawn. I squint at her. There's definitely something familiar about her but I struggle to work out who she reminds me of. I know it's not a dead ringer – just some key features, a clear resemblance, but it's definitely significant.

Then I realise who it is.

It's me.

Saeed nods slowly as he sees me come to that conclusion. I look at it again.

It's not exactly me. My history of not-entirely-legally-obtained hormone blockers, and then oestrogen and some laser hair removal, combined with the bone structure I was born with, means there are still some elements of my facial appearance not likely to be replicated in any other era. But I don't think you could hold up pictures of us side by side and not think we were related. We could be siblings, perhaps, or even the same person at different points in their life. Either way, the resemblance is staggering.

I pause, trying to formulate a question.

"Who... who is she?" I ask, not sure I want to hear the answer. Saeed has prepared, of course.

"Her name was Hattie – we can assume that's short for Harriet – Casswell. She was the direct descendent of the younger brother of William Casswell, who we otherwise know as the ghost eater. And... I'm rapidly coming to the conclusion that she's your great great... maybe a few more greats... grandmother."

I stare at the picture. I don't know what I had been expecting Saeed to find, but it definitely wasn't this. My nan always did say that we came from money somewhere along the line. I thought she was making it up, or at least that it had been exaggerated over the years. Well. Maybe I owe her an apology.

"In any case," Saeed says. "I want to find out."

With my help, Saeed sketches up a rough family tree for me. I give him my parents' and grandparents' names, those of the one great grandparent I remember, and I think through details that indicate ages and where they lived.

Meanwhile, I'm questioning everything. Not about my family – this is different to what I expected, but I didn't know the truth to be any different really either. No, I'm wondering how much choice I have. Did I decide to live here? Or has it somehow been my destiny, engineered by my past or something in my genes? Why can my family see ghosts so clearly when so few people can? I feel nauseous. What about my paranormal abilities? Does anyone else in my family have them?

Crap. Maybe I'm adopted.

I laugh and dismiss the thought. I am definitely not adopted. Firstly, I'm pretty sure both my parents would be far too honest in any social worker assessment to be approved to adopt. Secondly, everyone spots the resemblance between me and Dad. And there are all the inherited conditions and weird traits. That's some relief, at least.

"May I posit an unsubstantiated theory?" Saeed asks, increasing the speed of his fidget spinner.

"You're going to anyway, but sure, thanks for asking."

Saeed breathes deeply and begins the explanation he's obviously been rehearsing in his head.

"Okay, so. You're directly descended from Harriet Casswell who was the daughter of one of the owners of this house. As is one of your parents. There's probably not too much mystery as to what happened; stories get lost in families. You might be descended from a youngest son, his and his descendants' social and financial position becoming gradually lower over the years. It's possible you're descended from an illegitimate child which might mean your ancestor was simply never told who their father was and it was never recorded anywhere. Neither of those would be an unusual situation. No scandal or magic necessarily involved."

I digest what he's just told me.

"So how did I end up here then? Was I somehow psychically drawn to this place? I mean, I certainly don't have any legal claim to it, and I'm confident my parents would have said something to me if they knew anything about it."

"I don't know. I mean, part of it is they had a lot of ghosts and the family was very attuned to ghosts. It may be no more than that."

"But it could be?"

Saeed shrugs.

"I really don't know, sorry. I deal with documents. Pieces of paper or database searches. I don't have any paranormal abilities and my ability to see ghosts is less than that of anyone else here – they all seem fuzzy to me and sometimes I don't even notice them until one of you points it out. I'm just not the person to answer that type of question."

"I understand. You've found out a lot. It's been a bit weird but it's also been really helpful. Thank you, friend."

I try to work out who to ask next for help understanding this. I wonder if this is where my telescope came from. I know that this whole thing is only just beginning.

I'm about to check if anyone's still outside, and if not head up to my bedroom, hang out in the warmth with Mallard. Instead, without really trying to, I end up in the room I'd found myself drawn to before, the room with faded and chipped blue paint on the walls. We've planned to plaster up the cracks in the walls and give all the unused rooms a couple of coats of paint at some point, but it's low down our priority list.

As I open the door, I start seeing the lines of writing from my dreams in front of my eyes. Endless line after line, and any time I try and make my brain focus on them they slide away, unreadable. I shake my head until my hair beats against my face, forcing it from my mind.

I sit down in the middle of the floor with my legs pulled up in front of me. It's cold but I'm not really thinking about that. After all the stress of before, I'm bordering on dissociating. It's not something that happens to me often – much more so for Araminta, but I think that's mostly trauma based – but me, not so much.

I'm not really thinking anything just now. My mind is heavy and empty as I start rocking backwards and forwards. The names of ghosts come to me as if they were floating past in the cold air, and I say them out loud, watching clouds form from the moisture in my breath. They speed up. Ghosts that live here, ghosts I've met elsewhere, ghosts I saw in my childhood. I start repeating them over and over and over. Names. Dates of living, dates of death. Where they were found, causes of death. I slip into a rhythm that almost becomes a chant.

I know, deep down, what I'm doing. Even in this state I don't entirely lack self-awareness. But at the same time, I can't consciously think this through. The chant is carrying my mind along with it as if along a swollen river and I can't break out of it enough to think, let alone to do something else entirely.

The rhythm is both comforting and troubling all at once. I repeat the lyrics, quietly, over and over for hours, until eventually I lull myself into much-needed sleep. I wake only hours later to the sound of Theo yelling down the corridor that dinner's ready, and then I pick my aching muscles up from the cold floor. I've had a lot of practice pretending to be okay.

1707

A t night, or when he travels and does not ask her to go with him, Isobel copies his book by candlelight into one of her own. She copies lists and descriptions of ghosts, observations, results of experiments.

She's put the book together from stolen pieces of paper they write letters on, near empty pages that she has carefully ripped from books in the library. Paper is expensive, but it's easier to come by in this house than anywhere else she knows.

Learning to read hasn't demystified writing for her; it's made it even more magical.

She doesn't know what she will do with it, not yet, but she knows it's more powerful than anything else.

She keeps it tied in an apron under her clothes. It will stay with her no matter what happens next. And perhaps one day she can give it to someone who can use it in a way she cannot.

CHAPTER FOURTEEN

The noise starts just after 2am, just as I'd got to sleep, and doesn't stop. At first I try to will it away, holding my pillow over my head and tight over my ears, scrunching my eyes shut as if that would block out the sound. No such luck. Annoyed, and frankly a little afraid, I pull on my dressing gown, force my feet – still in their thick bed socks – into my boots, grab the torch I keep by my bed and head downstairs. The corridor is dark and uncomfortable. I keep seeing shadows in the light of my torch; more than once I swing round expecting someone – someone or something – just outside my range of vision, only to find a pile of forgotten laundry or an overly large spider caught at just the right angle.

It's an odd sound, a mixture of banging and wailing, but all mixed up together to the point it's impossible to distinguish one part from another. A childhood of listening for oncoming trains has given me good directional hearing. I head down the stairs towards it. It's quiet now and I can hear my own footsteps, my own breathing in the still dark. No-one else seems to have woken, not even Saeed, who has a downstairs bedroom.

By the time I reach the bottom of the stairs I can see in my torchlight half a dozen ghosts, perhaps more, congregating together, swirling around each other, like a crowd at the fair if that crowd – heaven help us all – could float through each other. I swing my torch around. There might be as many as ten ghosts here.

I feel uncomfortable walking through them, as if I'm physically barging people out of the way only more personal. I don't think I have much of a choice this time.

My feet are leading me back to the same room, the empty one with flaking blue paint. I see signs of destruction before I even get there; splintered wood flung across the hallway. When I get to the doorway I gasp even though I'd already expected this. Every single board of the floor has been ripped up and thrown haphazardly across – or out of – the room. I take a moment to survey the damage. Every board seems to be broken in at least one place and some are in fragments, but thankfully the window is unbroken.

I look down at the floor ahead of my feet. The basement level only extends to a small part of the house; it's what we now use for laundry and storage, though I understand it was originally the kitchens. In this part of the house we're on the lowest level, the foundations digging into old earth. I pick my way over the exposed beams, the soil and broken boards and other debris that might have been here centuries, thankful I put on my boots. Jodie Keane swirls around me. She's one of our most recently dead; would be younger than Alison and Denny if she were alive today, and yet right now she's paler than our Regency era ghosts, much paler. We shouldn't be able to notice ghosts fade. Normally it happens too slowly.

From down the corridor I hear something wail in anguish. It's dark outside and I can hear something tapping on the uncurtained window. I don't think about the fact that there are no trees round here, no plants beside the house. I stand, my feet on either side of a floor beam, and look at the light coming in from the corridor, the shadows across the near-destroyed room.

Oddly, this is the exact point I stop being scared. I can almost feel something click inside me, an understanding that there is no time to be scared. This is a house filled with some strange history, yes, but more importantly it's a house filled with people, living and ghost alike, who I love. I have work to do and that work is far more important than any feeling I might have.

I survey the damage as well as I can, but I reckon even a forensic investigator would throw up their hands at trying to make sense out of it. It looks like what would happen if I suddenly developed super strength and a vicious grudge against the floorboards. All I can see is destruction.

I struggle to even guess why any ghost might have done this. As a display of rage and anger, it's near unheard of in its destructiveness; most aren't even sufficiently corporeal to affect their environment in this way. Even for those who are... imagine ripping up the flooring from a whole room with your bare hands, how painful and damaged your skin would be. Now imagine doing that as a semi-corporeal being. If it was from anger, it was an extreme level of anger.

Or was it a violent attack? Were the ghosts going after the ghost eater or fending off his attacks? But every other room remains untouched, right down to the crockery in the kitchen, a vase on a table just outside. A fight of this violence seems unlikely to stay in just one room.

There's one other option, of course. That they weren't trying to destroy the room, that the aim wasn't destruction. They were looking something, something hidden under the floor, perhaps for centuries.

I get down, carefully, on my hands and knees, making sure I kneel on my dressing gown and not the splintering wood. I shine my torch around, and almost miss it, but there's definitely something wedged under one of the boards.

Carefully, one hand steadying myself and the torch in my mouth, I retrieve it. It's a book, very old, handwritten. I'm just starting to take a look through when I hear footsteps upstairs, and I shove it into my dressing gown pocket. It just fits.

Logic tells me that there's no reason to hide it, and that given how concerning things are I should be telling my flatmates anything that will help them work this out. But this is getting uncomfortably close to parts of me I don't fully understand, to my dreams and to my heightened abilities, and I feel nauseous at the idea of someone else getting too close to them.

Holly, woken by the noise, appears in the doorway. Her hair is tightly plaited and coiled on her head, her eyes heavy with sleep. Her slippers are visibly tight on her feet and her dressing gown is a soft baby blue and, like her coat, also too small. She stands at the door and we look at each other from either side of the destroyed room. I half expect her to break down in tears, but instead her fists are balled with anger. There's no need to speak. We both know exactly what the other would say.

Sometimes I feel that just as Holly is at once both strong and vulnerable, she's also young and old at the same time. I've always felt responsible for her, protective of her, but between us now is a relationship of equals. A friendship. And a need to work – and perhaps to fight – side by side.

The others arrive one by one, in dressing gowns or pyjamas, worn-down slippers. Vinnie swears a lot and then goes back to bed, dragging Theo with them in spite of his protests. Saeed mumbles apologetically about his health being difficult and really needing the sleep.

"Yep, we get it. Go! Sleep well," says Alison, and the rest of us nod tiredly in agreement. We know no-one else is going to be sleeping much tonight. At least most of my housemates tend to get an earlier night than I do. Alison gets together some snacks, because if we're not going to get sleep we should at least have some nourishment.

Araminta and Denny take a look at the flooring. I hope they'll be able to see something I missed, come to some conclusion, but there's nothing.

Before long, though, we're in the dining room and tucking into pizza squares that Alison just got out of the oven. There's chocolate on the table too and Araminta pours out tea. No-one says much. Perhaps because we're all half-asleep, or perhaps because there isn't much to say; I'm not sure.

Sitting on the high-backed dining room chairs, we see distressed ghosts all around us. Exhausted, we half-heartedly try and interact with them, console them, try and see if we can get them to communicate what's wrong in a way we can understand, but they always drift far away from us. Some of them are being dramatic, wailing and poltergeisting all over the place, but most of them are quietly withdrawn, sitting in corners or leaning into the walls, floating away from us. There's a sense of sadness hanging through the whole house and it's hard for us to tease out what's happening – what is them projecting an emotional response, and what is something that is affecting us as well as them.

We keep talking through the night. We talk about books and we talk about what we need to buy for the house and we talk about unexplained disappearances and unsolved crimes. The latter are particular interests of Alison's but it seems we all know of a case we've gotten lost in reading about. When we struggle to focus we show each other YouTube clips of cats that think they're other animals until the dawn starts to glow through the uncurtained window and the headlights of the cars from the townhouses starting their commute shine white and then fade as they turn the corner.

Our conversation is slow and full of long pauses, some of us leaning forward and propping ourselves up on the table. We could move to the living room but I suspect in the comfy chairs we'd end up falling into an unproductive half-sleep. At this point I think we all feel it's better to stay awake, stay together, and wait for morning.

Joseph and Henrietta float through the room at various points, but they seem distant, as if they don't even know we're here. We don't even try to interact with them, and not just because we're too exhausted but to give them some space in their obvious distress. It's what we'd want for ourselves after all. They show no signs of the earlier rage or panic or whatever it was that caused them to tear up the floor of that room. I think of the book lodged in that tiny cavity under the floor, and all I can think about is blood seeping through the wood. I try and distract myself, think about the conversation at hand, but the image overwhelms me.

Everything is about the book now. As soon as I manage to make it up the stairs, I shut myself in the bedroom, close the curtains, put on my noise-cancelling headphones, shut out the world. I turn the lights on low, a soft warm orange, using my torch to illuminate the pages of the book more clearly.

It's slow going. I have to look up samples of old handwriting, memorise how certain letters looked, work through the first page letter by letter, and line by line, writing each into a note file on my phone. At this rate it's going to take forever.

I don't have forever, but at the same time this is the closest thing I have to a clue, and I can't do nothing. The ghosts either wanted me to find this, or wanted it for themselves, and the fact there's no-one floating through the walls in search of it makes me think it's the former.

The first few pages seem to be a long and boring outline as to the author's personal theories about ghosts. Actually, it's more about the fact he has theories than the actual details of them: he goes on and on about how he's the foremost natural philosopher of his time and how deficient the works of others including – erm, excuse me, Isaac Newton himself – were. He's an asshole, in other words.

I skip a few pages. I can come back to this later. The long drawn out sentences give way to tables and lists and diagrams, and I instantly feel more at home, almost physically relaxing into my bed. That's despite the fact that everything seems to be in a sort of code, as shorthand rather than for secrecy because the codes are outlined in keys on subsequent pages.

After some flipping back and forth, it becomes clear that this book is a record of ghosts. It includes locations, ages, estimated years of death – the sort of information we also like to keep a record of, but also some categorisations and rankings that seem to relate to certain qualities of the ghosts like their corporeality and movement.

There's something else too. *Date secured*.

I feel ill.

I read it again. It's not entirely specific, but there's no good interpretation that can come from that. And then I hear the door creak open. I feel adrenaline surge, hastily try to put everything down under the covers. I'm not even sure exactly what I'm panicking about, but the memories of every time I've been in trouble are flooding back as panic.

It's Araminta, heading in carefully. She's close to me and I don't want anyone close to me right now, not even her.

"Can't you knock?" I say, angrily.

"I did. Three times. I..."

My headphones block out background noise, but not the sharp staccato of knocks at the door; at best, they'd muffle it. But annoyed as I am, I don't think she's lying. I must have been that hyperfocused on what I was doing that I didn't hear it at all.

I look at Araminta in the dim light. I can tell she isn't happy right now, that something's wrong, but I can't deal with it, can't even express the fact I can't deal with it.

"Sorry," I say. My mouth feels dry. My mind diverges in two directions: to justifying myself, telling myself that it's Araminta's fault for interrupting, and to hating myself for treating her that way. In any case, she's already gone, her footsteps faded to nothing down the hallway. I think of chasing after her but I don't feel like I can move very easily.

I pull extra blankets over me and carry on. This is one of those times people could easily say I don't care about other people, only my interests. In truth, I'm not coping and it is puzzling through the book that gives me my only chance, small as it is, of holding things together.

I keep translating. I find references for many ghosts, and some slightly improbable tales about the author's journey to find them. And with a sick feeling I recognise some of the ghosts being detailed.

It's not certain, perhaps, but I know this is true. I realise with a sickly feeling that four of the ghosts documented are the same four we released from bottles.

I've found the documentation that Saeed was so desperately hoping for. And I'm not sure if I'm going to tell him.

CHAPTER FIFTEEN

Araminta's message is short but tells us everything we
need to know.
>> help now please
>> my studio
It's my turn on dishes so I'm downstairs. I catch up with
Saeed walking along the corridor, and we catch the old
lift up together, pulling the metal grill shut. I never feel
entirely comfortable in there, even though we've had it
serviced within the past couple of years and they told us
reassuring things about how many cables hold even an
old lift.

I'm not sure Saeed has ever been in Araminta's studio.
It's a long time since I was, and whatever's going on must
be serious if she's willing to invite us all in. I breathe in
deeply as I spin round and see the scene of destruction
that covers the room. It's not just the paint squeezed
out of tubes and splattered across the room, the tubs
of pencils and brushes turned upside down, the pastels
broken and ground into the carpet, the stain of paint
water pooling across the lino. Those would be simple
vandalism. It's something else which catches my eye.

The canvases, some on easels, others propped against
the walls, are covered in words written in thick strokes of

paint – most of them red, but thankfully obviously paint rather than blood. One reads YOU WILL BE KEPT AS PRISONER in a deep burgundy on a white canvas, and another – smaller but painted in thick brush strokes – says, perhaps most disturbingly, YOU WILL DIE AS WE HAVE DIED. I suck in air between my teeth. A third, face up on the floor, is streaked as if painted with red and yellow on the same brush, mixing to orange in the middle, with the words WE WILL ALL FADE AND GO.

I spin around on my heels, shuddering, to see in a purple-red font:

GET OUT. YOU DON'T BELONG HERE.

"Charming," says Vinnie. Their voice makes me jump. "Pity I'm thoroughly desensitised to being told that at this point." Their facial expression indicates that right now they're anything but.

Saeed leans forward on his crutches, glaring at the text. The room is a disaster. The one mercy is that most of the paint – other than that used to write these horrifying messages – remains in the tubes. Still, much is broken and almost nothing has been left where it should be. I survey the carnage, unsure if I'm sad or angry or afraid.

"I can't afford to replace these," says Araminta in horror. "My paints... my canvases... I just don't have the money." It's the last thing the rest of us were thinking about, but Araminta's clearly in shock, focusing on the only part of this that makes any kind of rational sense. That, and her art really is that important to her, and to make art she needs materials, which cost money. This isn't self-absorption; this is her life.

"I think we can sort most of this with a little tidying and attention," Vinnie says pragmatically. "We'll help you when we're all a bit calmer. You know some of the greatest works of art are painted over something else? I imagine we could get these to a usable state for you, but if not I can buy you some replacements."

"No you can't," Araminta says, sounding very distant. "None of us have much money."

"I get decent child support and I have wages most months on top of that. I'll get you some canvases, Araminta. Please. It would be my pleasure."

Araminta shakes her head and says nothing more. We survey all the damage.

"Bit of a stereotypical haunting, really," Vinnie says. "Hope it's none of you having a laugh."

They say it expectantly, as if hoping it's a joke gone way too far. But we all know how private Araminta is about her space. Sure, some of us misjudge sometimes, but I can't see anyone breaching that boundary. And there's not a single person among us who wouldn't have apologised and tried to make it right when they saw Araminta's distress.

"Two of these tell us something about who wrote it," Vinnie continues. "They're saying, one, that they are dead and two, they will fade and go. Doesn't mean they're telling anything resembling the truth, of course, but it's pretty clear that these were written either by a ghost or someone who wants us to think they're a ghost."

"Or otherwise non-corporeal and fading," says Saeed.

"You're thinking of the ghost eater?" Vinnie says. "I guess so... But then who's we? Him and the ghosts? Or does he have some kind of sidekick? Heaven help us, I hope not."

Denny's arrived silently, listening to our conversation from the doorway.

"I don't know," he says. "But when someone says 'you don't belong here,' that sort of implies they think they do belong here. Which is consistent with Saeed's theory that the ghost eater was one of the family who owned the house."

Their voices fade out as I look more carefully at the canvases, and then between them and Araminta's work which is now strewn around the room. With a sickening feeling, I'm beginning to recognise her handwriting. The way she rounds the tops of her capital A's. The way the bar across the H is slightly diagonal. I... still don't know much about art, though I've learned a lot in the time Araminta and I have been together, but I fancy I can see something about the movement of the brush-strokes in these letters and it looks like her hand.

I feel instantly guilty that I could think she would ever do such a thing. It's not in her character, not at all, and yet it's nagging at me. The undeniable feeling that what I'm witnessing might not be what it seems.

I spend the night feeling more alone than I've felt in years. I can't get warm, even though the thermometer shows a reasonable temperature, and I'm under piles of blankets, though more for the weight than for the warmth.

But come morning I'm around others again. Coffee is brewed, and attempts to find solutions and make plans of action begin. As I make a stack of toast for all of us to help ourselves from, and smear mine thick with marmite in the way Araminta usually frowns at, Saeed creates a shared spreadsheet. Ghost Log, he calls it. He connects it to a web form – whenever we see a ghost, we're to select that ghost's name from the drop-down field and make a brief note of the location. It auto-completes who made the report, and the time and date. Then he sets up a monitoring sheet that shows him the names of all the ghosts, colour coded by how long it's been since they were seen, with that length of time in the next column. I recognise how I can help, making a button to go on our home screens so it opens like an app.

We nominally go about our usual routines. I try to push my worries about Araminta to the back of my mind, but I'm struggling. I thought I knew her better than that but perhaps if something's going really wrong for her... perhaps if she needs help but can't ask for it...

None of it makes any sense. I make another big pot of plunger coffee and hang out in the kitchen for a while. We log the ghosts, in between our breakfasts and our showers and our preparations for work and school. Alison is taking a walk outside the building – the ghosts mostly stay inside but that's not always the case, and right now nothing is sticking to the established norms anyway.

Saeed forwards an email wanting our help with the Pittlow campaign. I want to put it aside, to focus on dealing with what's going on in my own house which is more than enough for me, for any of us to deal with right now, but my mind is moving in all directions. So I open it and I read it. The Pittlow crew have also received a message from a ghost, scrawled with charcoal on the wall. I look at the attached photograph; grainy, in poor light, but clear nevertheless.

BRING BACK MY SISTER FROM CASSWELL PARK

I breathe with relief. They're asking us for a real reason, something relevant to us, not just because they want more work from us when we're already overwhelmed. And some other ghost is writing on walls. That means it might not be Araminta that...

From upstairs, I hear Denny crash into walls at least twice. He laughs at himself. Probably walking round with a phone in his hand and distracted by ghosts isn't the best idea for him. Still, I think he's been injured so much at this point that he just bounces back.

But despite our lack of coordination, we manage to cover the whole house. Another important thing about Casswell Park is that it has surprisingly good WiFi – Holly and Alison set it up a few years back. It's slow in places because when you have to cover an area this big and have no money, some of the equipment is inevitably going to be a bit old and dodgy, but it works pretty well overall, and I have an ethernet cable running to my bedroom so I get a high enough speed for gaming.

As we make our logs, Saeed watches the combined data and a bit later, after those with school and work have left, but still early by my standards, he messages the group chat.

>> Important everyone. Please think back and tell me the last time you saw these ghosts.

He types a list, and we all start typing at once. I don't envy Saeed having to sort through the various overlapping replies, but sorting information and data is basically Saeed's thing. It does"t take him long, and then we get the message that I've just started to dread.

>> Thank you all. The following ghosts have not, based on your reports, been seen at all for over a week:

>> Lydia Martin, Tim McCabe, Gregoria, Joseph, Jodie Keane, Hannah

>> Can you all please think carefully and let me know asap if you have any updates on them.

Between us we manage to conclude that we have seen Jodie and Lydia more recently; and Gregoria is not often spotted even at the best of times so her absence is of less concern. But the others seem to be truly missing. We'll search, of course, and we do, going through the attic rooms and the passage between the old kitchens and the back of the ballroom, the cupboards and all the unused rooms and storage spaces, the semi-outbuildings that are technically part of the house but can only be accessed from outside. But we know even before we begin that something is likely very wrong.

I feel nauseous. This isn't normal. I know people are used to the idea of ghost sightings being rare, perhaps only emerging on the anniversary of their deaths. Perhaps that is because so many people have only a weak ability to see ghosts. But round here, we usually see most ghosts between us most days. They're simply here. We don't consider ourselves as having had any encounters, any more than I would consider passing Alison in the hallway an encounter.

Only Vinnie has to go to work today. A stack of books are delivered for Saeed, each in an individual padded envelope as if they were presents, for the start of the semester. He looks delighted. We spend some more time looking for the missing ghosts but they're nowhere. The ghosts we do find seem withdrawn and unhappy, but calm. Fortunately, all the remaining floorboards stay in place, at least for now.

It doesn't really feel like we can ask for much more at this stage. How low our bar seems to have fallen, I think, and then I laugh to myself.

The next interruption is a knock on the door. I'm on the staircase, and head to answer it. It's Keira. The green streak in her hair is brighter than before – she's obviously had it redone.

"Hi Morgan!" she says. She's clearly been practising this speech, and her cheeriness is very forced. "I saw you'd been posting on the forum about reading some old text."

I want to kick myself. Even though I was very vague about the text I was reading, I should have known talking about it on the paranormal forums would have led to something like this.

"Well I found this book really useful and I thought maybe you wanted to borrow it."

The book is imaginatively named *Interpreting Handwriting through the Ages.* I'm sure I could have got it from the library and there's probably nothing in it I couldn't have found online. But it will probably be helpful just the same.

I look back at Keira. If she was hoping I would invite her in, she can hope all she likes. But I do take the book, and I nod and smile a thank you to her. Just as I'm about to close the door I hear footsteps and see Araminta joining me. Keira, already turning to leave, stops and turns back.

"Um Keira, if it's about meeting the ghosts... look we've got a lot going on and we can't do it right now but it doesn't mean it won't happen. Just bear with us, okay?" Araminta says.

"Oh no, that's okay. I understand." Keira is decidedly distracted and I'm only just starting to work out why.

"Um, my face is up here," Araminta says.

I watch Keira's face flush, as both of us realise she's been staring intently at Araminta's chest. Keira is immediately panicked, mumbling her words and apologies, almost in tears.

"It was just... I mean, I didn't mean to... I was looking at the pendant... I'm sorry... I wouldn't..."

And then she turns and flees, footsteps frantic on the driveway.

"Well shit," Araminta says, as we close the door. "I almost feel bad now."

"Yeah," I say. My fingers are curling up in my pockets, as I feel some of Keira's deep shame start to edge into me.

Later we're chatting in the hallway, because no-one has the focus to get on with anything today. Alison takes a look at Saeed, propped up on his crutches, obviously exhausted despite having gone back to bed last night, obviously in pain despite trying not to show it. She assesses him and perhaps she speaks without thinking, or perhaps she doesn't know how hurtful her words will be until she says them, but either way the effect is the same.

"Have you thought... this is physically dangerous for all of us at this point, but for you... I'm sorry to ask, but might you want to... well, is this the best place for you to be? Would it be good for you to stay with your family for a bit? You're close to them, right?"

Saeed looks at her for a long time before replying, as if weighing up every possible word and phrase, the consequences of every possible response, before speaking.

"Sure I'm close. My whole family is. But I'm an adult and this is my home and you're sure as hell going to need me. Also, when any of you dislocate a joint you whine and scream like a baby. I put it back in and keep fighting. Maybe you should go and stay with family."

"I'm sorry," she says. "I shouldn't have suggested it."

"No, you shouldn't," says Saeed. "Can you help me double check some data now?"

It's taking him effort not to cause conflict, I can tell. I wonder whether to say something to Alison on his behalf, or to operate on the basis that he's got it handled and can speak for himself. I'm not sure what the right thing to do at this, but I'm annoyed at Alison for fucking up like this at such a fragile and difficult time for all of us.

As Saeed and Alison head to look at his computer. Holly comes walking down the corridor, updating us on the fact that she and Denny have searched basically every corner of the house, and not only the grounds – small though they are – and driveway, but also walked every street of the development on the old grounds, and all the streets within a hundred metres of the house in every direction. Checking the former grounds is important for those who lived here when they were still gardens; they might feel drawn to them, they might be confused as to what has happened.

Their conclusion is that if the ghosts have left, physically left, then they have gone far away from here, in a way that is previously unprecedented. The alternative conclusion is not one any of us really wish to contemplate.

I instantly feel careless, careless and guilty. Ghosts can be powerful, but in some ways they're often really vulnerable. I feel like we should have been looking after them better. I feel we've failed them, possibly with devastating consequences. It's true we may not have been able to prevent what happened to them, but we're entirely to blame for how long it took us to notice. There's no escaping that.

But the battle isn't over. There's still something we can do. I head back to my bedroom, set the lights to the warm red tinge that helps me focus. On one side of me, I have the book. On the other, my screen displays the words from Pittlow.

Who is this ghost's sister? Could she be the ghost who turned up at her door, who still seems to linger, not quite accepting the invitation to come inside but not leaving either? And what else can the book tell me?

I haven't experienced direct written communication from the supernatural before; the closest has been those who can point at letters or words, but they haven't been able to physically put pen to paper, or paintbrush to canvas as the case may be. I've heard of cases of ghosts writing though; words written in condensation on windows and things like this.

From an emotional point of view, this whole thing is horrible, but communication with ghosts is an ongoing interest of mine and this development is fascinating.

There's a lot of research and discussion out there about making initial contact with ghosts, and very little about interpreting ongoing communication. And not much of that treats ghosts as individuals, discusses the need to reciprocate communication and understand the variations in how different ghosts act and the importance of context.

If things were different, if the stakes were lower, this would be a fascinating research moment for me. As it is, I have to focus on the practicalities, be pragmatic and sensitive, and not get distracted. But even so, I still make some notes as I go, observations, in the hope that I'll be able to follow them up later and make something of this, something better than survival, something positive when the fight we all know we're heading for is fought and won and in the past.

CHAPTER SIXTEEN

I 've been distant with Araminta and I'm uncomfortable about it. I tell myself that if she really did make those messages, she must have had a good reason for it, that I don't believe she would do it out of malice, that perhaps some old trauma is rearing its head. She's been sleepwalking more lately, and I wonder if she could even not remember having done it.

And at the same time I'm angry that she can't just talk to me about it.

I just want my old life back. Sure, I'm always broke and the house is freezing and I don't really leave it much, but things were, if not comfortable, at least stable? I don't think that's just in comparison to how they are now; I was genuinely happy. And now I'm on edge all the time, I'm scared for the people I love, feeling like I've let the ghosts down, and questioning myself at every turn.

We need to get out of here. Away from everyone. It's a crisp, still day, hinting at spring. I remember the gardens my family sometimes used to drive to for a day out. They'll be quiet at this time of year.

Alison drives us to the station. It's only once we're on the platform that I start to relax. Everything falls into place. Everything runs on tracks and I know where those tracks go. There are timetables and maps, and the world is comprehensible again. It runs to patterns; it goes back and forth and it circles round. It repeats.

When we arrive, we step down to the platform not saying much; I think both of us are feeling a bit dazed, as if the extent of what's been going on has suddenly hit us. But we're also feeling closer to each other, holding hands as we walk down from the platform and along the winding road to our destination.

We spend the afternoon walking through the gardens. Most of the trees are still bare but the snowdrops are out, and though it's still cold we have good coats and gloves and it feels pleasant, a gentle breeze on our faces. As we hoped, we have the place almost to ourselves. We sit for a little while in the Japanese garden and Araminta sketches while I watch.

In the tearooms, a near empty conservatory, I have a chocolate brownie, Araminta a slice of lemon cake, and we share a pot of tea. I can't handle the overload of leaving the house too much, and I can't safely walk far alone, but sometimes I think I should go out more than I do. Even though we're doing this because I'm over stressed – we both are – I like outings like this, doing things together.

We catch the train home late in the afternoon. Sometimes we just need to be moving. I need the rhythm and the movement to feel even a little bit okay. I watch towns fade out and fields flare in, country stations momentarily there with their surrounding villages and park and ride spaces before they disappear into emptiness, over and over. We see rabbits running alongside the track, the occasional squirrel making its way hastily up a tree.

It's dark and starting to rain when we get home, and Vinnie collects us from the station. I say nothing on the drive. I'm calmer, yes, and glad to have spent time with Araminta, but what's happening at home is affecting me on a deeper level than I can really understand. As usual, I can work out everyone else's reactions much more easily than mine. I think it's because I can look past the detail rather than getting caught up in it.

I don't understand why this is affecting me so viscerally. Yes, the unpredictability is difficult, and yes there's a sign of possible danger to the ghosts, to my friends, to me. Those are good reasons to be stressed. But there's something more to it, some level more fundamental than the emotional on which this is affecting me, making me feel continually nauseous and ill at ease. I think about Saeed's theory, that it was my own family who once owned Casswell Park. He hasn't been able to prove it, not yet, and it may not be true. But one way or another, I know I'm far more deeply involved in this than simply living in Casswell Park. Today has eased this feeling somewhat, but I know it will return.

"Um, folks, one of the ghost hunters is here," Denny says from the doorway to the dining room. We've been playing Catan – Araminta found the 5-6 person expansion on special, so we can finally get a good group of us together. The table is spread out with cards, bowls of cookies and corn chips, cups of tea. We all look up at the interruption.

"Shit," Saeed says. "I totally forgot to talk to Roderick."

"Well they couldn't exactly complain if they knew what we've been dealing with," Araminta points out.

"It didn't sound like she wanted to talk about that," Denny says. "She says she has something that might help us, and she's happy to meet up outside if we'd prefer."

Vinnie sighs dramatically.

"Invite her in. We need all the help we can get, even from ghost hunters. And I guess now is a time to be building bridges rather than walls."

"Feeling like building an entire fucking castle with a portcullis and a moat right now," Araminta mutters under her breath, but no-one objects to Vinnie's point of view and Denny goes to let Keira in. We leave our game in progress and head through to the living room where Alison is watching a home renovation show on her laptop. As if she didn't have enough of a project all around her; I'm not really sure why she wants to be watching anyone else's.

"Sorry Alison," Vinnie says. "Need to take over this space. One of the ghost hunters has something for us, apparently."

Alison pauses the show and raises an eyebrow.

"I hope you're right," she says. Her voice implies that she's not at all optimistic, but nevertheless she puts her laptop away and repositions herself to sit upright on the sofa. Keira looks smaller, shyer, less sullen as Denny leads her in and invites her to sit on one of the large arm chairs. It engulfs her slight frame, and even her bright green hair seems dull.

"So," Araminta says. "What have you got for us?" I'm leaning against her on the couch, my hand in hers. I can tell she's having to work hard to suppress the hostility in her voice. We all exchange looks. It's clear Keira needs to start talking and fast, prove she hasn't been bullshitting us.

It's me she turns to look at. I had been almost warming to her, but I'm feeling differently right now, like she's pushing things too far. This is her second visit in a week, and I see literally no-one I don't live with that often.

"I saw your pendant," she says to Araminta, blushing. "And I thought I'd seen some of that symbolism before. You don't know what they mean, do you?"

None of us reply.

"Neither did I," she says. "But I thought I'd seen something like them before, so I did some research, and I found this."

She hands over a small stack of printouts. I take them and hand them to Saeed, who will digest them much faster than I ever could – and enjoy it rather than considering it a chore. I can see Saeed frowning with concentration as he starts to read.

"One sentence summary," says Alison. "Please," she adds after a pause.

"Alright," Keira says, clearly forcing herself to think quickly. I can tell this is still going to be far more than one sentence, but hopefully, we can get there without going through the stack of documents. "There are really two parts to what's written but essentially they're both spells, not spells you read aloud but spells you need the object they're written on to perform. The first one helps you to locate ghosts. I'm not completely sure how that works, but given that you said it was found with a collection of ghosts, it makes sense. The second one, it refers to control and corporeality."

"And that means what?" says Vinnie, sharply. They're clearly beyond making the effort to be polite, and I can understand that.

"It could be an ability to control how corporeal a ghost is," says Saeed, leafing through the papers quickly. "But I think it's something more. More like drawing control from corporeality."

Keira shrugs awkwardly. "Yeah, I think it's something like that. I researched it a bit more, and I think I know who created the pendant, probably by order of a man who once lived here. Perhaps he paid him to do it, but more likely they were colleagues of a sort, or Barnabas was his mentor. Their terminology gets a bit mixed up. He was a scientist, or natural philosopher as they said then, and some sort of mystic. Possibly considered himself a bit of a theologian as well, though I don't think the church at the time exactly agreed. Name of Tristram Barnabas."

"I've heard of him," Saeed says. "He was alive at a similar time, or a bit earlier than the person who's been giving us so many problems. They perhaps knew each other?"

"Yeah they could have done. So he's come from and working in a Christian context, though he rejected what many Christians would consider essential tenets. In his writing he's basically talking about a journey to heaven or hell. According to him a ghost is a temporary stop, a lingering on Earth ahead of an afterlife."

"I wouldn't disagree with that," Denny says. "I know most of you are atheists, but it makes sense to me."

Keira nods, continues.

"He had this theory that corporeality is a definable thing, not a physical thing but like energy or a force like gravity. Something that can be measured and has particular laws applied to it. He believed that corporeality was what takes your soul to the afterlife, and that process uses it up. Ghosts still have some corporeality because they haven't yet passed to that after life. They're on a slow progression towards it, and their corporeality is the finite resource that's pushing them over and being used up in the process. And I think what they were aiming for, was to make one ghost more corporeal at the expense of another."

"Like energy," Holly says. "You all know about the law of conservation of energy, right? That energy cannot be made or destroyed but only converted from one form or another. So you can't just make something more or less corporeal, but you can transfer corporeality."

"And if there is no afterlife," Alison says, visibly thinking. "The idea still works, if we consider it a destructive force, or one that is consumed in the process of destroying existence."

We talk a bit more, back and forth, and Saeed starts sorting the printouts Keira brought on the coffee table. It's Denny, who has at once been welcoming of Keira and yet also seems clearly uncomfortable, who brings the conversation to a close.

"Thanks for bringing this to us Keira," he says. "We appreciate it. Are you okay getting home?"

She nods.

"I'm parked just around the corner. I hope you find what I've told you useful and that things work out soon."

Then she turns and heads out, down the corridor, towards the side door. Denny follows and locks the door behind her.

"So," Alison asks, as we return to our seats and close the door to keep in the little warmth we have. "Do we believe that?"

"I believe it," Saeed says. "It's consistent with what I've come across in my own research. The question is – is she genuinely trying to help us or is something more going on?

"Plus is Logan feeling this helpful, or any of the ghost hunters we dealt with before. Does he even know about it or has Keira done this secretly, like some kind of renegade?"

"Traitor to the ghost hunter cause," says Araminta laughing, even though it's far from as funny as we'd like it to be.

I stretch myself out on my bed and get back to the book. I flip through looking for mention of an afterlife, something that correlates with what Keira was talking about but there's nothing immediately apparent. I think I'm just going to have to go about this the hard way, transcribing everything letter by letter, word by word

And the worries I have make it far harder to concentrate. Normally ghosts fading is imperceptible, but every one I've seen in the past couple of days has faded noticeably, far faster than they should.

I've planned to do another patrol tonight, in the late hours when everyone else prefers to sleep. I don't want to. I feel like one of the ghost hunters. They're all about their kit and their strategies, and right now I'm assembling torches and phones and ensuring I have a set of keys handy and my phone is fully charged, and we've talked about strategy and signals. It feels like a game or a job or a hobby when in fact it's everything I care about most.

Right now I'd give anything to just be hanging out with Araminta, and for things to be how they used to be.

It turns out I'm exhausted and fall asleep over this ancient book. I can't remember the last time I slept before midnight, the last time something like this happened. I wake with a start, convinced something's wrong, but everything is quiet and the house is sleeping.

I grab my phone and torch, feeling the weight of it in my hand, reminding myself I can use it as a weapon, hoping I won't have to. And I creep down the corridor.

So often, walking through this house, I'm reminded of how much I love it. It's still a mess. We've managed to get most of the flooring sorted, though the newer boards are a cheaper pine and the varnish doesn't match. Some of the walls still reveal exposed wiring or pipes, other are flaking plaster or ripped layers of paint and wallpaper. Chunks of the ceilings are missing. The pipes make strange noises. Some of the windows have gaps around the frames stuffed with newspaper.

The house I grew up in was old, and undesirable because the train line went right past the back garden. We didn't have much money to work on it, but as both my parents are good at DIY we managed well enough. I love that house too, but not in the same way I love this one. That was a place I spent a largely happy childhood; this is a home we have made together and are responsible for. Either way, I could never imagine living somewhere new. Somewhere without a past. Without ghosts.

There are fewer ghosts than usual active in the house, and while I already knew that to be the case it's chillingly apparent as I walk. But there are no other signs that anything is amiss, and so I head back, my torch lighting the splintered floorboards as I go.

I've just got back into my bedroom and into my pyjamas – which are actually a set of leggings and an old t-shirt – when I hear Araminta's door creak open. She's possibly going to the bathroom, but I fear she's sleep-walking again.

I slip my feet into my slippers and grab my torch. I want to see if she's doing anything more than just walking in her sleep.

I keep my torch on low, pointing at the ground. The corridor outside is pitch dark but I know it well; how many paces to the stairs, its width, the parts where the floorboards creak. I can hear Araminta's footsteps ahead. I look up and...

...I shouldn't be able to see her in the darkness, but there's something about her that's glowing, something fuzzy and indistinct. Is she walking with a ghost? I can't tell from here. I creep forward, light down, careful not to wake her.

I follow her past the main staircase and to the section of corridor where most of the rest of our housemates have their rooms. It's the best restored section of the house, which is partly the cause and partly the consequence of so many of us having rooms there.

On my right are Alison and Denny's bedrooms, with one empty between them; they're the ones with the balconies and views, which means Alison's near-hermit cats get some sun. On our left is Holly's suite, which allows her to have both a bedroom and a study. Right at the end of the corridor is the two-bedroom suite which is partly over the front part of the ballroom. Within it, Vinnie and Theo have a bedroom each, and a shared sitting room. I'm not sure if she's trying to get to one of them.

I blink and try and make out what's going wrong. I can see her, see her still in her work uniform as if she hasn't slept, her hair is in the pigtails she uses to stop it tangling while she sleeps. But around her, illuminating her, encasing her, is something else. Something partly corporeal, partly not. I trace the outline mentally, the black cloak and the pale face.

"Ghost eater." I breathe.

My first instinct is to get Araminta the hell out of there, to fight him with everything I have. I stay quiet and I stay silent, inserting myself into an alcove, turning off my torch. She turns, he turns. I don't know what's going on, but they turn together and look, and I don't think they're looking for me.

Gregoria is walking down the corridor, a slow, contemplative walk as is typical for her on the rare occasions we see her.

As she approaches, Araminta – no, he, the ghost eater, no, both of them together, her hand enveloped in his, reach out to Gregoria and I think Araminta's trying to take her by the hand, but she turns and grabs her by the shoulder, pulling her upwards in a way that should be impossible, and her mouth is open, his mouth overlaid, and she pulls her into her mouth and swallows her whole.

I back myself against the wall, clutching my torch, and scream silently. Whatever I had been imagining, it was not this.

When I force myself to look, Araminta and the ghost eater have separated from each other, and I can only just see her in his glow. I shine my torch on them, not caring now about being seen, and I watch as both of them change visibly.

The ghost eater grows more corporeal; the black of his cloak becomes darker, the red brighter, every line is sharper and I can see only the fuzziest of outlines when I look through him; he is not so far from opaque. He's taken something from Gregoria, swallowed her, and now he is more powerful than ever.

And he's used Araminta to do it.

It's Araminta who changes the most. I watch it happening and yet my brain can't fully process it until it's done. Only then can I look at her properly, and begin to understand just what has happened.

She's suddenly a dull version of herself. I can see the colours of her red hair, her navy work pants and turquoise polo shirt with the company logo, but they're muted, as if they've been through the wash too many times. Not only that but I can see through them. See through her.

I think for a minute I'm seeing a ghost, that she was somehow killed in the scuffle, but there's no body. This is her, and yet she's not as she was.

The ghost eater, solid as I am now, stamps his foot on the wooden floor and white flames emerge, surround him, and then vanish with him into nothingness. I force myself to look at Araminta, taking tentative steps towards her, horrified and yet wanting nothing more than for her to hold me.

I have this bitter ridiculous thought about how, if she had to be stuck in the same clothes for eternity then she should at least have had the option of wearing an outfit she loved. The dress with the snails all over or the skirt with wave patterns and ships and the tiniest hints of sea monsters lurking beneath them. Her olive-green winter coat or her red knee-high boots. Her striped rainbow tights. Anything, anything, but her work uniform.

She reaches out, her hands raising slowly as if in a state of confusion, but then she drifts away. I scream and run after her as she drifts through the wall, seemingly lacking all control over her own movements. I'm watching a fear worse than my worst, the worst fear I never knew I had, unfold right before me and I run through rooms trying to track her but fall ever further behind as I have to run around walls and use the doors until eventually I've lost her entirely...

I've lost her.

I've lost Araminta.

I beat my fists against the wall and howl as if there's no-one else around, as if nothing else matters because right now it doesn't. Araminta is gone and if there's a way to get her back then I don't know it.

1707

She is still here to rescue Tobias, of course, but weeks have turned into months, into years. It is not the comfortable bed and the room all to herself, nor the meat and fish she eats at every meal and sweets after, that keeps her here.

She's found a comfortable rhythm, and she craves knowledge and order. Her brain is zipping from words to concepts to classifications, all blooming in front of her. She's taken to meet other scientists and they visit Casswell, and though she has to stand in the corner of the room like a servant and not speak unless spoken to, she's absorbing everything she's hearing. She can't imagine going back to the mill. She can't imagine being anywhere but here.

One day she takes the bottle she knows Tobias is encased within and hovers near a window. She can drop it and it will break and he will be released. But she doesn't drop it. She puts it back on the shelf where it belongs. She tells herself she will do it next year. That with a little longer and a little more knowledge she will be better placed to help him and herself.

CHAPTER SEVENTEEN

The doors are opened and lights are flicked on and I barely notice the whirl of people around me, in dressing gowns and pyjamas, as I run around frantically. I feel someone's hand on my shoulder but I push past it.

Eventually, Vinnie stands in front of me firmly and does not move. The others take a few steps back when I stop. I spot Theo watching from the corner of his room, having clearly been told to stay away, and his look of sincere concern as he swings forward, one hand on the doorframe, makes me burst into tears and I can't stop myself.

Vinnie puts a hand on each shoulder and holds me steady as I cry. They know I don't do hugging at a time like this.

I shake my head, trying desperately to stem the tears. Only Vinnie's hands, firm, are keeping me from completely going to pieces.

I catch a glimpse of something on the floor. Glinting in the light. The spot where the ghost eater – and now I know how true that name was – had disappeared. The pendant I gave Araminta. Could that really have been where everything started? Am I to blame for all of this?

Vinnie follows my gaze but it's Holly who darts through and grabs the pendant. No-one reacts to her.

"Morgan? Has something happened to Araminta?"

I nod, numbly.

"Was it the ghost eater?"

Again I nod. I don't think there's anything else I can do. But Vinnie directs me to the private sitting room that sits between theirs and Theo's bedrooms, gets me Theo's school Chromebook, and directs my hands to the keyboard.

I can't do it. Everything is too awful for me to tell this story.

"Type the words you can," says Saeed, who has come up from downstairs and wedged himself on the other side of the sofa next to me. "Leave spaces for the rest for now."

So I type Araminta and Gregoria and Ghost Eater and book, line breaks between every word, frantically hitting the enter key. I can't type words like possessed and eaten. I can't write the whole story. But they fill in the gaps. They ask questions. And I type words like yes and no and maybe and sometimes they gently pull my hand away when I've held my finger down on a letter too long.

Somehow between us we tell the story. That the ghost eater has been able to possess Araminta because she wears the pendant. He's been doing it for days, maybe weeks, and I'm not sure if she knew about it. When she was sleepwalking, he was controlling her. When her studio was destroyed, the messages painted on canvases, that was him controlling her too, and she probably didn't even know he was doing it. Possibly he was making us think it was the ghosts. Trying to reduce our sympathy for them.

And Saeed's figured the last bit out. The eater bit of the equation. He's been maintaining immortality by feeding on the corporeality of ghosts. He used Araminta – she ate, she *ate a child, oh god* – to eat them for him, and that gave him enough power to steal corporeality from Araminta as well and now... now he's a person and apparently one with magical powers, and she's non-corporeal. I don't know if she's dead exactly, but she's not alive like she should be, and I can't find her.

Once again, no-one's sleeping. Saeed and Denny are scheming in the dining room, researching, trying to find out what we can do to make things right. Alison has gone out for burgers at the one chain that's open at 2am. Vinnie is keeping me from falling apart completely. Theo has been returned to bed, though he's not happy about it. And Holly... no-one's exactly sure where Holly has gone.

I'm calmer now, but I've started walking, looking for Araminta again. People ask if they can help but I shake them off. I'm not sure what I want from anyone. I'm not sure what I'd do if I could hold Araminta to any one place. She's been hurt enough in her life by those who claim to want to help her. I don't think I could live with myself if I kept her, not sure I could live with myself if I didn't. In an odd way, it's a relief that it's a moot point, but I can't feel anything but anger right now.

Eventually, my frustration turns to tears and I'm walking numbly around, tears running down my face until I can't cry any more and I start to feel not so much sad as hopeless. I slide down against a wall until I'm sitting alone in the corridor, and finally I message the group chat.

>> need alone now

>> please

is how I finish what must be one of the hardest attempts at communication since I was a child.

There's a pause and then Vinnie's reply comes.

>> If we leave you alone will you be safe? Take care of yourself?

My finger hovers over my phone.

>> y

>> Alright, we'll give you some space for a bit. Please tell us when you need us.

After an hour or two I make my way downstairs, linger outside the dining room where most of my housemates are gathered, debating whether to go in, but I've no idea how to interact with anyone, not even the people I love most. And that's if they don't hate me for how I've behaved. Just as they realise I'm there I panic and start to walk fast down the corridor, self-conscious about how loud my footsteps sound, speeding up, not able to deal with anything.

Denny follows me down the corridor.

"Morgan, please come and eat at least?"

Reluctantly I head into the room and pull out my chair – we're a household of mostly autistic people, of course we have assigned chairs. My throat feels swollen and I can't imagine eating, but I'm also suddenly exhausted and don't think I can do anything useful right now either.

Alison pushes some fries in my direction. They smell good but make me feel nauseous at the same time. I shake my head and push them away, even though I have to admit they do look pretty good. But I can't. It's less not wanting to eat and more feeling like I'd be giving in, that I'd be letting Araminta down, that I wasn't strong enough to put aside my own needs and wants for her.

"Nuh-uh," says Vinnie. "None of this not-eating nonsense. If you don't eat you're not going to think clearly or effectively, and you're going to let her down and fail to save her. I know you love her, and I know you don't want to abandon her, so you're going to eat, right?"

Vinnie knows how to guilt me. It's blackmail and we both know it and yet I say nothing because they're mostly right. I gnaw on a fry. I confess it does taste good. There are tears stinging my eyes. I am realising that I'm actually hungry. Once I get eating it doesn't take me long to finish the serving.

Saeed and Denny are frantically talking about corporeality, plotting how to save Araminta. I want to help but it's going over my head. It sounds sufficiently close to physics that I want Holly to... Holly... where's Holly? Alison and Vinnie are talking about safety and defending ourselves. Theo is making an unholy mess with the sauce. There's no sign of Holly and with every minute that goes by I'm terrified for Araminta. I don't only fear for her life, but for what she is going through right now. I don't know how conscious she is, how much she understands of her current situation.

Vinnie motions for me to drink water. I know there's no arguing with them. The water is heavy and cold, and tastes implausibly bitter. I'm just finishing it when we hear the side door slam. All of us are on our feet instantly but it's just Holly, red-faced and out of breath.

Holly shakes her head in response to our questions and collapses on a chair. It's only when Denny has handed her a two-litre bottle of Coke and she's swigged a large amount of it straight from the bottle that she manages to explain.

"The pendant Araminta's been wearing, right? The one that came with the bottle? Well, that was on the floor where it all happened. And when I picked that up... well you know how you just know that something's bad sometimes. That happened here. And I needed to get it as far away from here as I possibly could."

A hint of a memory flashes past me, of something red amid broken glass, a stone in the middle of the pendant, but then it's gone.

"I would have driven..." Vinnie begins, but Holly shakes her head.

"No. I didn't want anyone else near it. And don't ask where it is now. None of you want to know."

CHAPTER EIGHTEEN

W e have all these strands we need to untangle, and it's hard to keep any kind of focus on them when things feel so urgent. The house seems eerily calm and still right now, which is so at odds with my mood that it makes everything seem even more discordant.

We all want to stay together for as long as we can bear it, for safety, so we've spread ourselves out in the ballroom. Holly and Denny are lying on the floor around a big sheet of paper. They're trying to measure corporeality and the changed speed at which it has been reduced, and they're looking for factors in common among the missing ghosts.

Meanwhile, Saeed and I have returned to the book, have decided we need to finish transcribing it together. My hands are greasy and covered in salt, and it's bothering me. As if she could read my mind, Alison hands me a wet wipe. I thank her and it's amazing how getting the sensory horribleness off my fingers helps me feel like I can cope.

Before we look at the book, we look at the logs of ghost sightings. Saeed adds what I saw happen with Gregoria, because I really don't want to, and then we open the list. And in that research, I find something I really didn't want to hear.

Two of the missing ghosts have been located, but they are faint, so faint as to be near invisible, and on top of that were sufficiently terrified of the ghost eater so had been hiding themselves as much as they could. That's concerning enough, but there's worse. There's every indication that Hannah and Tim have completely faded away.

Gone.

And once a ghost has faded completely, you can't get them back. It's the ghost version of death, basically. The fury I had managed to dampen a little comes rushing back. He fucking killed two ghosts. He murdered two of our ghosts. Ghosts who did him no wrong. Ghosts who had already been through more than enough, and never deserved this.

"That piece of shit fucking killed them," I say out loud. My fists are balled and I can feel my face heating up, red spreading across my normally pale cheeks. That doesn't normally happen to me. It's Araminta who gets the freckles and the sunburn and the flushed cheeks.

Araminta...

"They were already dead," says Denny. "That's why they're ghosts."

I know he's not actually being heartless, that he's just not able to handle the technical inaccuracy in my statement but still, I have to swallow the fury that rises in me at him. I don't care whether this fits a technical definition of death or not, only that they were once here and now they're not. They had, if not dreams and a future, then at least those who cared about them, a home where they belonged, a time they had forged a place in even if it ignored them.

I wonder whether they went to parties in halls like this, or if they drank at the local pub, if they liked to dance to folk music or piano or bawdy songs at the bar, or if it was they who were playing the instruments, making the whole room come alive as they played their fiddle or harpsichord or harmonica.

I wonder whether they met loves here, here in the ballroom or secretly in the gardens or in the woods. I know so little about their lives. There are so many possible questions, questions I wouldn't think to ask even if I could.

I wonder if – if Araminta is now a ghost – will she still be here in decades to come, centuries, after we're all dead, reminiscing about a time of oil-paint and Instagram in a drowning world, or a world where humans are uploaded to virtual systems and are themselves non-corporeal, or a world being abandoned for other planetary systems. Will she be drifting among it all? And will she still remember us – will she still remember me – so long after I'm gone?

I force myself to stop thinking about that possibility, and focus on what Saeed is telling me. And for the first time, it seems like we have something we can really make use of. And together we start to put together a plan.

I thought dealing with the ghost eater and recovering Araminta was more than enough. As usual, the universe decides to throw even more at me. A day and a night have passed since Araminta disappeared, and we've only had very fleeting signs of her since. I've been in the ballroom most of the day but it got too much, and I've barely been back in my room for an hour when I hear Theo's footsteps – running, rather than wheeling, down the corridor, then the sound of banging on my door.

"Holly's really sick!" he says. "Please come quickly. It's an... I think it's an emergency."

I'm not always good at doing things at short notice but when I need to I usually can. Fortunately, this time I stop myself freezing and follow Theo, still in my bare feet, to the closest bathroom where Holly is bent over the toilet bowl. I touch her on her shaking shoulder, and then I scan the room, spot the empty pill packets on the floor.

Oh FUCK.

My internal shouting bursts out of my head before I can calm myself. I know I'm really not helping. I take a deep breath and try to keep calm.

"Holly... Holly, what did you do?"

The words are coming without too much difficulty right now. I imagine when – if – we get through this, though, I won't speak for days. And probably finding more than the occasional white hair.

I turn to Theo, who is staring wide-eyed at the whole situation.

"Theo, I need you to find another adult and send them here. Tell them it's an emergency. Then I need you to go to the kitchen and get a glass and the bag of salt. Can you do that?"

He nods as if words are hard for him too right now.

"Is Holly going to die?" he asks.

I look him in the eye even though it hurts.

"No," I say. "She won't die."

Somehow I manage to get out of her how many she's taken, using the empty packets as a guide. Counting half-digested pills in her vomit is one of the less pleasant things I've ever had to do, but I'd rather that than any harm come to her.

"I'm sorry," she sobs. "I'm really sorry. I didn't mean... I'm sorry. I know you..."

"Fuck's sake Holly. Stop apologising and tell me what's happening."

At that point, Theo runs up with the salt and glass. I make her a glass of warm salt water and persuade her to drink it, and then another, and she vomits until there's nothing left to throw up. I help her sit down on the floor and, as Vinnie and Denny arrive, she begins to talk.

"I hadn't slept," she says. Her voice sounds hoarse and empty. "I hadn't slept in days. And then I had this biology exam and I sat there and I looked at the questions and I kept reading and reading them over and over and none of them made sense and then it felt like all the time had disappeared and the test was over and I'd hardly written anything."

"Oh Holly... Oh Holly... was this a real test or a mock?"

"Real. It's part of the in-class assessment."

"Okay, and how much of your final grade is it worth?"

Holly thinks. Talking about percentages and course structures has distracted and calmed her. She's stopped crying and seems mostly dazed. She's shaking a little and I wrap a towel around her like a blanket.

"We have six modules," she says. "It's worth fifteen percent of one of those."

"And what do you need to pass?"

"To pass..." she says, like she's never even considered the possibility. "I mean, a pass is a C so you get fifty percent for that but I need..."

"Okay," I say, quickly calculating in my head. "So even if you got zero in this, you need to get uh a little under sixty percent in everything else in the module to pass. You can totally do that. And I know it's not the mark you want. I know you want more than a pass, but it's not a disaster, okay??

I raise my head and speak gently to Vinnie and Denny, who have paused in the doorway but are looking desperately concerned.

"Overdose," I say, compressing so many things into a single word. "She's thrown more or less everything up, though. She'll be okay."

"It's just school..." Denny begins. I know he's trying to be helpful but it's all I can do to not turn around and say 'dude, not helping'. Everything is so fraught. It's Holly who responds, and she does it dramatically, howls, and the noise echoes down the corridor.

I pull my arm tighter around her and she sobs.

"People act like I'm this highly-strung perfectionist and..."

"You're not?" I ask, a deliberate tone of surprise in my voice. I'm taking a risk but she makes this indescribable sound that seems to be laughter coming through the sobbing in spite of herself. She reaches out and grabs more sheets from the roll of toilet paper and blows her nose heavily, tries to wipe away her tears. Her voice sounds weak and exhausted.

"I know you all mock me for it and don't take it too seriously, and I know that's friendly mocking, but it's not that I'm being obsessive or focused on the wrong thing. It's that it's all I have. It was the only thing that saved me. The only thing about me that people were okay with, the only thing that compensated for what I was, what I am, and if I fail at this, the only thing I have, then..."

She shrugs in despair. I want to tell her that she's one of the best people I know; that she's not only smart but she's the sort of person who keeps a group together and smooths out tension, who will play ridiculous games with Theo and yet protect him as if he were her little brother, which I suppose in some ways he is. I want to talk about how she can notice and fix the small problems, quietly and without any praise; it's always her who notices when a tap needs a new washer, and she's the first to leap up when a fuse blows, as they do so often in this big old house. I want to say all this and more but I can't find the words so I just hold her tighter and let her cry.

To my surprise, there's part of me that's angry with her as well. I don't want to be feeling it, don't like myself for feeling it, but it's there. The thing is, Araminta is smart as hell, and she mostly managed to keep out of what they called the Shelter Class at school, but it definitely didn't save her from abuse or what they called therapy which was basically just more abuse. Holly could fail a dozen tests and still have options I don't, just because she can speak reliably. What seems horrifying to her is still miles ahead of reality for many of us. She's had it tough, yes, but she has possibilities none of us will ever have. And she was on the verge of throwing them all away.

But I say none of that, because none of it will help.

I think Vinnie's going to say we have to get Holly to hospital, tell us not to be so stupid, especially as Holly's technically still a minor. I almost want them to just decide so I don't have to be responsible, to say it's the only option, so confidently I have to believe them. I want other people, professional people, to take care of the situation. It's not the work of taking care of her that scares me, but the responsibility, the knowledge of how terrible the consequences could be should I get this wrong.

I want to live in a world where we can trust doctors. A world where hospitals aren't overloading and dangerous, where we aren't always seen to be the problem. A world where we don't have to fear Holly being pushed back into the hands of her abusers, because people who aren't blood or marriage related aren't seen as family while violent abusers are. A world where doctors don't see our existence as an attitude problem and take their frustrations out on us.

But we don't live in that world, and even Vinnie's strength and decisiveness isn't going to get us there.

People who aren't us get to make easy choices, like calling an ambulance when someone is ill. People like us have to make difficult choices, imperfect choices, and accept the guilt that may arise from whatever decision we may end up making. And right now, I'm making a difficult choice.

And the one thing that keeps me going is that we may not have the back-up most people have. We may not be able to rely on systems others can count on, but I'm not on my own either. And Vinnie surprises me.

"Fine, well, we're already on ghost-watch, and evil-ghost-eater-who-looks-like-a-vampire watch, so we may as well be on suicide watch as well. Never rains but it pours, doesn't it? Both of you go eat a food and drink a water, as the young people say."

I set about making things as safe and as manageable as possible for Holly, and for all of us. It doesn't really help that even as I take anti-depressants and painkillers from her to dole out as needed, and send a message round to everyone else to keep any medication they're on secure, I can't ignore that Alison, Denny, and Vinnie have assembled a whole fucking weapons cache downstairs. Terrible fucking timing, which seems to be the theme of things lately.

With Holly tucked up in bed, and Saeed checking in on her, I take a look at the preparations people have been making. There have been three strands to this. One, we need to find a way of returning Araminta to corporeality – fortunately no-one is saying this is impossible, just that we haven't worked it out yet, and no-one is using past tense or talking as if she were dead. I think I'd lose it if they were. Two, the ghost eater seems to have magical powers, so we need to find out what they are and, at best, how to neutralise them. Three, as he's now corporeal, we need to fight him physically.

For some reason, it's the third that feels most intimidating to us.

The weapons are out on a table. It looks like a scene from a paranormal TV series, not my reality. Whatever they could get their hands on without looking suspicious. There are two BB guns but no real firearms; not like anyone with our diagnoses would ever get a gun license, and I'm personally relieved because guns scare me. But more or less everything else I can imagine, and quite a few that I couldn't have. There are kitchen knives, some taped to sticks. The axe which has been sitting in our storage space, possibly for decades. A small canister of pepper spray – fuck knows who got hold of that and why they've been keeping it, but I'm certainly glad they haven't been caught with it.

Then there are some things I wouldn't have thought of as weapons. Aerosols – deodorant and fly spray, I assume to spray in someone's eyes to buy a few extra seconds. Other supplies too: rope and matches. First aid supplies. A pen knife. A torch.

Alison has told me there's a reason for them to be focusing on this; the more corporeal the ghost hunter becomes, the more effective conventional weapons – and, for that matter, good old hand to hand combat – will be when fighting him. In some ways it's a reassurance that things seem to be moving back into the rational domain, a space where the laws of physics apply once more. But it's also looking like one of those situations where things have to get worse before they get better. We need him to become more powerful and more corporeal in order to win.

I can only hope the authorities don't get any hint this is going on. I can't see any scenario in which autistic people with weapons fighting a supernatural force would get treated well by the police. I'm particularly worried for Vinnie; Black, autistic, trans, solidly built. I feel sick when I think about how bad it could be for them, so I can't even imagine how they'd feel. Saeed... well young man with an Arabic name and a weapons cache is going to be any tabloid's dream. Meanwhile, I'd get stereotyped as loner who tried to hack the Pentagon or something. But even someone like Holly is at risk; I can imagine a scenario in which she'd be dragged back to her abusive parents, subjected to court ordered therapy.

But we're kidding ourselves if we work on the assumption that we can somehow exempt ourselves from that danger by doing the right thing. We can't escape the world we live in, only do our best to live in it.

So I'm looking at all these weapons, and it seems like there's going to be a lot of direct combat in our immediate future. And maybe some traps and other obstacles set up. That makes it sound like a kid's book but it's all sounding very real.

I have to say I'm not feeling good about having all this here when Holly is in her current state, but I suppose needs must, and there are no perfect choices when you have an evil recently-corporeal ghost eater lurking round your house, trying to harm your ghosts.

We're going to need every bit of strength – mental as well as physical – that we possess. I can tell that now.

CHAPTER NINETEEN

I sleep only with the help of meds my housemates pool for me from their various prescriptions; a zopiclone from Saeed here, an ativan from Denny there. Even then my dreams are filled with following Araminta around this house or other houses, along railway lines, through abandoned tunnels. Always she slips from my grasp just at the last minute, and I wake covered in sweat, willing the minutes and the hours to pass quicker so at least I won't have to be alone any more.

When the day comes and I'm around others, I long for solitude.

Vinnie, more than anyone, is keeping me at least partially functioning. This time they've handed me a pair of rubber gloves, turned the tap on, and directed me at the dishes we have somehow managed to accumulate despite us living on take-aways and toast for the past few days. I force myself to go through the motions. I don't know what I'm feeling. I don't know how to feel. Vinnie grabs a tea towel and starts drying.

My mind has been darting around possibilities for saving Araminta. It's landed, for now, on paranormal abilities, and for specific reasons: namely that my own abilities seem to be changing, seem to be growing.

It's not as unusual as many people think to have some form of psychic or paranormal power. It's unusual for it to be strong; even a moderate ability like Denny's is unusual. But most of those who, like me, have mild powers, attribute their experiences to chance, or to confirmation bias, or to picking up on non-verbal cues. If you understand what's going on you can strengthen your abilities a little, or at least become more adept at using them. I've done this. But most people never do.

I suspect there's some kind of genetic link underpinning such powers, but it's not a simple one and I suspect multiple genes are involved. I do know that while neither of my parents have abilities, my grandfather had a form of telepathy.

I finish the dishes and start to scrub the large cast-iron frying pan. Irrespective of the whys and hows, I'm increasingly getting a sense of this house's past.

I've always been sensitive to spaces. To buildings and rooms and walls; to stone piled upon stone and wood nailed to wood. To the mosaic floors of churches and metal beams holding up old factories, to high mill windows and canal locks. And to the rails, always the rails. I've been sensitive to fields and woods and the pond where we caught frogspawn when we were children.

But now my ability not only seems heightened but qualitatively different. I can tell the ghost eater's details when he's not visible; it's not like a vision or a hallucination, but I get a shape in my mind, a sense of where he is and which direction to go in order to become closer to him.

"...with the head." Vinnie's voice booms out of nowhere. I must have visibly jumped because Vinnie looks instantly apologetic.

"Sorry," they say. "I didn't mean to scare you. Are you okay?"

I nod. I have words to say but today is not a talking day. I circle my hand to encourage them to continue.

"Just wondering what on earth was going on with that severed head business? It's clearly fucked Holly up even more than she is already, so I for one would really like to know what exactly they thought they were doing."

For an instant my mind flashes back to that initial horror. So much has happened since then, and not much of it good. I feel a bit nauseous. But then everything starts to come together. We'd assumed the stress of what had happened had been, if not the cause of Holly's overdose, at least what finally tipped her over the edge. I try to talk to Vinnie, to tell them, but in the moment of realisation everything's tumbling in my head and there's no way I'm going to get the words out. But it must be visible on my face because Vinnie's looking at me, their hands still on the tea towel.

"What is it?"

I signal to them to wait a moment, dry my hands and pick up my phone. I have an AAC app I'm learning to use but until I get used to it typing is easier. I type the words in and show them.

>> Not trying to harm us. Trying to WARN us.

It's all making sense now, and I feel stupid and a little bit guilty for not having worked it out earlier. There are some malevolent ghosts, sure, but they're far rarer than most people would have you believe. There are some that cause you distress, but it's in the same way a screaming baby distresses sleep-deprived parents; there's no malice there. And none of our ghosts have really fit into either category, not for a long time. Yet even I, with that knowledge and all my experience and comfort with ghosts, still jumped to the stereotypical conclusion the first time things went outside our established patterns. I saw a threat when I should have seen an attempt at communication between two groups of people who cannot easily communicate.

They were not trying to threaten Holly with danger. They were trying to warn her of upcoming danger. It wasn't gentle or subtle, but it was the best they could do.

And perhaps scaring people is one of the ways ghosts most communicate. I can see how a recursive pattern could have developed. Their presence scared people so they used the way they could have the most effect on people as their means of communication. And sometimes we've interpreted it better than others.

It doesn't explain everything, of course. But this is a start.

"Well," says Vinnie. "If you're right, we might have been a bit slow on the uptake, but I think we can consider ourselves warned on all kinds of fronts now."

I shake and nod my head all at the same time. I can't say it, but it's not all bad. We know now that some things we thought were a threat no longer are. And that the ghosts we had begun to be scared of were on our side.

And there are times when there is nothing you need more than to have people, alive or dead, on your side.

A thing Saeed is much better at than me, especially when I'm in a state like this, is to break things into component parts. He's been dictating and Alison's been writing and when I see the results I calm a little, because at least we're doing something. At least there's a line between here and things being okay, even if I don't know how long it is.

One of the large sheets of paper in the ballroom is headed MAIN STEPS in red marker pen, and below it four bullet points:
—FIND ARAMINTA
—MAKE ARAMINTA CORPOREAL
—STOP GHOST EATER DOING MORE HARM
—RETURN GHOSTS (if possible)
I wonder if this is what team planning days are like at one of those office jobs that would never hire someone like me. I'm thankful no-one put '(if possible)' after the

second bullet point. Even if they don't believe it, they are at least willing to act like we can get Araminta back.

Finding Araminta is not that hard. I keep looking for her; any time someone doesn't manage to keep me distracted, I'm looking for her. Like a ghost, which she isn't exactly but isn't too far from either, she seems to be tethered to this house, to never go far beyond these walls.

I catch glimpses of her endlessly; her work uniform, her bright red hair, her face that I desperately long to make smile again. It's making her stay that's the issue. Every time I get close, she slips away from me. I don't know if she's doing it deliberately. I'm not sure if I could bear the answer to that question. Only once has she seemed to communicate with me, tracing her fingers round her neck. The pendant. Why was it left solid and fallen to the floor when not only her but her clothes were stripped of corporeality? How does this piece fit into the puzzle?

When we split up duties, mine is not to find Araminta. It is to find the ghost eater. It might be because I'm angry enough; it might be because I can't focus enough to do research. Either way, the job is mine, and I'm going to do it.

The plan is to try bargaining with him. And if that fails – as I can't help assume it will – the plan is to gain more information about him and learn how to fight him.

While I begin to plan, Holly asks to be involved, to help me from the start, as I draw the ghost eater from his hiding place. She's looking superficially a lot better: her face is no longer puffy from crying, her clothes are clean, and her hair is neat and pulled back into a long ponytail rather than her usual plait. But I know her well enough to tell she's not quite her usual self either. Her skin is pale, her eyes dull, and everything she does seems to be slightly slowed, not enough so that most people would notice. But I do. Her speech, her thinking, even her breathing is not as fast, not as sharp as she usually is.

That's not why I'm worried about her involvement. Even in this state, she's one of the smartest and most practical people I know; someone who is willing to turn her hands to almost anything and never afraid to put everything she has into the task at hand. It's not her competence that concerns me here.

She's not yet eighteen, though, and that makes me feel particularly responsible. I can't fight this ghost eater alone, much as I'd like to, which means that whenever I ask other people for help or get them involved, there's a risk of them getting hurt. When they're adults, I don't like it, but I also know they have the right and responsibility to make that choice for themselves. But when they're not, when they're as young as Holly, that changes the equation.

But I also know that if we didn't get involved and someone got hurt or worse because we didn't have enough people working on it, there's no way she'd be able to cope with that either. So she's working with me. I reason that having her where I can see her, having her engaged and distracted, can only be good for allowing the rest of us to get on with things without being too worried about her, whether or not she's any help herself.

But once we are working on it, I have to reconsider. She may be young, and her current moment of crisis may be terribly timed, but she's not one to avoid responsibility either. I run through the plan a few of us had been working on and she spots some holes in it, details that don't quite make sense. I realise that much as I need to take care of her, she'll also do her best to take care of me. And that she's not just going to be useful; she's going to be essential.

In the end we don't find the ghost eater, though we search in rooms and cupboards and staircases.

In the end, the ghost eater finds us.

We've headed up into the attic space when all the lights start flickering. That in itself is not unusual; we know the electrics in this house are dodgy. I switch on my torch and shine it down to help Holly navigate the last few steps.

Then our mobiles ring at once. Vital piece of information here: this is a household of autistic people, *all* of us have our phones on silent. I don't even recognise the ringtone as my own.

I look at Holly.

"Shall we, uh, get out of here?" she asks. She doesn't need to suggest it twice, and I turn and follow her down the stairs. The lights are flashing on and off and there's a draught coming from nowhere in particular that quickly grows into a movement of air strong enough to make me grab the handrail. A ghost – I can't even tell who, flies screeching over our heads, which makes me think perhaps we're going in the wrong direction, but there's no time to turn back now and so I jump the last few steps behind Holly and into a corridor that doesn't feel like home.

It's like being in a wind tunnel. Items of clothing, newspapers, even books, are being blown past us and there's dust and grit in my eyes. I hold Holly's hand and we steady ourselves on each other and turn to face the direction the blast of air is coming from.

And we see the ghost eater.

Sometimes, the human is more terrifying than the paranormal, and this is one of those times. He is, after all, just a man, shorter than I expected, his skin pale but no paler than mine. He's dramatically dressed as before, his cloak around his shoulders, his boots firm and black.

To my right I see Denny making his way up the staircase, pulling himself up desperately by the bannister, one step at a time. Much as I want to yell at him to get away, I'm so glad to see him.

Holly and I, meanwhile, are frozen to the spot. We can do nothing but look at him.

The air is still. His voice is quieter than I would have anticipated.

"You're in my house. It's time for you to leave."

I step forward in anger.

Part of me has always believed that when I really need to speak, I will be able to do so. Turns out that's not true.

It's lucky I don't just rely on myself. Holly steps forward with me.

"You need to give us back Araminta," she says. Her voice is shaking but she elevates it with every syllable.

The ghost eater waves his arms forward. The air starts to move, stronger this time. Before I know what's happening we're falling and we're tumbling down the stairs and I'm trying to grab onto Holly, Denny, the bannisters, anything, and there's pain growing in all my body as it hits the stairs on the way down and I want to scream but I'm moving too fast for that, and the main doors fling open and we are all blown out, tumbling into a pile, lying on the wet gravel outside our home.

CHAPTER TWENTY

T he park at the centre of the housing development is pretty enough on a good day. For those who live there, with their small slivers of gardens, it provides space for kids to run around, or to read a book beside the old fountain.

For a group who have been thrown out of their home – for some of them the only place that's ever truly felt like home – and with the horizon promising rain, it feels less comfortable. I look back and see Casswell Park rising above the modern houses; a building bordering on dilapidated, and at the very least in need of some fresh paint, a building of centuries ago, and yet everything in me wants to turn back and run towards it, throw myself at its dual staircases and wide corridors, its balconies and the ballroom with the wonderful high ceiling.

I'm sprawled out on the grass beside a bench, my legs in front of me, propping myself up half-heartedly on my hands. I'm not going anywhere.

"Morgan, any injuries?" I hear Alison say gently. I turn and pull up my trouser leg to reveal an ankle red and swollen. Holly passes me one of those chemical ice packs, the ones where you burst open a compartment inside and it turns suddenly cold. I nod with gratitude, pull up my sock and place the ice pack over it. I hadn't realised how badly it was sprained until I tried to put pressure on it and found my leg unable to support my weight; I limped most of the way here but perhaps everyone had something else to focus on and didn't notice.

It soon becomes clear that all of us are injured. Denny is also pretty beaten up from his fall downstairs and Alison is worried he might have hit his head, though he denies it. Holly weathered the incident better than us, and seems to have escaped with only bruises – nothing that stopped her sprinting to the chemist by the railway station and back in what can only have been twenty minutes or so.

Saeed is unsurprisingly struggling, but the others who were on the ground floor are generally in better shape. I learnt that everyone had emerged from various rooms to see what was happening, and the ghost eater's powers swept them along the corridors and out just as we were too.

It seems like a lifetime ago. I start to shiver even though I'm in my warm hoodie.

"Okay," says Vinnie, and I turn to look up at them from where I'm still sprawled on the grass. "Tell me the essentials. I'll go back and get them for you."

Everyone who can talk is talking all at once, but Vinnie is insistent. And sometimes when Vinnie insists there's not much else to do but agree. But I'm still scared. We've lost almost everything. We only have each other. I don't think I could handle losing another of us.

But Vinnie is determined and we make a list: meds, laptops, Holly's school books. Half of me wants to go with Vinnie, to protect them; most of me is terrified. But now the problem is not just mine alone. I'm coping better. I'm much better at organising what needs to be done for someone else; much less likely to fall apart when someone else needs me.

Case in point: I've jumped into the shared to-do list Saeed has set up and while Holly helps him apply tape to stabilise his joints, I'm working out what we need to do to stabilise this immediate crisis and ensure that, even if we can't help Araminta just now, even if we can't go home any time soon, we are at least physically safe for this night and the immediate nights to come.

The sun is still setting early, and the sky is warning of rain...

Those of us who are up to it pool the few ideas we have. It's not that we don't have options, even when you factor in our lack of money. I can go back to my parents', and they wouldn't complain if I brought a friend with me. Alison has adult children she can stay with. Saeed has parents and siblings. Vinnie and Theo have Caleb. But they're scattered across the country and Holly has school and Vinnie has a job that might be turning permanent and...

...and if we split ourselves up now, it would probably be forever.

Contrary to stereotypes, most of us do have local friends. Not me, really, because I mostly talk to people online, but others do. But there's a difference between a friend you can hang out with at art shows or study with, and a friend you can turn to for help when you've been kicked out of your haunted house by the re-corporealised form of a wannabe scientist slash magician from the seventeenth century.

Without even thinking about it, I've navigated to Keira's number in my directory. The fountain is running behind me, endless circles of water. No-one is speaking. Having dealt with our initial injuries, everyone seems to be quite dazed. I'm no exception to that.

I look at the time. Little more than an hour or so has gone by since we were evicted from our home. It doesn't seem like forever. It seems like it's raw and painful and I want nothing more than to be curled up amid a blanket in my bedroom with Araminta by my side, with pizza, M&Ms, and a trashy TV show in front of us.

Vinnie drives over and I get up to head toward their car before I realise my ankle will struggle to get me even that far. They look unscathed, at least. Small mercies.

Probably more mentally exhausted than physically, Vinnie sits down heavily on the bench next to Saeed.

"Did you...?" Denny asks.

Vinnie shakes their head. "Nothing. No sign of him. And no sign of the ghosts either. I was going to offer to take them with us, wherever we're going, but I didn't see a single one. Place is so quiet it's eerie. But I think I got everything you all asked for, and I tried to get a bit of clothing for you all as well. I put some food out for the cats, and fed Arabella in her tank. The cats will probably make themselves scarce for a while though." Vinnie pauses, and reassures us the animals will be okay, but I think they're more reassuring themselves.

Part of me wants to go back. To let him kick me out again and again, to refuse to leave unless forced to. Perhaps if it were just me, I would. But there's more than just me to think about. I text Keira. I'm above pride at this point. I'm above refusing to make compromises on principle. I'll do anything to get Araminta back, and to make sure everyone else is safe, even if it means not only asking for help – one of my least favourite things to do at the best of times – but asking someone who I feel not entirely positively about.

We can't stay here all day. Vinnie leaves to drive Theo to his grandparents', commenting that with any luck they'll fill up his bottomless stomach with chicken curry and peas and rice. I know they'll be back but if feels like our numbers are being depleted by the day.

And then there were five...

We head to the library, Saeed barely getting by on his crutches and me steadying myself on Holly's shoulder. There's a bit of time until it closes. We're looking at pooling our money, how long we can stay in a motel or Airbnb. We're almost there when Keira texts me back:

>> I think I know somewhere. Give me an hour or two.

An hour or two seems endless, and Saeed and Alison are not entirely happy about me having involved Keira, but they mostly keep quiet about it because we all know how limited our options are, how little choice we have.

Keira arrives at the library dressed in smarter clothes than usual; a pale pink blouse, an A-line skirt, her hair – though still streaked with green – is pulled back from her face. I'm suddenly struck by how young she looks, younger than Holly, though she must be at least a few years older.

She spins around her phone to show us Google Maps.

"It's a school," she explains. "Two rooms, pretty much, an old village school that was abandoned when rolls dropped. They keep saying they're going to pull it down but... well... there's a situation with the ghost of a teacher who is... she won't be any trouble to you, but she's essentially blackmailing the local authority."

"Good on her," says Denny with a grin. We chuckle.

"So it's basically two classrooms. I've brought some blankets and camping equipment, a couple of foam mattresses. There are toilets and there's a shower. The water and electricity is still connected. Does it sound okay for now?"

We agree. We have little choice.

I climb into the back of Keira's car, Holly squashed in the middle between me and Denny, and Alison in the front. Saeed is in Vinnie's car, who is following us close behind. No-one is really saying anything. Keira puts music on, and I can feel all of us tense, but we don't say anything. Another reminder of how the space we designed for ourselves, our one space in a world so hostile, is no longer ours and may never be again.

The school is tiny, set back from the road on tarmac broken through with grass and weeds. It's built with stone blocks, half the windows boarded up, the sign that once announced its name completely unreadable. There's no sign of a ghost, but that doesn't surprise me.

Those of us who can unload the car. We set up spaces, dividing ourselves between the two classrooms and what seems to have been a small office. Denny offers me the latter but I insist he takes it, and Saeed and I share the smaller classroom, with Vinnie, Holly, and Alison in the other. I put down a camping mat in a corner for me and Holly salvages some pallets which together with the best of the mattresses make a bed for Saeed.

It's a home of sorts. A home for now.

Alison and Keira are talking out by the car. I'm not sure I'm up for talking – wonder briefly if at some point my voice will wither away from lack of use, wonder if I'd even care – but I head over to join them anyway. As I approach I hear Alison asking Keira when she first got interested in ghosts.

Keira shrugs and gets out her vape. Clouds of apple scented smoke fill the air.

"When my sister died. I was seven, she was nine."

"Your sister... she stayed?"

"No. She didn't... we were on holiday and Logan and Elise got caught in a rip. Someone rescued him but she... they never found her body. We never saw her dead, and we never saw her ghost."

"I'm sorry."

Keira nods, acknowledging the nicety. "Logan and I read everything we could get our hands on about ghosts. When we were a bit older, we'd search for them everywhere. At first, it was because we wanted to find Elise. Or even just know she could be out there somewhere. But over time... I guess we grieved and started enjoying it..."

I stretch up and hug Keira without saying anything. It's pretty uncharacteristic for me, but I suppose it's been a long day. And I couldn't just communicate nothing after her telling us all this.

Back in the school, we're discussing how to take back Casswell.

"...when Morgan and I finish translating the book..." I overhear Saeed say as I sit down.

We all look blankly at each other in concern.

"Sorry," Vinnie says. "I didn't think to grab it."

The book... Something I had clung to as our main hope in solving this. I should have asked Vinnie to get it for me, can't believe I could have been so *stupid* and so *selfish* as to prioritise my laptop and my favourite hoodie over what might end up to be my only hope of saving the woman I love.

"Good thing I photographed all the pages and backed them up to cloud storage, isn't it then?" Saeed says with a grin.

I don't even know what I feel but suddenly I'm crying, hot tears that don't stop coming and flood the pillow I've been clutching.

"That's okay," Saeed says, as Alison passes me a tissue. "You can thank me later. Preferably by buying me a burger... you know that place near Holly's college that does chicken burgers with hot satay sauce?"

I somehow manage to laugh through the tears, which turns into a rather unpleasant snort. I suppose we all have our priorities.

And so that night we begin working through the book. Saeed is not usually nocturnal like I am, but it's unsurprising that tonight he can't sleep.

We sit outside, ostensibly so we won't disturb the others, but in reality I'm craving the night air. It's a cold, clear night, edged with frost, and so dark the stars are brighter and we can see the glow of the milky way. From photographs of old pages, we make words, and we keep going until dawn until we have transcribed and read everything, and we start to understand what we must do to defeat the one who has taken so much from us.

1708

The longer Isobel stays, the more absorbed she gets in her work.

The longer Isobel stays, the more she knows she can't continue to let this happen. Every day she witnesses experiments, ghosts being tortured in the name of science. She sees their bodies – such as they are – ripped apart. He tries to burn them, to submerge them in water.

She doesn't think he gains pleasure from the cruelty of it. It's just that he'll do anything for knowledge.

She has challenged him gently, cautiously, but he's dismissed her each time as just not understanding the importance of his research. She understands it far more than he could know. And she's learned from it.

The incantations and the metals that take and give corporeality. The powder in the bottles that sucks the non-corporeal in. She's thought about it for a long time, but she snaps one day, seeing him slice an elderly woman through the middle of her torso with a cursed knife, watching her expression as she looked down at what was left of her body.

If Isobel doesn't stop him, he'll be able to do this forever. To suck corporeality from both the living and the dead, to keep himself alive, if that is even the right word, indefinitely.

She rings him with his own silver in his sleep, the pendant he used for corporeality experiments. She jams his mouth with rags as she says the incantation quickly. She's been practising by reading the words out of order so they will have no effect. Now she says them as they're meant to be, and solidity flies from his body into hers. But there's too much. She feels heavy and nauseous and then she sees a glow in the middle of his pendant, that solidifies into a gemstone. He's in there. And she needs to contain him.

She takes a bottle from his collection and opens it, seeking to set the ghost free and have him take her place. But perhaps the ghost is intent on revenge or perhaps she is scared? Isobel isn't sure, but she rises out of the bottle to drag in the ghost eater, and the bottle bends and flexes to take everything in; silver and gemstone and one who is neither living nor dead.

She tells his brother just a few of the details. Tells him to keep the bottles closed and keep watch on them forever. He doesn't need much convincing. With his elder brother out of the way, Casswell Park is his, and he doesn't care too much about how that came to be.

He offers Isobel a place. A place of service, of course, but a favoured one. Or he can seek to arrange for her to be a companion for a spinster relative, if that would be better for her.

Isobel has better ideas. She's staying in Casswell, and she's staying on her terms. She dresses all in white. She rubs flour on her skin like the miller's daughter she is. And she goes to find the child that haunts the gardens, the child who used to play there until he was struck with fever. And she gives him his corporeality back, gives him back a life.

She's not exactly a ghost, Isobel isn't. But in every sense she could pass for one. And Casswell Park is her haunt.

CHAPTER TWENTY ONE

"**W**here the fuck are we supposed to get silver from? Couldn't they have chosen something cheaper, the fucking snobs?"

Denny's having little difficulty in putting all our frustrations into words. After too little sleep – but I'm way beyond caring about that – Saeed and I are presenting to the rest of our housemates what we've found. They're crowded round my laptop, the one with the biggest screen, sitting on mattresses or broken tables. Saeed's speaking, I'm skipping back and forth through our notes and through the photographed pages to prompt him.

After the endless classification of ghosts and their various properties, the ghost eater had clearly taken a more proactive role in his experiments than just observing. What I'd read last night, or early this morning, still makes me feel ill and I suspect I'll never get some of the images out of my head. So rather than subject everyone else to the details Saeed and I skim through them, talking in abstract terms with just enough examples to convey that he was doing something horrific.

I don't let myself think about what he might do to Araminta. I focus on the task at hand. It's the only way.

Saeed moves to the practicalities.

"The end of the book is most useful. It talks about transferring corporeality. It's magic, basically. There are all kinds of experiments but there's one that works. It talks about reciting an incantation, which I think is encoded into the book, but I haven't worked it out yet. And that someone needs to be bound with silver."

"So we need to get some silver," Vinnie says, practically. "I don't suppose silver plated would work?"

"I might have a necklace..." Alison begins, but suddenly Holly's almost jumping up and down with an answer.

"The pendant..." she says. "It's silver."

Everyone turns to look at Holly. Vinnie chucks a set of car keys at her.

"Let's go get it," she says.

Vinnie and Alison have been teaching Holly to drive – to Theo's annoyance, who considers he's quite old enough to also be given lessons, and insists, despite all evidence to the contrary, that everyone else starts learning to drive at his age.

Holly though, who is actually old enough for a licence, is learning methodically despite some anxiety. And it seems that even in this never-ending succession of crises, Vinnie is determined to give her some practice. Perhaps it will take her focus away from everything else.

With them gone, I shower. The water is cold but I don't really care. It's only really been a day, but I feel like I'm scrubbing off weeks of grime. Vinnie did a supermarket run last night, so along with some basic food, we have shampoo, and I run it through my long hair, untangling knots that seem to have built up impossibly quickly.

Vinnie got me clean underwear from the house, and in yesterday's jeans and my favourite hoodie, having poured myself Mountain Dew into a disposable cup, I'm pretty sure I'm ready to face anything.

My hair's still drying when Vinnie and Holly get back. Denny is spreading us sliced white bread with jam and margarine, which is a pretty tolerable breakfast given the circumstances. Holly is clutching the pendant tightly in her right hand. Fearfully, she places it in the middle of the table and we all lean through to take a look.

"It's definitely silver," Denny says. I'm not sure where he got that confidence from, but I'm willing to believe it. I'm not sure what the alternative is.

"Do we know why it looks like there was a stone in there but isn't now?" Saeed asks, taking notes. "I don't think it was just broken."

"Because the ghost eater's corporeality didn't go to someone else..." Alison says, understanding now. "It compressed into what would seem to be a gemstone. I think... I think he used it as a sort of battery for storing others, and then it somehow got used against him."

"And when I gave Araminta the pendant," I say with horror. "I... I bound her with silver. Bound her with silver."

The words keep repeating and I try to keep them in my head but I can't. I push my chair out because right now I feel like a freak even among freaks, and shut myself in the other bedroom.

Bound her with silver. Bound her with silver.

That's how he was able to take her. It was all my fault.

I force myself to stand up. To walk back in. Guilt solves nothing. If it was my fault then I have all the more responsibility to get her back.

When I return, planning is well underway. We're going to take back Araminta's corporeality from the ghost eater. He's corporeal now, so we have to fight him like a human, though he also seems to have powers, powers like Denny and I have, so he's dangerous on two levels. But then we'll have to resort to magic. And this sort of magic is unlike anything we've ever used before.

"It's a cipher!" Holly says, suddenly, out of the blue, and everyone turns to look at her. Saeed grabs the pendant.

"Of course it is! Each of these markings is two letters overlapping each other. And that's the key to what's written in the book. So if we just... does someone have some paper?"

I realise we're all grinning at them. They're in their element right now. Me, I'm not sure exactly what I'm going to bring to this fight, but everything I have, we'll use.

I want to go tonight. I want to fight that fucker with everything we have. But the consensus is that we need to be on our best form. We only get one chance at this. That means food and sleep as well as strategising, so Alison takes our orders and Vinnie's car and returns with both pizza and Chinese takeaway. I feast on sesame prawn toast and chicken cranberry pizza. I have my preferences and I'm sticking to them.

I debate taking a sleeping pill, but the hangover from it will probably affect me more than lack of sleep. I guess there's always caffeine in the morning. But surprisingly, despite everything, despite my anxiety, despite the fact I'm on a thin mat on a hard wooden floor and somewhat cold even fully clothed and with a blanket over me, I sleep soundly and when Saeed wakes me with takeaway coffee from a run Vinnie made, it's already morning.

All of us somehow manage to squash into the same car – figuring traffic accidents are the least of our issues right now - and we park a couple of streets away from Casswell, on its old gardens. No-one here has any idea what's about to happen so close to where they live, or that for the group of oddly dressed and determined people walking in unison down the road, so much is at stake.

Home still looks like home. It doesn't look terrifying or looming or anything else I feared it would. It looks a bit broken and a bit weather worn, and it looks like the place we're about to take back.

We pause at the door. I feel the knife in my pocket. Denny steps forward with a key, and we open the door and walk inside, into Casswell Park.

We're home.

CHAPTER TWENTY TWO

The ghost eater is waiting for us. There's no surprise there. The air around our feet begins moving but Holly has taken a leaf from the ghost hunters and somehow scaled the back wall and headed in through a window. She takes him by surprise, leaping and throwing him forward. It's not enough to do him real harm, but enough to stem the movement of air and allow us all to rush forward to meet him at the top of the steps.

It's a difficult balance we have to strike. If we kill him, we may never get Araminta back. At least, not in the way I want to. What I haven't told anyone is that I've decided if necessary, I'll drain my own corporeality to save her. But I'd really like for it to not come to that.

So it's with our bare hands we move on him now, as he stumbles to his feet. I wince the first time I punch him, not from pain but from the unfamiliar sensation of plunging my fist into semi-corporeality. Vinnie has no such reaction and is punching him repeatedly with every bit of fury and determination they possess. I try and shove him towards the door, being sure to aim for the doorway and not the walls, which he could potentially slip through and escape in the time it takes us to run around and through the doorway.

I feel like I'm half-inserting myself inside his body as I slip through the semi-corporeal skin and muscle and fat and bone, and I'm not comfortable with it; not comfortable with the sensation I feel, and not comfortable with myself for executing it against him; it seems more intrusive, even more violating, than simple violence. But there's no other way to fight him, so I continue.

Saeed and Denny are putting together our next bit of the plan in a downstairs room. I only hope they hurry. I'm not sure how long things are going to be this easy.

The ghost eater doesn't respond initially. I don't know whether it is due to surprise or a tactical decision, or a physical inability to do so. For a while, though, our attack has little effect but also comes with no retaliation.

Then he fights back.

His eyes are bright and his cloak swirls around him. He might be a bit of a stereotype of a villain, but knowing that doesn't diminish the effect. I take in our current location and the route back to the stairwell, focusing on letting him win in our interactions just enough to keep him from advancing towards me. I fight back just hard enough to prevent myself from sustaining any significant damage, or him growing suspicious of my motivations. He has to think that we don't have much of a plan.

Once Holly picks up on how I'm provoking him, she adds verbal mocking to my gestural taunting. We don't know for certain if he can hear her, but in any case, I can tell we're both silently cracking up at each other which is giving us a bit of extra confidence, so it's certainly doing some good.

I had expected to be scared, but my anger takes over. I don't bend and I don't break. I stand up and look straight at him. Holly stands up too. Sometimes the most vulnerable people are also the strongest. We have a job to do and we're not going to fail. We can only do what we need to and hope everyone else in the house is prepared.

The ghost eater is more corporeal than I have ever seen him. He may not be able to form intelligible words, but when he opens his mouth noises that resemble them still emerge, sounds that seem to be him attempting to yell at me. I hate being around yelling, but I don't waver.

I see Denny running towards us, and he gives the signal we've been waiting for. Holly moves towards him while I distract the ghost eater.

I pull the pendant from the pocket of my jeans, hold it out mockingly to him. It's a risk, but we've prepared. Holly takes out the wax-sealed bottle Denny passed to her. We spread out and the ghost eater wavers between us. I know he will choose the pendant, but just a few seconds indecision are all we need. Those few seconds are enough for me to run a few paces down the corridor, drawing him further.

Holly holds the bottle above her head and hurls it down to the wooden floor below. The bottle smashes. The ghost eater turns and looks at it in anger and confusion; as we have guessed, his collection is what's important to him. The bottle is in fragments but no ghost emerges from it. The look of confusion on his face turns to rage. He dives at me, but I'm prepared, already a few metres back, and I scoot back even further as he approaches.

'Good job, Saeed and Denny,' I think to myself. Their replication of the wax that sealed the empty bottle that we had released Joseph from was convincing even to the man who had first sealed the bottle all those hundreds of years ago.

As the ghost eater rages at both of us, seemingly unable to work out who to target, I grab the metal lock box Alison has slipped into place. I visualise the steps in my mind, a clear sequence of movements. I only have one attempt, and if I dont move quickly enough then I'll be right back to the beginning. I hold the pendant just long enough to be sure he's seen it. Then I slam it into the lock box and quickly scramble the combination. I think he has been appropriately taunted; at least I hope this will work. It had better, because we don't have a backup plan and the stakes couldn't be higher.

He immediately goes for the box, pushing into me – which has a more literal meaning here than it usually does – and proceeds to try and desperately get the pendant out of it. But the corporeality that has been in his favour now counts against him; not sufficient to handle the delicate task of undoing the combination, even if he has seen it, but too high to put his hands right through the box.

I charge forwards and kick the box between the bannisters, bending back my swollen ankle until I almost scream with pain. It crashes down onto the steps below. The ghost eater flings himself over the rail and I stand with my back to the stairs, my heart racing, knowing that I have done what I can for now, and yet my body is still flush with adrenaline, and I can feel my pulse through my whole body. The battle is far from won, and Araminta is not safe, but I have done what I need to for now, and while the fight continues downstairs, Holly and I take a few moments to rest.

Something feels different in me, something that changed once I had the pendant in my hands and is now lost again. My paranormal ability is back to where it was, very mild, not of much use in practice. There's no time for worrying about that, though. I don't think I need it any more.

Sitting on the top step of the stairs, I wrap my arm around Holly's shoulder. Her eyes are shining and I swear she's almost laughing, not because it's funny but because she's on fire with the exhilaration of having finally done something that doesn't rely on the approval of others. I don't think she's even scrapped with anyone before this, much less fought; she's an only child and probably responded to school violence by running away and hiding in the library. I can tell that, at least on some level, she likes it.

We sit together on that step for a while, too exhausted even to respond to the noise and commotion downstairs. I know I have to trust my found family. I already trust them with my life. The question is whether I can also trust them with Araminta's.

The sounds we hear below us all blur into one. I hear running feet. I hear yelling. I hear something crashing and something falling. Soon, I will join them. Soon, but not right now because every part of my body seems too heavy to move and my brain is spinning its wheels and not going anywhere – or to put it more technically, my executive function is completely shot.

Saeed brings me a cold compress, by which I mean a towel soaked in ice water. He obviously prepared for just this scenario. I don't feel like I need treatment, but I hold it to my leg anyway and the cold numbs the pain I didn't know I was experiencing.

The fighting erupts on the lower half of the staircase. Alison and Denny take the lead, with Vinnie not far behind them. When we see them tiring, Holly and I run down the stairs towards the ghost eater. Despite everything we've read, everything we've observed about ghosts, we're still surprised about how his lack of corporeality works. When he attacks Alison and she fights back with a knife, his blood only half flows out and then sort of lingers around him, not subject to the laws of gravity.

Another thing that surprises us, but shouldn't, is that the ghosts arrive to help. Whether they planned and communicated with each other, or if one followed another, we don't know, but they swarm towards us right when we need them most. They may not be able to physically fight in the way we can, but they are more help to us than I can ever express.

Three ghosts join hands and dance in a circle around the ghost eater. Their faces are all smiles and deliberately performative glee; if they could speak I have no doubt we would hear a taunting rhyme coming from them. They get in the way of the ghost eater, distracting him, while keeping out of ours, seemingly completely in tune with our needs and our unspoken plans.

We don't always know what ghosts do and don't understand, but there's one thing that's perfectly clear right now: they know exactly who their enemy is.

When the ghost eater bursts through their circle, trying to attack Denny, Roderick appears as if from nowhere. He skips up and down from the ceiling, keeping always just a few metres ahead of the ghost eater. Even as one of our most corporeal ghosts, Roderick can't slow him down that much, but he does serve to distract him, reinforce that he has no allies, that he's totally outnumbered.

I watch the ghost eater as I hang back for a moment while Holly and Denny take the lead; we'll swap places when they start to tire or if they get injured. Despite how outnumbered the ghost eater is, I'm also worried about how powerful he seems to be right now. He's looking confident, despite the taunting of the ghosts, and I can barely see through him; only shifts of light and dark as he turns. He doesn't look exactly like a regular, living human, but he's not far from it, albeit in a rather dated outfit.

I'm not sure if that makes him more intimidating or less. But it does make him easier to fight, even as in some ways it makes him more dangerous.

We know it's going to be hard. We know that we have to do it anyway.

I move forward and I fight. It's not like fighting a human, a living human. As I lunge forward, and as he lunges at me it's as if everything's cutting through me at once; heat and cold, darkness and light, pain and numbness, as if the extremes of everything had gone so far they'd curved right around to meet, became one and the same. I feel like

I'm squinting in the brightest sunlight and flailing around in pitch darkness at once.

In the middle of this, all I can do is push forward. There's no time for strategic thinking, no time for any kind of thinking at all. I rely on Holly to pull me back and push forward when it's her turn and it's only then, though I'm still exhausted and in pain, that I can begin to think at all.

I'm not sure how this is going to end; I just have to believe it will. I'm not even completely clear what the ghost eater wants. Does he want to kill us all so he can have the house to himself? Does he just want the pendant or does he want something other than that? Or is all the joy in the fight, him taking some sort of twisted pleasure in harming us, scaring us, disrupting our lives?

I'm not sure of the answer to any of these questions, and I know I can't fight forever. But for now, I have to keep fighting.

We move forward and back, trying to stick to the formations we'd practiced. But this is very different; we're scared and exhausted, all of us have minor injuries, and around us are flickering lights and confusion. Still, we fight. We fight with fists and improvised weapons. We shield each other and we shield ourselves, ducking behind barriers and then leaping up, walking straight into the danger when we need to, without flinching. We keep it up for as long as we can, knowing that when we tire or falter the ghost eater will take his chance.

We fight and we hope we can win, because right now that's everything we can have, and everything we can do.

The ghost eater goes for Alison again. I'm not sure if her actions in fighting him have put a bee in his bonnet, or if there's some other reason he's singling her out, but I realise – we all do – that we have to make an effort to protect her. We close in a protective circle around her, my heart thumping.

It's not enough.

I hear Alison yell, fall over backwards, catching herself on something as she goes down. I'm not sure what it is that hurts her, but she has visible injuries and appears stunned for a few moments. I hope it's not a concussion.

I help her up. She's bleeding from the side of her face, blood running down and then splatting on the wooden floor. Absurdly, I find myself thinking about what a big clean up we're going to have ahead of us.

"It's okay," she says, inspecting her bloodied hand. "It's just superficial. Worse than it looks."

There's not really much I can say to that so I don't. I only nod. Afterwards... afterwards we can talk firmly to each other about self-care and about not taking sufficient care of our own needs. Afterwards we can make oxygen mask metaphors. Afterwards we can be angry and fearful all at the same time. But right now, I'm not even sure I could have helped Alison even if she had asked.

Alison's back fighting in far less time than I feel comfortable about, but she seems to be doing okay. I don't think there's much choice to be had in the matter, in any case. After a while she and I step back together as Holly and Denny take the lead. I'm trying to get my breath back, trying to calm myself, when I hear a familiar sound from the upstairs corridor. I raise my eyes upwards. Vinnie does the same.

"WHAT IN THE LORD'S NAME ARE YOU DOING HERE?"

I know exactly what the sound is now. The sound of heelys along the wooden floor. I swallow dry air. The last thing we need right now is for a child to be caught in the middle of this. But Theo takes the stairs two at a time, heading straight into the unfolding violence.

This was exactly what we didn't want to happen. But I don't think any of us could have predicted that he would sneak away from his grandparents' and somehow make his way home. Theo has many good qualities but... well, when it comes to staying away from the action, he's still a very impulsive ten-year-old.

I don't want to have to worry about a child as well as everything else, but I don't get to make a choice because now he's leaping down the steps two, three at a time – and yes, still in those same shoes. Honestly, it wouldn't need a ghost eater's intervention to break his neck; the only wonder is that he hasn't already done so.

He goes for the ghost eater with absolute fury, punching and kicking him with energy like I've never seen until Vinnie grabs him around the waist and hauls him backwards, still yelling and kicking his feet in mid-air.

I don't know what Vinnie says to him but he calms quickly and goes off with Saeed without too much fuss. That's some relief. I'd like him to be further away, out of the house entirely, with his father or grandparents, but just being out of the ghost eater's immediate reach helps. And his burst of relentless energy and fury has not only done the ghost eater a bit of damage, but given us all a boost, a boost of contagious energy and a reminder of what we're fighting for. So, newly energised, we push on.

It's not just punches and kicks, relentless fighting. If only. That would at least be straight forward if nothing else. But just as we are working from plans and strategies, the initially startled ghost eater seems to be working from them too. He calls on all the tools at his disposal. These are not physical weapons; he would struggle to hold those, much less use them effectively. But he's summoning powers that I can only describe as magic.

Magic is an imprecise term, one that covers a range of possible mechanisms, and if this were any other time, I'd interrogate that. But for now it's all I can do to be aware that he has a small arsenal of unpredictable abilities, and try and account for that – and think and react quickly when he does deploy them.

Alison charges at him with what I suppose you might call a homemade bayonet and he sends out what seems to be a tiny horizontal tornado, twisting blue air that wraps around and dismantles and blunts the bayonet all at once. When Denny retreats, Saeed blows the planned whistle from down the corridor and then triggers the mechanism which releases the pepper spray from the rigged canister, just as all of us, having heard the warning, have covered our faces.

I hadn't thought it would work, and it's true that it doesn't have as much effect on the ghost eater as it would on a fully corporeal human but it still has an effect, causing him to stagger backwards. He covers his face too late; his skin is red, his eyes watering, and he's coughing silently. That buys Holly enough time to leap forward and grasp at his legs, tugging them backwards until, despite being less influenced by the laws of gravity than the rest of us, he falls forward.

I see Joseph fighting against invisible bonds, becoming more visible. I worry I might be making a mistake but I leap up just the same and hook the silver chain Alison found in her jewellery box around him and then I reach out to touch my other hand on the ghost eater, somehow cling on to his cloak. Without the incantation, it's not much, but it's enough to save the child. He becomes more visible, gradually growing in corporeality until he's almost as I first saw him, his face returning, his head looking only slightly damaged. I look at Joseph and then I look at the ghost eater. The corresponding change is less noticeable in the ghost eater but I can see it all the same; as Joseph has gained corporeality, the eater has lost it.

There's a long way to go, but saving a child ghost from the eater's grip is a small victory all in itself. There's no time to soak in it though, because in some ways everything has just got harder. We'd be naive if we didn't expect that to unleash another bout of rage, causing him to fight back harder. But nothing's ending until he's completely defeated. He's shown no willingness to negotiate and as far as I can tell there's nothing to negotiate anyway. It's not like we can say 'hey, take half the ghosts'; we're dealing with sentient beings here.

His bout of rage comes suddenly and destructively, in a way I wasn't prepared for; turning the house into weapons. And he uses the ghosts to do it for him. The floorboards shake and move under our feet, leaving us struggling to keep our balance; Denny goes right over with a thud and the ghost eater laughs. Another ghost hurls chairs from one of the rooms at us. They're not doing us much harm, but it means all our energy is spent on them rather than directed against the ghost eater.

The way the ghosts turn against us confuses me initially. They've been fighting with us for a while, and given the evident harm the ghost eater has been perpetuating against them it would not make sense to align themselves with him and against us. It used to be clear they were on our side. Now that's all changed.

I think back, though, to the room with the ripped-up floorboards. I think about how ghosts anchor them to a place. I think about the spell on the pendant, the idea the ghost eater might control something via the ghosts' corporeality. Things start to make sense. The ghost eater, by means of a spell cast long ago, has some control over the ghosts, but only to the extent that it relates to the house.

This is entirely the wrong time for ideas and understanding to fall into place; I don't even have enough brain capacity to focus on the immediate issue at hand, let alone anything else. I'm not even in a state to think things through, let alone act on any conclusions.

Araminta picks up the broken bannister post and lunges straight at me. I duck and I realise I'm crying, repeating to myself over and over that it's not really her, it's not really her. It's not even the thought of someone

I love harming me that's distressing. It's more that I've never been able to shake the idea that our relationship was like some of my childhood so-called friendships, a trick all along. I usually manage to control that fear, but now – even though I know it's not really Araminta doing this – it's like my deepest, longest-held fears unfolding right before my eyes.

I breathe deeply. I cannot fall apart right now. I can't. People are relying on me. I stand up straight, just in time to see something worse happening.

It all happens in slow motion. Pipes being sucked and ripped out of the walls. Water spraying, hot or cold I can't even tell as I charge forwards, and then the ghost eater flings the piping forward. I seem to be moving in slow motion too; I can't do anything to stop them as they graze Holly's face causing her to scream in pain, can't do anything to stop them as they slam straight into Vinnie's chest and they don't stop or bounce but keep going, sharp edges of ripped copper pipes straight through their skin and then they fall.

They fall.

They fall in slow motion and then the moment they hit the ground time catches up and all the sound comes back and there's blood on the floor and I'm screaming, this desperate scream that surprises even me, and I have to fight every instinct to run to Vinnie, because I know where I'm most needed and I know, finally, that right now there is something I can do.

CHAPTER TWENTY THREE

E verything is a blur. I know Vinnie has been badly injured, but my mind is shutting down, not allowing me to think about how badly or the implications. It's a protective mechanism, I think. Consciously, I want to go to Vinnie instantly, but something inside me knows that there's no point unless we deal with the immediate danger.

We're down to non-stop physical combat at this point, most of it with fists and some of it with makeshift weapons. Most of the time it doesn't work like fighting a person does, not that I've exactly got heaps of experience in that. Most of the time, rather than causing him specific injuries, we're generally weakening him. We work in a sort of makeshift formation, taking turns to be at the front of it and then falling back for a few minutes rest.

I've just fallen back, exhausted and aching. I know there's something else I have to be aware of. I spin round. I know there's someone who shouldn't be here, someone who doesn't belong, but my brain isn't processing anything properly. I wonder if one of the ghosts have got out of the bottles, but it's not a ghost.

It's Keira.

Her green-streaked hair is straggly, her hands are covered in blood. Her expression is exhausted and yet she shows no signs of slowing down. I don't know how she got in and right now I don't have time to work it out, but when this is all said and done we are definitely getting some new locks. And strong ones.

But my attention is needed in five different places at once, and none of them are the future, so I park that plan and turn back to look at Keira.

"I told you I'm a nursing student, right? I can help with this."

"Okay," I say, managing to force out a grudging thank you before getting back to the fight.

From the corner of my eye, I can see her surveying the scene. She mutters terminology under her breath as she gets a handle on everything, then kneels down beside Vinnie.

"We're going to need an ambulance," Keira says. "They're losing heaps of blood."

"Come up with a cover story first," says Alison, breathless, looking at me rather than Keira. "And take them outside. I've had my fair share of issues with paramedics but I still don't want them ending up in the middle of a ghost fight."

That's easier said than done. Keira is a tiny, waif-like thing, and Vinnie quite the opposite. I want to help but I'm going in all directions, unable to turn away from the desperate battle underway, unable to pause for even a moment because the consequences could be fatal. I try not to think about Vinnie, hope that Saeed is still taking care of Theo. I hate forcing myself not to care, but it's the only way to keep going. I'll just have to trust that they'll be okay. It's the only thing I can do.

And for me... for me the battle's not yet won. If I can do anything for Vinnie now, it's to ensure they have a home and a family to come back to. Which may be easier said than done.

Still, I throw myself into it with everything I have. I have to. I swallow my nausea and my fears, I still the shaking in my hands. I've always been told I don't care much about others, that I don't have feelings like other people do. Most of the time, though, I think it's the opposite. Most often, the strength of how much I care overwhelms me to the extent that I can't express it well. That's even when things are quiet and uneventful. With everything going on now, and people important to me in serious danger, Araminta is... lost, and another is badly injured and I can't be with them – well, that's more than a little overwhelming.

That's what I have to push through even before I can start the actual fighting. No wonder this whole thing is draining me right down to the bone.

I think the way we all fight, our attitudes are influenced by the fact that at some point we've all struggled for survival in one way or another. And being in this situation has brought it all back up again. Surrounded by ghosts, you're surrounded by the idea of death and it's impossible not to think about your own mortality, and therefore your own survival. And now someone is literally putting our lives in danger.

In different ways, Casswell House has been integral to our ability to survive. None of us would say so outright, but I think it's clear to all of us that if Araminta had not come here she would have killed herself by now. The abuse and therapy she'd endured had eroded her sense of self to that point. Holly may have gone the same way, but I think a literal murder at the hands of a family member was also a genuine possibility. Alison was precariously housed, sleeping in friend's rooms and occasionally on the streets, unwilling to impose on her children and knowing that emergency housing never handles people who don't fit into their boxes.

For others of us, survival was a less immediate need. I didn't want to live with my parents in my twenties, but it was safe and warm and they gave me a reasonable amount of privacy and security. Saeed was in a similar position. But the question loomed, even when we were very young: what would happen when our parents were no longer able to take care of us? Could we do it ourselves? Would there be anything resembling a welfare state by then or would governments of both sides have ripped it to shreds? Would we end up in the group homes that pretended not to be institutions? It might not be that our bodily survival was always at stake, not exactly, but our future was. For Vinnie, they would have been okay in a way, probably, but they were miserable and at a dead end.

And Denny... Denny was also doing okay, in some respects, but I know weeks went by without him seeing another person when he wasn't working – and when he was, in a currency exchange booth, locked behind glass, the customers were the sum total of his human interaction. Maybe some people like to live like that. Some of us, me included, need a lot of time alone. But everyone I know needs more company than Denny was getting – and I know it wasn't enough for him.

What seems oddly cruel is that many of us were just getting to the point where some of our fears for our survival were just beginning to leach out. Our finances were and are a constant concern, and we may not have this house forever, but it wasn't that crushing fear every single day; sometimes we could just live. It's exhausting to have to fight for your survival every single day.

I suppose at least we're used to it. At least we're experienced in it. At least we know that sometimes, if only sometimes, we can win.

I can see I'm going to have to tell myself a lot of reassuring things over the next little while. I've done it before, I guess. I'm going to have to do it again.

I swallow my terrors and keep fighting. Not the first time, and I'd be foolish to think it could be the last. I try not to have too many feelings about that and just do what I need to.

It's hard to keep fighting. It's even harder to maintain the careful balance of believing that you are capable of winning while also not assuming it will happen. But just when I'm feeling almost depleted of everything, I realise something. Something important. It's just possible we may have more resources than we thought.

If the ghost eater has what some people might consider magic, we might have an equivalent. We have paranormal abilities: mild, yes, but enough to be effective when we truly need them to be. And never have we needed them more than we do now.

I catch sight of Denny. He's staring at one of the doors, the heavy wooden ones. I recognise his look, his focus, because it's something that I need to deploy from time to time, but I've never seen...

The door is ripped from its hinges and flies across the room. Saeed screams at Alison to duck, which she mercifully does, and the door sails right over her, angles down, and hits the ghost eater right in the stomach. Rather than bouncing off him, or falling to the floor, it begins a long slow slide into him that it's hard for me to tear my eyes away from. It's enough to incapacitate him for a minute or more, enough for the rest of us to catch our breath and quickly think through the next few steps.

I turn to Denny; he looks dazed but pleased. I've never seen him manage to move something that heavy, let alone do it so fast. The accuracy, I'm most likely to attribute to luck, but the strength needed... I didn't know he had it. He probably doesn't really. I've read about people, regular people, who could lift up a car when their child was trapped beneath it, and it's probably the same sort of thing. Your body naturally limits your abilities because of how much damage they could do you – except in those rare instances where the consequences of not acting vastly outweigh those of doing so. There's no reason that wouldn't apply to telekinesis as well as regular movement.

I'm feeling buoyed by this new display of power, just when I worried we might be on the edge of defeat. But it's no clearer how we win this. We don't know if we can kill the ghost eater, or what the consequences of doing so might be. We don't know if it's physically possible to restrain him long term. We don't know if it's possible to force him to leave – or who else he would wreak havoc on if we sent him elsewhere. We're fighting because we have to fight, but we have short term tactics rather than a long-term plan.

The use of our paranormal powers gives us a temporary boost, but it doesn't last for long. I can see this is going to be a fight in which it's hard for us to gain any clear advantage, the only compensation being that it may be equally hard for the ghost eater to do too.

There's some sort of charge in the air, and then swirling currents, even though we're inside. Something is happening. The air moves violently as if a strong wind was blowing through the house. The ghost eater's cloak flies out behind him, but it appears more comical than intimidating. Then more than just the air around us begins to move.

The ghosts swarm up and entangle themselves in objects, even parts of the house itself, lifting them up and breaking them, throwing them. Bannisters are ripped up from the lower part of the staircase, posts flying out like arrows one at a time, hitting us in a barrage, us fending them off with our arms, turning to keep our faces out of the way. We try to keep fighting and shielding ourselves at the same time. It's even harder than it sounds.

But Denny hasn't finished yet, hasn't exhausted his ability. I don't see him do it, don't see him lift it, but I duck and pull Holly down with me as the old wardrobe, the one we keep in the corridor for our winter coats, comes careering down the hallway, pauses seemingly impossibly in mid-air, and then it knocks the ghost eater sideways then lands right on top of him, pinning him to the ground.

The wardrobe is crushing the ghost eater. His own corporeality, that he has worked so hard to gain, that he sucked out of Araminta and a number of the ghosts, is now operating against him. Once he could have floated right through the wardrobe, as if it was, if not quite air, then at least some kind of fluid. Now he is as trapped as I would be. Alison seems to have hurt her wrist as she got out of the way, but that's the only injury, and she and Denny lean on the wardrobe. We can't maintain this situation forever, but there is a pause for now. After some flailing and resistance, the ghost eater has fallen still beneath the wardrobe and I can hear us all exhale breath we didn't know we were holding in, all at once and loudly.

Alison turns to Holly.

"You still got sleeping pills?"

"Morgan took them."

"Right, Morgan's going to give you one sleeping pill and you're going to take it and you're going to sleep. I promise that you will do more good if you get some sleep, and I promise you we will wake you if we need you."

"Or if there's news on Vinnie?"

"Or if there's news on Vinnie."

I fetch Holly the pill and she goes with far less resistance than I would have expected. Perhaps she's listening to reason, which would be a fucking miracle for her when it comes to self-care, or maybe she just really is that tired. I know I'm that tired too, but the adrenaline's coursing through my body way too fast. I won't get any sleep tonight, not until Araminta's safe, not until this whole thing is fought and won, but that doesn't mean no-one else can.

Right now, everything's about Vinnie. I feel sick over the whole thing, sick and shaky. The only piece of reassurance I have is that they're still talking.

"This is my favourite shirt," I hear Vinnie wail breathlessly, pain in their voice. "My favourite. Don't let them cut it off me, you hear."

"I..."

"PROMISE me."

"Okay, okay, I'll do my best."

"And when I'm out of it, can you soak it for me in cold water and salt? COLD water, nothing hot. Hot sets the stains. Can you do that for me?"

"Vinnie, I'll do everything in my power to save your shirt," I hear Alison interject. "Once we've saved you and dealt with this other guy. And if I fail, I will buy you a replacement shirt, I fucking swear. Have it tailored as well if need be."

"Do you know how much it costs, how hard it is to get good clothes for a body like this? And don't you go offering to... to..." Their voice peters out.

"Okay Vin, stay with us," Saeed says, somehow managing to take some of Vinnie's weight while also balancing on a crutch. I know he's going to pay for this with pain and injury, perhaps even more than those of us who have been at the front line of the physical fighting. I also know he'll end up in my room justifiably complaining about it, so I consider that to be the time I'll worry about it and not now. Survival mechanisms, and all that.

Keira heaves open the heavy door and a blast of cold air from outside hits us, makes me realise my eyes are heavily swirling with tears. Vinnie yells something about their shirt into the darkness and the night.

"It's shock," says Keira. Somewhere in the distance I hear a siren. "It's the body's defence mechanism to get stressed about the minor things as a means of distraction from the main trauma. It's a really common way of coping with things like this."

Alison somehow manages to laugh.

"That's not shock," she says, through the tears and the anger and the exhaustion. "That's just Vinnie."

1971

I sobel is there through the centuries. Not quite ghost, not quite living. The room that was a laboratory becomes a library, then a classroom, then it is abandoned, blue paint left to peel.

Still, below it sits the book that holds the key to all this. Wedged in beneath the floorboard, silent, waiting.

She is here when new ghosts come to Casswell Park. She is here to welcome them, to help them settle in. She is here when Henrietta dies, here with her as she watches her baby. And she is here when Roderick dies too.

They will think, in years to come, that he killed himself. It's not that he hasn't thought about it. But it was not his intention here. The world is terrifying for him at times, and shrunk to a smallness he's not sure he could ever escape, but it's also filled with possibility. The world is painful and uncaring, and yet he finds glee in it.

More specifically, he finds glee in messing with it.

It's not just him today; he's roped two of the younger boys into helping; they're impressionable, enthusiastic. After all, this is going to be the crowning event of the year, the prank that is a culmination of a year of pranks. This is prize giving. The boys have had their uniforms checked: tie done up properly, shirt tucked in, fingernails clean, blazers neat, and are sitting on long benches with their parents ahead of them on chairs. All of them except Roderick and his accomplices who are hiding on the ledge above the stage.

The fishing twine is near transparent, hopefully invisible to those in the audience. Carefully, so carefully, he drops the loop down, hooks it over one of the large trophies on the cloth covered table. The headmaster is droning on. The loop hooked around, he wobbles it a little. A few of the boys notice, smirking.

Then he raises it into the air. Now they fail to suppress their laughter. Some of the teachers look round but the cups are instantly still. There's nothing to see.

They extend down more lengths of twine. Soon they will have all the cups dancing in a row, one after the other.

Roderick can't loop the twine around the last cup.

He leans forward. He loses his footing. And he falls.

A fall like that shouldn't have killed him, but there was something they said later, in the position in which he fell, the angle at which he hit the ground, that broke him in just the worst way possible.

Roderick had absolutely no intention of staying at school forever; even the next three years seemed unimaginable. And yet you don't choose whether your spirit lingers.

CHAPTER TWENTY FOUR

I remember it as if it all happens at once. Araminta comes back. I can tell she's fighting against everything that keeps her drifting, fighting to stay in one place, to be close to us. Because she needs to be close to us for it to work.

I piece it together later: I'd sat in the corridor and fallen asleep right there, without meaning to, somehow in contrast to my usual stubbornness. Someone or other figured, probably rightly, that if they woke me up to get me to bed I'd never go back to sleep. So they put a blanket over me and a pillow under my head and let me get a few hours of much needed sleep.

When I wake it must be the early hours of the morning. I don't think I feel rested; everything aches and I want to just sleep for weeks, but I reason that I'm probably better for it. I'm pleased to find that the ghost eater is still under the wardrobe, unconscious and tied to the wardrobe for good measure. Denny is sitting beside him, a collection of cola cans, some full, some empty beside him.

"Alison's getting some sleep," he says.

"So it's my turn to keep watch?" I ask.

Denny heads in the direction of his bedroom and I sit in his place, open one of the cans, yawning loudly. And then Araminta appears.

I don't know exactly what she's experiencing; maybe she'll tell me one day, maybe she won't. I can only tell what I see.

I see Araminta. There's still colour in her hair, colour in her uniform, and even though I can see right through her she still casts a hint of a shadow. She's not a ghost. I refuse to believe she's dead, not yet.

When this first happened to her she was listless, unresponsive, seemingly confused by her surroundings, drifting away from me whenever I came close. Now, even though she clearly doesn't understand things in the way I do, she is focused and deliberate in every one of her actions, even when she doesn't seem entirely in control of them.

She seems to be struggling against some invisible force, something that is constraining her, something that has half enveloped her. She's fighting against something I can't see but is utterly real to her – and not just in her head, is my feeling – and I'm not sure if she's winning.

I know this is the time. I plan through the steps in my head. Put the pendant on the ghost eater, recite the incantation. Saeed and I have been practising it, the sentences out of order so it doesn't work until we need it to. I have the pendant. I know what to say. I can't say it.

I start feeling anger at myself return. Everyone who said I could speak sometimes, so I could if I really wanted to: I'm feeling that now. Maybe I don't really want to enough.

I look at Araminta. She's starting to drift. There is no time to get Saeed. I have to do this. I feel the pendant in my pocket. My phone is there too. I have a plan.

I think through the incantation. I work out how to type it phonetically. Then I force the pendant round the ghost eater's struggling neck with one hand and with the other, my phone in my hand, I reach out to Araminta. I can't hold her, she's not solid enough for that, but I can touch her with my hand and with the phone, and maybe that's enough.

I touch the screen of my phone. The words sound. The voice is practiced, American accented, but each syllable is close enough. I hold my breath, scrunch up my eyes, and hope more than I've hoped for anything that this works.

I dare to look at Araminta. She's slowly becoming more corporeal, solidity and then colour returning.

It's hard to avoid vampire metaphors right now. The ghost eater has been draining from others for his own sustenance, a process Araminta is now reversing. The only difference is that the human body makes replacement blood far more easily than it makes replacement corporeality.

Plus, that cloak? Kinda playing up the whole stereotype to be honest. If he's not a vampire, he totally wants to be.

And Araminta falls to the ground, catches herself mid-air so she lands on her feet, but her hands steady her on the floor so she doesn't collapse entirely. She seems dazed for a few moments, and then rights herself, shaking her head as if to dislodge something, and then she's finally back with us. Full colour: red hair, work uniform, fully solid, full corporeal.

I want to throw my arms around her, want it more than anything, but I'm cautious, aware that she's fragile, that physical contact may be too much right now. So I settle for a hand on her arm and it confirms to me that she's utterly solid. As solid as I am.

Even by her standards she's pale – even her freckles are mostly invisible, but her clothes, her hair, they're all as bright as ever and, more importantly, completely opaque. I'm crying but silently. When she tries to speak, though, no sound comes out and she shakes her head in frustration. It's okay. I think we know what we need to know for now. I hold her like I've never held her before, so grateful for her solidity, her realness. After a while she extends her arms around me and I know then that even though it might take a long time, even though things might be difficult for a while yet, she will be all right. And maybe, maybe that's all I need.

There's still a lot to do, but I'm confident now in a way I wasn't before that we will win this. I have Araminta back, and however hard it may be – and things are, I suspect, going to be hard for her for a long time – we can do anything.

But there's a consequence to what I did. The ghost eater is now much less corporeal than he was. And that means that he can move through the wardrobe which has, up until now, been holding him down, can move his wrists and ankles through the ropes tying him. He can escape.

I yell down the corridor and to my relief people come running; first Alison and then Denny who probably didn't even get chance to fall asleep. The sleeping pill has clearly knocked Holly out; we'll wake her if we need to, but not just now.

They realise what's happening all at once, rush over, but he's already breaking out, moving through the wardrobe as if it were a thick liquid, breaking the wood a little as he goes. The rope we tied him with already lies on the floor, and when he's out from under the wardrobe he moves quickly, like this forceful blast of air that throws us all a few steps backwards.

And before we can recover, he's got the pendant in his hands, and then he visibly changes, summoning just enough corporeality to drag it out, the box shattering as he does so. I watch in horror. Fighting this is going to require everything I have.

The ghost eater was in the bottle as a stone in the pendant, is the conclusion we came to. And when we opened the bottle he escaped. So we've decided we have to get the pendant back in the bottle. That, however, is far easier said than done.

The pendant is wider than the mouth of any of those bottles. We had to smash the bottle to get it out, but it must have been put in there somehow. And if it can be put in once, it can be put in again. We can trap the ghost eater like he trapped so many others

That might be easier said than done though. Alison is still fighting the ghost eater. It's easy enough to keep him from doing any real harm at this point, given how weakened he is. He's barely corporeal, and most of the colour seems to have leached from him and his clothing. But we can't seem to defeat him

Denny manages to snatch the pendant back and together with Saeed, we get to work, hoping that Alison can fend him off just long enough.

. I pick up the bottle and examine it, the pendant in my other hand, contemplating the situation. No matter how hard I force the pendant, no matter what angle I aim it at, I can't get it in. It's just not going to happen.

I hold the pendant and it feels like it's calling to me again. Feels like it's offering me power and comfort. As if it's humming, a song only for me, calling me home.

I'm already home. I give it to Saeed before the pull gets too strong.

Meanwhile, all around me I can hear clashes and shouting, screams. The ghost eater is fighting... well whatever the undead version of fighting for your life is, and he's giving it everything he's got. If we don't sort this soon, he's going to gain more corporeality, and we'll be right back at square one. Right back where we started – except weaker.

I turn my attention to the pendant. Even though it clearly won't fit, I desperately try pushing it into the bottle because I've no idea what else to do. I'm quietly crying with frustration but I can't let my feelings overwhelm me. I have to think. I have a need to do something and the obvious way of doing it isn't working. That doesn't mean I give up and it doesn't mean I keep repeating something that doesn't work. It means I need to find a less obvious way of doing it.

And fortunately finding non-obvious ways of doing things is well within my skill set.

The ghost eater has used forces from outside the physical realm against us, and if we're to win we have to do the same. And only two of us have known paranormal abilities, and we now need to take the lead, however hard it might be for both of us. I don't have strong powers, and I've never had telekinesis, but Denny does, and he can do this. We can do this together.

"Denny!" I scream, with no sense of how loud I'm being because it feels like the entire world is vibrating in my ears. "The bottle needs to be wider."

"Got it," he yells back. He takes the bottle from in front of me and in the midst of all this chaos he stares at it utterly serenely for a few moments. He's completely focused. The mouth of the bottle visibly shudders and flexes, moving to an oval shape and back. It's unsteady and it's not enough to get the pendant back in, but it's some movement. It's progress.

Now it's all just a matter of degree really. We need to increase the amount by which he moves the bottle lip, just a little, and hold it for longer. And that takes two of us.

In some ways, Denny's powers are the opposite of mine. Mine are detecting input, rather than changing or influencing, whereas Denny's is creative output, moving physical objects with the power of his mind. We've already shown that they can affect the solid bottle, change its shape, but we haven't been able to do so sufficiently to get the pendant in. It needs to be widened, perhaps flattened, sufficiently for the full width of the pendant to fit through the mouth, and it needs to be held in that shape for a sufficient amount of time but also be able to be returned back to its original shape in order for us to insert the stopper.

And I sense there's a way we can work together. There's no rule-book for this one. I'm most comfortable when I'm working to books and timetables and schedules, but this operates on pure instinct. I'm not the best person for the job anyway. A telekinetic, or just someone with strong powers, would be better. But there's only me.

As Denny holds the bottle, I place my hands over his. I focus on not thinking anything, allowing him to draw on my powers. I'm not very good at it. But I can tell I'm doing just enough for it to start working.

I don't like the sensation that comes with it. It feels like I'm allowing someone way too close to me, letting them see something private about me. But it works.

It seems to take forever at first and then it all happens at once. The mouth of the bottle expands and then flexes to a wider oval. It's enough, but only just. Saeed pushes the pendant right through it before either of us says anything, and we hear it clink as it hits the glass below.

With it comes the ghost eater, a wisp of a thing now, sucked along as if connected by an invisible thread, and then compressing into almost nothing within the bottle. I slam the stopper in quickly, the sound of glass against glass echoing all around. The ghost eater is back in the bottle. It all happened so quickly that I'm not sure it really feels like anything happened at all. Everything around is so loudly quiet, so busily empty and gaping, that I feel dazed.

I've instinctively moved back from Denny, shaking, the bottle in my hand. I want to be alone, though I know I can't be. I want to be so far from other people that I can't see or hear them or have any sense of their presence. I want to be entirely alone, in a way I've never needed to be before.

It's not over yet. I wrap my hands tightly around the stopper and the mouth of the bottle, one on top of the other.

At least I find the words to speak and I yell into this space, into the stairs and the shut door and the corridors around, that I need to seal the bottle. I'm heard, as if my cry was a prayer.

I live, now, with people who, once they know what's needed, never let me down. I knew they never would but I'm still buoyed by the instant response, the fact they all trust me to know what I'm doing, that I'm making the right decisions.

Alison leaves Araminta flopped on the step and runs, her footsteps light and fast above me. It seems like hours I'm there with my hand over the stopper, sealing down every possible gap. The ghost eater won't be able to push out the stopper but he might be able to fit through a gap around it, I think.

At last, she throws blue-tac down the broken stairs, which Denny characteristically fails to catch but picks up quickly enough and together we make sure the bottle is securely sealed and then I put it down on the ground and stand up slowly and then I can't do anything at all.

CHAPTER TWENTY FIVE

Everything is empty and open and blank.

The adrenaline of the fight has dropped off, and for some of us that's all that's been holding us together. For two days I can't speak a word, find even text chat difficult, and have shooting pains through my body that I think are only partly to do with the physical exertion and damage of fighting. Araminta gets screaming nightmares. Vinnie was operated on the night they were injured, and is recovering but needing to spend a few more days in hospital yet – which they'll hate. Denny is withdrawn, and both Saeed and Alison have broken down in tears more than once.

Theo never seems to sleep, going backwards and forward along the upper floor corridor on those shoes or up and down on the trampoline until his father collects him, until Vinnie is able to take care of him again. Caleb's apologetic about it, saying that he knows we've looked after him well but he feels responsible after everything that's happened. He's secured a transfer for a little while until things are more settled, and his mother will help out as well.

It's Holly who seems to be coping the best. She just does what needs to be done with minimal fuss; she orders pizza for us on the first night and makes a pasta bake the second, she covers one of Araminta's shifts at work. I'm worried that when it does all hit her, she's going to crash all the harder, but I reason that at least the rest of us will be closer to recovered and in a better state to catch her.

Still, I worry. I've seen how she's fragile in some ways, and that there are some decisions that can't be undone. But I try not to think about that too much. I'm not up to it right now.

We find our ways of coping. For some, that means sleeping. For others, it means work. For me, it means taking myself off to a virtual world. I feel a bit guilty like I should be spending every moment with Araminta now I have her back, but honestly, I need some time alone, my headset on, my hands on the controller.

I leave this world. I'm piloting a ship through space. Steering clear of the battles, I set it on exploration mode and touch down on a planet of blue-green sands and glimmering trees like golden weeping willows. I check the atmosphere and the radiation levels and both are safe. I collect items on my travels; a piece of wood, a discarded shoe. There are metal detectors you can hire in exchange for gold. I take one and scan the desert, and when I get a positive result I start digging. I find coins and artefacts when I'm lucky and rubbish when I'm not.

When I've had enough of this world, it's time for me to fly to a new one. Alien world bleeds into alien world. I am anywhere but here and that is how I need it. I lose all track of time, playing for hours on end, interrupted only to use the bathroom. Mallard perches on my lap. Holly brings me snacks – and proper snacks, asparagus rolls and carrot sticks with hummus, as well as the usual comfort food, along with a large bottle of cola. Maybe she really is coping better than anyone.

Afterwards, I sleep. I sleep for a long time, perhaps a day and a night, perhaps twice that. I may not be fully asleep all that time but never fully awake either. At most, I am only semi-aware of what's going on around me.

This is more than mere exhaustion. Sometimes I have a half-formed thought that I should be with Araminta, but I think we both need to be alone. At least I reason that's the case, and hope that I'm right.

I sleep more. I'm heavy with sweat and my hair is so tangled I fear I may just end up having to cut it off. I feel uncomfortable at the thought. There's nothing wrong with having short hair, of course, but for me it's so connected with those years I had to pretend to be a boy that I don't think I'll ever be able to escape those associations.

At least hair always grows again, is what my mother would say.

Meanwhile, we have a bottle with the semi-corporeal form of an early eighteenth-century ghost eater – not to mention a pendant larger than the mouth of said bottle, inside, and not a clue what to do with it. We keep it on the dining room table for a couple of days before someone delicately points out that given the clumsiness issues affecting some people in this household, and given how catastrophic it would be if the bottle was smashed and the ghost eater released, it may not be the best idea. It's now in a box padded with blankets and kept under Alison's bed. Rather her than me. I wouldn't be volunteering to have that guy under my bed in any form, trapped in a bottle or not.

I don't know when it is that I hear a knock on my bedroom door, but when I yell to come in, it's Araminta, and without saying a word she clambers under the covers with me.

"You probably don't want to do that," I say. It's the first time I've spoken since we got the ghost eater in the bottle, and I'm surprised I can. "It's been a while since I last had a shower."

"Don't care," she replies, her mouth muffled by my shoulder, her arms intertwining around me, and then mine around her. Her hair smells of shampoo though she's dressed in a onesie. Bit by bit, she's returning to the real world. And we lie there until I finally feel like things will be okay.

Eventually, I get up. I take a shower, rubbing off layers of grime and sweat. I condition my hair twice, and tease out the worst of the tangles. I make myself a meal — admittedly it's coffee and microwaved porridge but I reason that the porridge has apple and cinnamon and milk, which means it covers multiple food groups.

The worst of things may be over, but there are still unanswered questions for us. There is still tidying up to be done, both literally and otherwise. We haven't decided what to do with the ghost eater, what standards we should be bound by, how we stay true to our principles while also ensuring our safety.

I look around the kitchen, along the corridor. In some ways, the house is a mess, trashed and broken. In others, it looks very well cleaned.

In the time I've been non-functional, Holly has taken everything off the kitchen shelves, cleaned each shelf, and returned the contents to their places. She's also thoroughly scrubbed the oven and wiped down the cupboard doors. The tablecloths are not only washed but neatly folded as if waiting for the birthdays and celebrations that we will still get to have in years to come.

We all have our coping mechanisms; I can only wish mine were that useful.

I head to the room Araminta's been sleeping in, knock on the door. It's bare and plain-walled, with little of her personality. I think she's scared to add anything like that, scared of losing everything all over again.

"I need to say sorry," I say. "I'm sorry for giving you the pendant."

"You just wanted me to have something nice," she says.

"I know but..." My mouth is dry. "It wasn't mine to give but I let myself go along with the pull of it or whatever it exerted on me just because it felt comfortable."

She's not angry. She would be within her rights to be, and maybe it would be easier in some ways if she was, if all our feelings could explode and then fall away.

"We're okay," she says. "Or we will be. I love you."

"I love you," I say, feeling like I don't deserve her one bit.

I'm clearing some wrappers and Mountain Dew bottles from my bedroom when Keira messages me. We haven't talked to her properly since we came back here, and I still don't know how I feel about her. But I'm not sure we'd be here without her.

I grab my laptop, head down to the dining room where I make myself a cup of tea and jump on text chat with her. She has an offer to make, or at least a suggestion. But she checks on how we're all doing first and I pass on our thanks for her helping Vinnie. It's not just a social nicety; I really do mean that bit of it.

>> So the ghost eater?

>> In a bottle. Not getting out any time soon.

>> You know what you're going to do with him?

I try to work out what to say – the truth is I don't know and the lack of an answer to that question has been bothering me. It's almost a relief that Keira doesn't wait for a response before continuing.

>> There are a lot of old houses whose owners would love them to be haunted. He may not be a ghost exactly but we think we could bind him to a building, a strong bind. He could spend his time in relative comfort there, with a large house and likely gardens to roam, while you could be confident he wouldn't bother you or the ghosts that live there.

I pause, saying nothing. It's an appealing offer in some ways. It would not require us to destroy or even harm him, and at the same time ensures our safety.

And yet it makes me feel uneasy, even as another part of me is seeing white with fury. We've always objected to haunted houses, our ghosts being made a spectacle of, especially when most can't meaningfully consent. And I think having ghosts on show as an attraction harms other ghosts too. It sets a standard for people's attitudes, what they think is acceptable behaviour towards all ghosts. but all ghosts, in that it influences people's attitudes and what they think is acceptable behaviour towards them.

And yet I also think, even for those of us who aren't always opposed to prisons, there are some issues with sticking someone in a bottle for eternity.

I thank Keira for the suggestion, tell her I'll get back to her. I'm increasingly convinced she has a lot in common with us. And then I get another message.

I appreciate Callum asking before he visits, even if he doesn't ask until he's most of the way here. I warn him that things aren't how they normally are, both in terms of the physical structure of the house and our ability to be sociable. To his credit, he turns up with a carton of putty and a pack of sandpaper.

"I wasn't quite sure what you needed," he says. "But I hope you can use these."

I smile and thank him, making him tea. We will use them all in the months to come. But that's not what he's here for. He's here for Florence.

They would have loved to have taken down Pittlow, closed it for good, but that's not happening any time soon – and even I know that you can't win every battle. But they have a house where they've offered sanctuary to ghosts from there, and ghosts from an old orphanage being demolished. And he thinks she'll be happier to be around children.

We can't get a verbal consent from Florence, and she can't point at letters, but we don't need her to. We just have to tell her. And when Callum leaves, she follows.

Later, Saeed and I are sitting in the dining room again. We're idly playing Carcassonne; it's the best game for two players I've found, and even though our large table is made up of multiple tables of multiple heights, it still works out pretty well. There's a fan heater going – it's too late to light the fire and I haven't the energy – and I've microwaved wheat packs for both of us. Mine is sitting comfortably on my knees; I appreciate its weight as much as I do its warmth.

Our focus isn't really on the game. It's not even on conversation with each other. Mostly we're just not ready to go to sleep yet, and we're enjoying each other's company and the restoration of relative normality. I like these nights, when we sit together. Sometimes someone is doing craft or small chores at the table. Sometimes we talk or play games. Sometimes we just sit.

This time, though, Saeed has something he wants to get off his chest.

"Don't you think I'm like the ghost eater, though?"

I look up in surprise.

"How so?"

Saeed takes a deep breath, leaning back in his chair.

"I've been looking through that book the ghost left behind. It's the ghost eater's notes. And it's all these little charts and classifications, exactly how I write – or how I would if I had to do it all by hand. I like categorising things. I follow stories and leads and sometimes when I'm onto a batch of information or deep in an archive, I can't think about anything else. And hell, I'd love a cloak like that. Did you see that cloak!?"

"Bullshit," I say. "It had no sparkles and it was black, without a trace of purple anywhere on it."

Saeed forces a smile. "It's dramatic though, you've got to admit."

"Well, I'm pretty sure if it's the cloak you want, Araminta will help you make one." The thoughts are coming all at once and I switch to typing, letting Saeed look over my shoulder.

>>Everything you've been doing – all your research and organisation and classification, all the systems you've

set up for us, all the information you've found – none of it has been selfish. All of it has been about helping us. About working collectively rather than selfishly. Even when you're following your own interests, you are doing so in a way that understands other people have needs and aren't just to be ridden roughshod over. People and ghosts alike. You're like... it's the difference between someone who buys some nails to leave under his neighbour's tires and the person who buys them to make a playhouse for his kids. Buying nails isn't really the most important thing, if you get my meaning.

"Wow, Morgan, you're beating me for off the wall tortured metaphors, congratulations! I'm so proud of you."

"You know what I mean, though," I say, with my voice this time, feeling the edge of a warm glow travel through my body and the corners of my mouth creep upwards towards a smile.

"I use my powers for good, not evil, you reckon?" I see a smile creep into his face, a genuine one this time. He brings his fidget spinner to a halt.

"Yes, exactly. But it's not just about what you do. Your actions are because you're a fundamentally better person than him."

"Maybe. But how close was I to travelling down a path like his? Are we just very similar people that some random accident of circumstance sent in different directions? What if something changes for me? Will I become like him?"

I spread my arms open wide and breathe, indicating the breadth of the question we're faced with.

"Digging into the deeper philosophical questions, I see. I think we need sustenance for this."

I pour us hot blackcurrant with a little whiskey – you can't say we haven't earned it – and sit down at the table with my friend. I don't think I could ever rank the people I live with, and I don't understand why your partner can"t also be your friend, but I think the way most people would see it, Saeed is my best friend. Whatever words I use don't really matter – I just know I'm lucky to have him. I find a container of freshly made cheese straws – Holly seems to have been on a baking binge as well as a cleaning one.

"I don't know, Saeed," I say. "I really don't know except I know that you're a good person and if you changed so much that you could ever do things like what he did, you wouldn't be you anymore." I shrug. "We're all products of our environments in some way – nature versus nurture, etcetera, etcetera. But no, I think there's far more that separates you. And hey, you're not the one who's the direct descendant of the dude and got all enticed by his weird magical pendant and dragged the woman you love into it and..."

"Your family's totally different though..."

"I know. It still scared me, though, how much of a hold it had on me."

"You need to watch more horror movies, I swear."

I laugh loudly. "No, Saeed, I really don't. No more horror movies. Not for a very long time."

We consider what to do with the ghost eater, over and over; snatches of discussion around the dining table, standing out on one of the balconies, while we work out repairs. Araminta fills in some of the gaps of what happened, of how when the ghost eater destroyed her studio it was the ghosts who forced him to make her write those messages, those desperate attempts to warn us. And now we need to know what to do with the ghost eater.

The ideal, of course, would be a solution both which the ghost eater consents to, and where we know he can't harm us or anyone else. There are... at least three problems with this. The first is obtaining genuine consent, what with us having him in a bottle and all. The second is the risk of him tricking or manipulating us – it certainly wouldn't be the first time for that! The third is actually communicating with him at all – after all, he's almost entirely devoid of corporeality and trapped within a bottle.

It's Roderick who offers us a potential solution to the second problem, though not one that comes without its own set of quandaries. He's offered to act as a representative, to go inside the bottle, speak to the ghost eater on our behalf and report back. It's a tempting offer, but at the same time this brings up all the philosophical questions we've grappled with, and at a time when I don't feel very well equipped to deal with them. And now they aren't abstract; they're right here in front of us and we have to make very real choices with significant consequences based on our answers to those near unanswerable questions. I run through those questions in my head now; we all do. What responsibility do we have to protect ghosts? How autonomous can they be? And if the ghost is a child, do we consider them to still be the age they died at, or do we take account of all the years that have passed since with them as a ghost? Are ghosts just living on borrowed time that is of little consequence, a blip between life and eternity?

We don't even know if Roderick's plan will work and we don't know exactly what level of danger we will be exposing him to. Which doesn't make the decision any easier.

We've discussed how much capacity ghosts have to consent before. It's not just been an idle philosophical question – it has genuinely informed the world we have built here at Casswell Park. But we haven't had to grapple with the hardest questions; as we have made few requests of the ghosts, and they tend to just float off through the ceiling when exposed to something they don't want to be around, it doesn't seem terribly high stakes or high risk or high consequence.

But now it is urgent and difficult and filled with all kinds of pressing questions. What about those whose knowledge remains almost frozen in their own time, who cannot process more current knowledge and thus don't have a good context for their decision making? How much are they able to consent to something we may ask them to do, to take care of themselves, to be responsible for the choice of not taking care of themselves?

I worry about all the possible reasons someone might be vulnerable or unable to fully consent, and all the reasons I may not be able to adequately judge their capacity – them being a ghost chief amongst them. It worries me. Roderick is so many of these things. He died at fifteen – technically a child – but in terms of years he's existed, as human and ghost combined, he's about my parents' age. I would be uncomfortable, to be honest, with a human adult taking this risk on my behalf, but at least I could be confident of their understanding of the consequences. Roderick we can communicate with more easily than most of the ghosts, and yet he's still childlike, leaping around with a cheeky grin, and I fear the ethics and the consequences of him going into terrible danger on behalf of us.

And yet, firstly, I have to respect his autonomy and secondly, I know that if we don't resolve the situation – then it's not going to just have an impact on us, but it's going to affect all the ghosts, including Roderick. It's not an easy decision, but we end up making it.

Roderick, meanwhile, is visibly bored, wondering what is taking us so long, wondering why anything is even up for question.

At last, we decide that if he's sure, and if he can recount the risks back to us, then he can go in. It takes forever using the letter board, and all of us have had enough, especially Roderick who doesn't understand why he can't just do it, why we can't just let him, but at last we get through it.

The bottle rattles with the pendant a little when we shake it – and I wonder if I shouldn't, if the ghost eater is sufficiently corporeal for that to be incredibly painful to him. Part of me doesn't care and feels like he deserves it, but the thought of casually and callously hurting someone I have captive doesn't exactly sit comfortably with me either. So I stop. The stopper is still in place from that terrifying time when I pushed it in and sealed it. It's not a moment I wish my mind to transport me back to, but my mind isn't exactly doing what I want right now – it rarely is, to be honest.

I take a deep breath in. Roderick is ready to squeeze himself through the narrow neck of the bottle, but it's terrifying me to open it even though I know that the necessary precautions have all been taken, even though I know that it's going to be okay. I feel nauseous. Visions of the ghost eater re-entering our world and attacking swirl in front of my eyes. Words start repeating in my head: I can't. I can't. I can't. I can't. In the end I give the bottle to Denny and fly from the room like I'm a child, fly along the corridor and fling open the side door and stand there looking out at the world outside, tears pricking my eyes and the still-winter air cold against my throat with every breath I'm forced to take in.

CHAPTER TWENTY SIX

I'm smashing up the broken wardrobe with a hatchet when Araminta comes to tell me that Roderick is out of the bottle. I leave my work for now; I can finish it later and then at night Denny and I can sneak around and deposit the results in other people's skip bins. It's not being very neighbourly, I'm sure, but needs must. And it's not like no-one has ever chucked trash over the hedge onto our driveway.

We grab Saeed from the laundry room where he's spent the day with his e-reader, washing linen and curtains, a cleansing of sorts for this house. We've been scrubbing even the unaffected areas. To be honest, the house needed a good clean even before that day that seems so long ago when an elderly man showed up on our doorstep with a box of bottles. Now, it's comforting in a way. And it means we can work together without having to speak.

As we walk, I wonder what it was like for Roderick within the glass, whether it was more prison or adventure, a chore or an activity that came with satisfaction. I've often wondered what it feels like to be a ghost, how different it is to being human. I suppose one day I'll either find out or I won't.

We're relieved, though, that Roderick is seemingly unharmed, and equally relieved to find that the ghost eater has not emerged with him. But the news he reports, pointed letter by pointed letter, is somewhat more troubling.

>>Not interested in options. Wants to end.

I roll my eyes. I think almost everyone around me makes the same gesture. I'm not making any pretence at approaching these discussions in good faith, and nor should I have. I'm doing what my conscience feels is ethically required of me; no more, no less.

"Well, I hope he has a happy life in that bottle then," says Denny, with more bitterness than I've ever heard from him before.

The whole thing feels a bit anticlimactic, a question I'd wanted a straightforward answer to returns just more complications. I'm exhausted, and every muscle in my body aches. When, having thanked Roderick, we sit down to discuss it, I can't formulate thoughts into a sentence. I just want to sleep.

We're not sure if this is a genuine decision or a tactical manoeuvre. And we're out of resources for fighting and out of energy for dealing with bullshit right now. I'm not the only one who is pretty tempted to keep him in the bottle. Perhaps all that's discouraging him is that it might leave a chance he finds a way to get out himself. Or more likely he'll be let out at some point; perhaps deliberately, perhaps by accident.

I wonder if the man who brought the bottles here inherited them from someone who had been told by an ancestor to keep them sealed, to never let anyone out, and to always pass that on, and the message got lost or thought of as unimportant.

I don't really believe in prisons, but he rejected our only good solution, so maybe he does need to be kept in the bottle. We're not dealing with a typical human lifespan either; we're talking about functional eternity.

It would be simplest to kill him, simple and easy and I'm exhausted. But I can't let the fate, the life and death, of anyone, even someone who has done me and those I love great harm, balance on what I have the energy to do. If I do that, I've given up on everything that is important to me, everything I believe in.

The room is warm and the fire is crackling. I don't think I can think anymore. I slump in my chair and half close my eyes.

Even though I'm dozing, the conversation continues. I do my best to follow it, although frankly, I'm longing for my bed. No-one would actively object if I left, but I know no-one else wants to be here either and I have an obligation just as anyone else does. I'm not going to flake out on them just because I'm exhausted. After all, we're all exhausted.

"The other problem," Alison says carefully, "is that we only have his word for it that destroying the pendant will destroy him. It could all be a trap. It could release him or make him more powerful. And I'm not feeling great about taking that chance."

Several of us nod in agreement. We're feeling rather risk-averse right now, given everything we've been through. It may not be possible to avoid risk in this one, though. But if there's an easy solution, I've no clue what it was.

Araminta nudges me. "You okay?" she whispers.

I yawn, shamelessly performatively. "Sleeeepy."

"It's been a long day. Go to bed if you need to."

But I shake my head, forcing myself to keep my eyes open. I pour myself a glass of chilled water from the fridge in the hope it will wake me up. It only half works. Meanwhile, Saeed is coming up with alternative suggestions.

"What about putting something into the bottle? Something that will harm him directly but not risk releasing him? At least if we pour it in properly."

"Oh no," says Denny. "You already had me ask the vicar for holy water once, and it didn't go well. You're not taking advantage of me like that. Besides, it's a pretty bad premise given that most of our ghosts are at least nominally Christians."

"Well, I'm not going near a church," says Araminta definitively. "Last time I did that I burst into flames."

"No dear," says Alison. "That's just your hair."

I worry for a moment that Araminta will be upset by the comment. Her hair was often linked to her behaviour when she was a child, and she's definitely in a sensitive place right now. But after a moment's pause she bursts into laughter.

"Sometimes I turn round," she says, "and I'm like, shit, what's that creature lurking around my head? Scares the life out of me if I don't put it in braids."

We all crack up. It's good to have some laughter in here again; it seems like so long since that was normal.

I'm not a very patient person, though, and I'm particularly bad when the time needed or the endpoint is undetermined or vague. I'm not the only one here who struggles in that way either. I straighten myself out, consciously shifting and stretching each muscle in turn. Everything aches and I don't know how long I can keep going before I actually fall asleep at the table rather than just dozing. I wrap my hands around the cold glass, trying to stop myself falling into sleep.

The conversation continues. I'm honestly not sure if we're getting any closer to a solution right now. I can only hope, because I have little capacity to contribute.

Eventually, I can stay awake no longer. I make my apologies, heat myself a heavy wheat pack, force myself through the routine of cleaning my teeth, switching off my computer, wiping my face. It doesn't matter that I can barely stand, because if there's one thing that;s going to keep me going right now it's re-establishing my routines.

Then I crawl into bed, hugging the wheat pack and clinging to every bit of its warmth. Sometimes when I get this tired I paradoxically can't sleep, but fortunately, I'm experiencing none of that tonight. I sleep quickly and deeply, avoiding the tormented dreams I might have expected.

And when I wake up, the others have decided. And they've left me a job to do.

Glass is easy to destroy. I smash the bottle on the pathway outside, letting the green-brown glass splinter on the driveway until it becomes just old, broken, glass, nothing more magical or powerful at all, just rubbish. Some of the bigger pieces I pick up carefully and then smash again, even more forcefully. Then when all those are destroyed into tiny shards, I reach down, careful not to cut myself, and pick up the pendant. I can still feel its pull, a desire to wear it, the sense that it somehow belongs to me – or I to it.

It's never been strong enough to force me to do anything against my will, but the connection I felt to it was comforting, enticing. I wish that I"d known then, when we opened the bottle, when I first picked up the pendant, when this all started, what I know now.

I know, now, that it was designed for a family line that includes me. That it's designed for something within me, something passed down through the generations. Perhaps it is as-yet unresearched genetics, or something less tangible entirely. Perhaps the ghost eater wanted to pass it on; perhaps he wanted to restrict its powers to his own family.

But I know one thing. The family he felt was his, that's not my family. My family may see ghosts, even have paranormal powers, but we're not a family of wealth and classifying ghosts and evil sorcerers. The ghosts are our equals, not our subjects. My family is a family of railway workers, teachers and nurses; not occult scientists and certainly not aristocracy.

And I know this also: this pendant is not for Araminta, and it is not for me. Perhaps for a descendant that someone imagined hundreds of years ago, a person they imagined in the place of me, but not me. Not the me I truly am. It might give me abilities. Over time, it might allow me to use them in ways that benefit me or the people I care about. But the feeling of home I got from it... I know that's all a lie. The wish to connect it with someone I love is not me either. I'm better off without it.

It's harder to destroy than the bottle, but that doesn't mean it's beyond me. I smash the gemstone with a rock and it disintegrates into shards and then fades and disappears right before me. Then I start work on the metal surround. It's bent and then it's broken, folded back and forth until it breaks, and then I break it again. I don't know how many pieces it needs to be in but by sheer force of my hands, I get it into eight. I could have used tools to do this, even clamped it between rocks, but I needed to do this myself.

It's the closest thing I've ever done to killing someone, and yet it's easier than I thought it would be. I keep going until I am confident the pendant is functionally just small pieces of metal, and all the harm it could do, all the harm that could be done with it, is fully destroyed and destroyed forever, until my hands are bleeding and sore and I feel dazed and exhausted by the effort.

Then I sit down, checking the path for glass shards, and ruin my fingernails by unpicking the chain link by link by link.

2018

Isobel isn't a ghost, not exactly. She did not die. But though she has gained enough corporeality to pass for human, though she can speak and her focus is growing stronger by the day, though her mind is not locked in the past like those of many ghosts are, she will fade and she will go. It might take one year. It might take ten.

But between then and now she has many days, and she has a world full of new inventions and old ghosts.

She is not a ghost; she is not tethered to a house. She starts walking. The world is welcoming her back.

CHAPTER TWENTY SEVEN

I t's early March. The sun is starting to warm and the frost in the air has lifted completely. The little strip of grass outside is green and growing near out of control, and I take the lawnmower out of storage. It's an old, heavy, manual thing, with a handle too short for me to push comfortably. I do it anyway. I drag it to the start of the grass and push it along the whole length, turn and push it back again. I form a rhythm, a pattern. It's almost meditative. Birds are gathering on the gutters, which are heavy with water. Holly and I will have to head up there to unblock them, which isn't my favourite job but it's a normal, routine job, and I don't plan to complain about normal and routine any time soon.

I put the lawnmower away and brush the grass off my ankles. Back inside, Holly is nailing together a temporary banister. It doesn't look good, but it's enough for those of us who need to use it on the stairs until we can get something better sorted. Walking down the corridor and I can smell cooking. Alison is making pots of soup that we can portion, freeze, and defrost, because things are better now but organising and eating food can still be difficult. Like repairing the house, repairing ourselves isn't an instant process.

We've taken stock of the damage. Saeed has set up a shared to do list app with categories for each area of the house and tags for the level of expense involved. We split into two groups going through and logging everything broken or damaged, assigning a priority level to each item. Now we have that information we can make a start on the repairs we are able to, and make a plan for those we need professionals or significant amounts of money, or both, to complete.

I try not to worry about those right now, but I can't help but worry. Some things we can fix ourselves without too much trouble, some are going to take time and energy a bit of strategising. But some, especially the plumbing, are going to need a professional, and we're really not sure how we're going to pay for that. We still have no water in the upstairs bathroom, and both the hassle of going downstairs, and the pressure on all of us sharing just one decent shower is definitely less than ideal.

It's not that we aren't tremendously lucky to have this large, historic property for essentially no rent – we are. But we're also all unemployed, underemployed, or students, and there's nothing to fall back on. We have no revolving mortgage, we certainly don't have savings of note, much less investments, and we're basically living day to day. Vinnie hasn't left their bedroom since they got back from the hospital. I tell myself that healing takes time, but every day they're in bed my anxiety grows that perhaps the damage done is irreparable.

I just have to believe that we'll find a way through. We always have before.

Halfway down the corridor and Araminta sees me, runs out of the spare room she's been staying in, kisses me briefly, grinning. What she experienced would have been hard for anyone, but for her it's ripped open so much trauma that she'd worked so hard to get a handle on. I suspect there will be hard times ahead for her too, but I'm determined to do whatever she needs to help her through them, and now, right now, she is smiling, her hair braided and her dress flying out around her as she twirls round.

We burn the clothes she was wearing when her corporeality was taken from her, right down to underwear and socks. They are tainted for her and I enjoy burning things, so it makes sense. We put them in the fire and shove them with the poker until they are entirely gone. She'll tell her manager her shirt was damaged in the wash, and hopefully he won't charge for a replacement.

After that Araminta and I go looking for Saeed and Denny. We find them in the room where the ghosts tore up the floor, just weeks before and yet it feels like it was so many years ago.

"We're taking another look at what to do about this floor," says Saeed. "It's one of the biggest areas of damage, so we want to make a plan and price it up, even if it will take some time for us to put it into action."

I nod in understanding, assessing the situation.

"The boards are mostly broken. It's not just a matter of nailing them down; most of them are going to need to be replaced. And that won't be the biggest expense we'll be facing, but when we have so little in the way of funding, it's still significant."

Denny and Saeed look at each other like the clear co-conspirators they are, and it's Denny who responds.

"Replacing the floor... nah. Want to hear my idea?"

I truthfully don't see how there can be any other options, except possibly plan to replace the floor at some indefinite point in the future and never actually get round to it. But hey, I'm prepared to listen to anything that doesn't involve spending money we don't have on flooring, of all things.

"Go on then."

Denny actually, literally, rubs his hands with glee.

"Okay. So, it's about fifty centimetres deep there. We leave some around the edges and ensure everything is stabilised, and then we dig a central section down to a metre..."

"I'm not sure I like what I'm hearing," says a voice behind us.

"Vinnie," Saeed yells, as we all turn around. "You're up!"

"Woah, gently," Vinnie says and Araminta pauses and then hugs them slowly but gently. Alison's walking just behind them. I can't stop grinning. I grab a chair and put it so Vinnie can sit down, which they do, and they're visibly in pain as they bend.

Soon we're all here, crowded around Vinnie, who finally, finally seems to be recovering.

"I think you've got an audience for yourself," Saeed says to Denny. "Want to tell them all your grand plan?"

Denny's eyes light up. He's definitely been scheming.

"Ok, so we dig out the centre of the floor to a depth of one metre. And then instead of returning the floor, or a new floor more likely, we brace it around the sides and add in some support to the foundations, we can remove the existing supports, then install some kind of moisture barrier..."

"Ohhh... kay?" Araminta says. I have to admit, this does rather sound like making everything worse rather than improving it. But Denny clearly has plans.

"And then we install a floor trampoline. Like, most of the floor one big trampoline floor level. It will cost, of course, we won't be able to do it immediately, but I reckon that's a good long term plan. After all, our whole purpose is to make a space that is designed for people like this, and this will be some good out of everything."

Plus, I think, but do not say, we can get rid of that thing of Theo's that creaks and squeaks every single time he bounces on it. That would more than make any cost involved worthwhile. I'd go through this all again for that.

Well. Not really.

"Campaign for people with ADD to get trampolines on the NHS!"

"Yeah, good luck with that," is Saeed's response. "If I have not yet ranted to you about the need for approval to get wheelchairs and some of the shitty designs people end up with then congratulations! That rant is always on tap and you're welcome to it any time you like..."

"Or alternatively," Vinnie says, "when you've just got home from a long day's work and have finally sat down to some peace and quiet."

"That too!" says Saeed. "I'm always at your service with my rants."

Vinnie recovers over the days that follow. They have some quite dramatic scars across their stomach, which they are only too happy to show off, as a result of the surgery to extract the broken pieces of copper pipe, which shattered inside the abdomen in a way the surgeon had never seen before. I'm not sure how much of it is bravado and how much of it is that they're genuinely feeling okay about things, but I guess if it's the former then I've no doubt the latter will follow.

Araminta spends quite a lot of her time in Vinnie and Theo's living room. Holly brought her a pack of pencils and a good hardbacked sketchbook – and by brought, I mean she stole them from the art room at school, which is an unusual act of rule-breaking for Holly and one I wholeheartedly endorse. Araminta spends much of her time in there sketching, while Vinnie reads or watches TV – and I assure you, their taste in television is terrible; I didn't know quite how bad. It will allow me snarky retorts and good-natured jibes for years at this rate.

In time, when she's ready for it, we'll sort out Araminta's studio, perhaps move her to one of the other two room suites in the corridor. But only with her consent, and she's not quite ready yet. The important things are she's still drawing and she's not isolating herself. Recovery is happening, for both her and Vinnie. The rest can come later.

We're starting to fall back into old routines where we can, and make new ones where we can't.

Araminta goes back to work; she showed up at the doctor's office looking like death itself and got anti-depressants which she didn't take, an iron supplement which she did, and a suitably vague sick note. I thought we'd have to ask one of the ghosts to haunt her manager but fortunately he didn't give her any crap. Maybe he was scared of Holly, which is fair enough. Sometimes I wouldn't want to get on the wrong side of that quiet fury Holly can occasionally be driven to.

I'm looking at what I can do for a bit of money. I can't be outside the house that much and I'll never get a proper full-time income, but Saeed's suggesting I start a blog of game play thoughs and strategies, and see if I can make a bit with advertising and donations.

I'm not sure. I shall see. But it sounds like I could at least get some review copies of games that way, and that certainly wouldn't hurt.

We've re-budgeted, and Saeed has got himself an emergency financial hardship grant based on accommodation issues, which is not a lie. He missed, though, the small detail about a ghost eating evil sorcerer from the 18th century destroying our water pipes – and we're putting that towards the plumbing bills, along with a loan from Theo's father. With any luck, the upstairs bathrooms should be operational before too long.

Things are coming together, piece by piece. I feel like even though it's still hard now, we'll get there.

Today most of us are in the living room, though. Denny has picked up his chainmail for the first time since... since it all began, and I'm watching the even, repetitive motions of his fingers, transfixed by them; they're calming. Theo and Holly are at school, but Saeed is studying, with a large book propped up on cushions so he doesn't have to put more pressure on his wrists. Araminta is also reading, but a novel – she's put aside her sketching for a bit. I'm the annoying one; I've discovered one of my yoyos, prized possessions of my teenage years, and it's a good one, with a proper clutch and everything. They'll tell me if I get too annoying. Vinnie and Alison are playing chess; Vinnie lying on the sofa, still not back to full health, and Alison sitting on a cushion on the floor so they can play on the low coffee table. Things are getting back to normal. Slowly, but they're getting there.

Just a few days later, and Keira is running the sander over the wood. It's been needing doing for ages, but we'd reasoned it wasn't a priority. Now, with the effects of the fighting, not to mention doors and random items of furniture being hurled by forces not entirely natural, it's become a priority – and now we have someone who has offered to do it for us.

Keira hired the floor sander and won't accept anything for reimbursement. She says she'll come back with a couple of hand sanders for us to do the stairs, if one or other of us who can stand the – far lesser – noise of those can help her with it. I've volunteered, though I'm planning earplugs under my noise cancelling headphones and frequent breaks. Then Araminta, definitely, and whoever else, can work on the varnishing – we'll need a lot of varnish, probably too much to get a mis-tint, but I'm hoping one way or another we'll find a cheap option.

Though I still have some issues with Keira, I have to admit she's being incredibly helpful doing this, and she's not making a fuss about doing it either. And it is useful, because there's no way in hell I'd let our hyperactive ten-year-old loose with something like that; it's a few years before he'll get his hands on the lawnmower, though likely both of us are looking forward to when that moment comes.

When she finishes the ground floor she lugs the sander to the lift and works on the upstairs as well. Theo – our resident sensory seeker – is sitting on, and periodically jumping up to dance on, the stairs, while the rest of us are at the other end of the house with headphones, except for Vinnie who is back at work part-time, and Holly who has gone to a friend's place to study. Bit by bit, we're working out how to put our house, and ourselves, back together. Mallard is sitting outside, sulking, but he'll deal with it. He's dealt with noise before. If only they made noise cancelling headphones for cats.

On the wall of the corridor hang three portraits, Araminta's first real paintings since this all began. They depict Hannah, Tim, and Gregoria, the ghosts who were lost to the ghost eater. They may have died long ago, but they didn't deserve to go like that. We won't forget them.

The house is full of people and it is full of ghosts. It is a world where we live separately and together. A world that – even though it's hard sometimes, when money and the limitations of our own bodies work against us – we fashion. That works for us when the outside world is hostile and inaccessible. It is a world where there is no shame in tape markings on the floors. In wearing headphones around each other, in eating alone or together. It is a world where ghosts and humans are both welcome. A world where it is totally reasonable to convert a room into a trampoline.

It is a world where we are almost ready to open more bottles, to allow new ghosts to leave their glass confines, to do our best to calm their fears, to offer them the best place we can to be for the years, decades, even centuries until they eventually fade away.

It is a world which, despite everything, I would not change for anything.

A world where we are friends and family in multiple different configurations, where we build the relationships that work for us, and understand that some relationships may be closer but that doesn't mean certain types of relationships automatically take precedence. Where we laugh and go on tangents, where there's space for what interests us. Where things are safe for both humans and ghosts.

Where we feel at home.

And yes, I know we're idealistic in some respects, but we're building our ideals right here and now, in these old brick walls, in rooms that have been classrooms and the bedrooms of the wealthy and monastic cells, in rooms that have seen learning and pain and love and death. We know how important the world around us, and specifically our environment is for all of us. And we understand that means both built environment – the ramps and the terrifying lift and the sound proofing on the walls and the coloured lights I have in my bedroom – but also how we live together, how we support each other and enjoy each other's company, how we give each other space the space and boundaries we need.

And this world is a rundown home, once one of wealth and privilege, now the residence of a rag-tag bunch of near squatters who desperately try to keep it from falling apart. And mostly, we do that successfully. Mostly. A rundown building with heaps of bedrooms and very little in the way of grounds, with who knows what nesting in the roof – and I'm not talking about the ghosts here. That is rumoured by all the local children to be haunted, and they're both very right and very wrong all at the same time.

It's not bad, as worlds go. I'll take it.

As Keira leaves, promising to come back and finish the sanding tomorrow, Denny calls after her and invites her round for our Equinox dinner. Keira pauses, and then accepts. We're not committing to anything else. We're all cautious with people, and our reasons for being so are little to do with our neurology and everything to do with our experiences. But Keira... we know Keira is more like us than she is like the rest of the ghost hunters.

And this is also part of our world, because some people can change and some people will not. Some people prove their character despite their actions. And this is, if anything, always a place for change, a place not just for us but for those who need to be here in the future.

I turn, closing the heavy door behind me. There's a smell of pastry baking in the kitchen, and upstairs I hear the squeal of wheeled shoes over the freshly sanded floor. I smile, and for now, just for now, I leave the door unlocked.

ACKNOWLEDGMENTS

Thank you first and foremost to the beta readers, editors, and expert advisors whose work helped bring out the best in *Sanctuary*, and in doing so supported the development of my craft. Thank you to my crit group and other writing communities for so much encouragement, resource sharing, problem solving, and friendship.

Thank you to my cover designer for working with a tricky concept and making things *glow*.

Thank you to my parents for surrounding me with books from a very young age, and to the teachers and others who continued to do so.

Thank you to all those who have taught and edited and mentored me since - it feels like so much of it has got me here in indirect ways.

Thank you to those who have done so much work that came before this.

Thank you to neurodivergent and/or disabled communities that have welcomed and challenged me.

Thank you to the crew at Robot Dinosaur Press for the framework I needed to get this out into the world, and for both personal and practical support.

Thank you to Kelly, for everything.

And thank you to you, the reader, for picking this up
and giving it the chance to be read.

ABOUT THE AUTHOR

Andi C. Buchanan lives among streams and faultlines just north of Wellington, Aotearoa New Zealand. Winner of a Sir Julius Vogel Award, their genre-blending novella "From a Shadow Grave" explores a historical murder, the legends surrounding it, and what might have been. Andi's short fiction has previously been published in Fireside, Cossmass Infinities, Apex, and more. You can find Andi at https://andicbuchanan.org or on twitter at @andicbuchanan.

ALSO BY ANDI C. BUCHANAN

From a Shadow Grave

Wellington,1931. Seventeen-year-old Phyllis Symons' body is discovered in the Mt Victoria tunnel construction site. Eighty years later, Aroha Brooke is determined to save her life. Urban legend meets urban fantasy in this compelling alternate history.

This Other World

When her son reached adulthood, Vonika made the decision to emigrate to Kami, settling in the nation of Temia. In the years since, she's found the sense of belonging that she, as an autistic woman, struggled to find on Earth. But the approach of old age brings decisions that Vonika knows she can't avoid forever. As Temia teeters on the edge of war, Vonika finds herself a reluctant emissary for peace.

ALSO PUBLISHED BY ROBOT DINOSAUR PRESS

The Silent Fringe
by R J Theodore

After Ehli inadvertently exiles herself to the extra-dimensional realm known as dimspace, she discovers a planet full of iscillian who are scheduled for the same life she recently escaped. Can she save more of her people from that fate without losing her ship, her freedom, or her life?

Underway: The Phantom Travelogues
by R J Theodore

Jayess chronicles the strange worlds visited by Harrow's Tusk in this illustrated travelogue.

The Bantam
by R J Theodore

When one of Ehli's bantam sisters turns up dead, she tries to figure out what happened before she's blamed for the murder, and before the real killer strikes again.

The Wolf Among The Wild Hunt
by Merc Fenn Wolfmoor

A disgraced knight must survive a night among the most deadly hunt ever known.

The Midnight Games: Six Stories About Games You Play Once
edited by Rhiannon Rasmussen

An anthology featuring six frightening tales illustrated by Andrey Garin await you inside, with step by step instructions for those brave—or desperate—enough to play.

The Stars and Green Magics: Season One
by Novae Caelum

The Stars and Green Magics is an unabashed space fantasy serial with shapeshifting royals, vicious politics, complex aliens, and queerness everywhere!

Hero's Choice
by Merc Fenn Wolfmoor

Never get between a Dark Lord and his son. Who needs destiny when you've got family?

They Dreamed of Dead Ships
by Byron M. Kain

A terrifying plague sweeps the world, and there is nowhere safe...for it comes to you in a dream about a ship. And then it is too late.

A Starbound Solstice
by Juliet Kemp

Celebrations, aliens, mistletoe, and a dangerous incident in the depths of mid-space. A sweet festive season space story with a touch of (queer) romance.

Friends For Robots: Short Stories
by Merc Fenn Wolfmoor

An upbeat collection of short science fiction and fantasy stories featuring many good robots and their friends!

CPSIA information can be obtained
at www.ICGtesting.com
Printed in the USA
LVHW081317170922
728616LV00015B/883

9 780473 600488